Cater
TO YOU

Dear Reader:

We were introduced to Riley Ryan in Shamara Ray's most recent novel, *Rituals for Love* (an excerpt is included in the back of this book.) Now Riley's a personal chef and once she's asked to cater a retirement party for the powerful Carlyles, her life will never be the same. After her debut family catering event, she makes such an impression the couple requests her to cater a weekly Sunday dinner.

Little does Riley know that the dinners will be more than serving. They will include four Carlyle sons who attempt to woo her: twins Hutton and Dutton, totally opposite personalities and lifestyles; the youngest, Preston, and the married Grand. Watch how she manages to mix business with pleasure, although it was never in her original plans. Like her culinary delights in the kitchen, Riley is tempted with treats offered from all of the sons, who each have positive traits and exude extreme confidence that they have the upper hand in this game.

Prepare to see how this chef balances her kitchen skills while handling these men who are in hot pursuit. Shamara first enticed readers with her romantic novel *Recipes for Love*, which included some of her own personal recipes.

As always, thanks for supporting myself and the Strebor Books family. We strive to bring you the most cutting-edge, out-of-the-box material on the market. You can find me on Facebook @AuthorZane or you can email me at zane@eroticanoir.com.

Blessings,

Zane

Publisher
Strebor Books
www.simonandschuster.com

ZANE PRESENTS

Cater TO YOU

SHAMARA RAY

SBI

STREBOR BOOKS

NEW YORK LONDON TORONTO SYDNEY

Strebor Books
P.O. Box 6505
Largo, MD 20792
http://www.streborbooks.com

ISBN 978-1-59309-588-8
ISBN 978-1-4767-6190-9 (ebook)
LCCN 2015934968

First Strebor Books trade paperback edition January 2016

Cover design: www.mariondesigns.com
Cover photograph: © Keith Saunders/Keith Saunders Photos

10 9 8 7 6 5 4 3 2 1

Manufactured in the United States of America

For information regarding special discounts for bulk purchases,
please contact Simon & Schuster Special Sales at 1-866-506-1949

The Simon & Schuster Speakers Bureau can bring authors to your live event. For more information or to book an event, contact the Simon & Schuster Speakers Bureau at 1-866-248-3049 or visit our website at www.simonspeakers.com.

For Mia the Intrepid

CHAPTER ONE

bustled through the living room toward the kitchen, glancing at Tyler perched on my sofa watching television. I grabbed my knife roll and packed it in my tote bag, while mentally checking off items on my list. I had my clogs, aprons, kitchen towels and mitts; the only thing I needed to get was my chef jacket. As I rushed back through the living room, I stole yet another glance at him. He seemed oblivious that I was gearing up to leave and would be gone all day catering an event.

I headed upstairs to my bedroom and took a chef jacket, still draped in plastic from the dry cleaners, out of the closet. I tossed it on the bed and started to get dressed.

I slipped into a pair of black slacks and a fitted black tee shirt. I pulled my shoulder-length bob in a bun, securing it with pins. I applied natural earth-tone makeup to my eyes and cheeks with a neutral lip. I didn't like to wear heavy makeup when preparing food and cooking for special events. Too much heat or too many hours spent in the kitchen could have the most beautifully made-up face looking like clown paint in the end.

The event I was getting ready for was indeed a special one. When I received the call from Miriam Carlyle, I was astonished that she was inquiring about my business. She let me know one of the clients to whom I provided personal chef services was her sorority sister and recommended me. I held on to the phone, my

heart racing, as she asked if I was available to cater a retirement
party for her husband, Louis Carlyle—one of the most prominent
money men in Atlanta. I didn't hesitate to accept the event.

The offer from Mrs. Carlyle could not have come at a better
time. It had been about a month since I had resigned from a position
as executive chef at Eden2, a hot new restaurant in Atlanta. Eden2
was an unexpected opportunity that I pursued at the suggestion
of a friend. I thought it was a one-of-a-kind chance to exercise my
culinary chops and enhance my resume. I landed the dream position
after a week-long residency in New York, only to step down two
weeks later. It was a difficult decision, but one that had to be made.
I shook my head, trying not to dwell on what could have been.
Immediately after resigning from my post, I returned to my personal chef business. Luckily, I managed to recoup all of my clients.
They were elated that I could resume providing their services after
my brief hiatus. I even added two clients. The entire experience
with Eden2 had left me a little down, however, the Carlyle event
was exactly what I needed to lift my spirits.

I was a professionally trained chef having studied at Johnson &
Wales and also Le Cordon Bleu in Paris. Although my primary
profession was as a personal chef, I also catered affairs on occasion.
I was honored to be catering the retirement party for Louis Carlyle
and intended to dazzle him, along with his guests, with my cuisine.
I checked the clock, snatched my chef jacket and hurried downstairs.

Tyler peered at me when I entered the living room. "You look
good."

"Thanks," I blandly replied. "You know I'm going to be gone all
day, right?"

"What time does the event start?"

"The party is this evening at six."

"Why are you leaving so early? It's barely after eight."

"I have quite a bit of prep to do once I arrive at my client's house. Everything that I'm serving tonight, I'll be preparing today."

"What time will you be home?"

"I don't anticipate returning until the wee hours. I hope you have something planned for the day."

"Actually, I don't."

"It's Saturday. You're just going to sit around here all day?"

"I didn't get off work until eleven last night. That was after going into the newsroom at seven a.m. Then, I came straight here. So, yeah, I pretty much planned on doing absolutely nothing today."

I shrugged and headed toward my bag. I didn't have time to start a discussion that we'd been over many times before. "Well, enjoy your day doing nothing." I started for the front door.

"Can I at least have a kiss before you go?"

I sighed and turned, walking back over to the sofa. Tyler puckered his lips, eyes never shifting from the television. I reluctantly graced him with a swift peck and breezed out the front door without another word. If Tyler wanted to squander away his day, then so be it. I, on the other hand, was about to make the most of mine.

CHAPTER TWO

My navigation guided me through a neighborhood in Sandy Springs I was certain I had never before visited. The homes I was passing on my drive were definitely not houses. I lived in a house. The homes I was passing were estates—monolithic mansions set upon acres of land, secreted away behind high fences. I turned off the main road and approached the Carlyles' access gate. A red light glowed on a small surveillance camera as I reached out the car window, apparently motion-activated. I had barely pushed the call button before the gates parted, allowing me entry to the property. I traveled slowly up the road to the mansion, taking in the decadence and splendor. The manicured grounds were impeccable with lawns that appeared as thick and lush as carpet, an abundance of flowers and bushes architecturally positioned, and trees that were as stately as the grounds they adorned. I knew before I even saw the expanse of brick and stone that the Carlyle home would be a sight to behold.

I walked from my car to the front door, gawking at the ornate stonework. The sheer volume of windows made me pity whoever was responsible for cleaning them all. A classic Westminster chime rang out when I pressed the doorbell. I was greeted by a middle-aged woman in a spotless black uniform. She introduced herself as Melba, the Carlyles' house manager. She escorted me from the entrance foyer down a long hallway to the kitchen. I managed to get a glimpse of the living room, dining room, library and what appeared to be a sunroom. I silently marveled and speculated how many rooms there were in the entire mansion. I wished I could see more than a mere fraction. I had never seen so many chandeliers hanging in one home. The light was reflecting off the sheen of the perfectly buffed hardwood floors.

During my conversation with Mrs. Carlyle, she assured me that her kitchen would be more than adequate to accommodate my prep and cooking for the evening. As I followed the house manager into what would be my workshop for the remainder of the day, I realized Mrs. Carlyle had not exaggerated. The kitchen was larger than some commercial spaces I had previously worked in before starting my own business. I slowly surveyed the kitchen. Two full-length islands and stone counter tops on both sides of the room would absolutely provide ample workspace. There was an eight-burner range with a grill and double oven, a full-size built-in refrigerator and two additional under-counter refrigerators.

Melba showed me where all of the pots, pans, bowls, utensils and anything else I would need could be found. "The refrigerator has been stocked with the food you ordered for the event. Your spices are located in the cabinet next to range and you'll find your additional items in the pantry."

"Thank you, Melba."

"I'll bring the platters, serving trays and dishes that we'll be using for the evening in shortly. In the meantime, the kitchen is yours. Please let me know if you need anything. Just pick up the phone on the wall next to the pantry and your call will be routed directly to me."

Melba left me alone. I took a minute to do another walkthrough to acclimate myself with the space. I observed the top-of-the-line appliances, fine cabinetry and made a mental note to avoid any spills on the stone flooring. The kitchen was simply amazing...

and spotless. I wondered whether Mrs. Carlyle ever cooked in it.

I looked at my watch. I had work to do and it wouldn't get done if I continued standing around taking in the magnificence of the kitchen. I audited the contents of the refrigerators, freezer and pantry to ensure everything I ordered had arrived. I retrieved an apron from my bag and put it on. The kitchen was equipped with cutting boards of all sizes. I grabbed a few I intended to use, opened my knife roll and began the task of prepping food. I started with the vegetables that would serve as the base for more than one dish—peppers, onions and celery. As I chopped, diced and minced, I ran through what would be prepared in which order. I had beef and chicken to trim and marinate, as well as seafood to skin and debone. There were sauces to be made, hors d'oeuvres to assemble, vegetables to roast, bisque to puree and desserts to bake. I glanced at my watch again. I had eight-and-a-half hours before the party started and I would need every minute.

When I cooked for my weekly clients, the amount of food I needed to prepare depended upon the number of meals they required for the week. I spent approximately three to four hours at each client's home. I typically wouldn't provide services for more than three clients on any given day. However, on occasion, I have worked for four clients on a single day. That meant long hours and a lot of cooking.

Aside from creating delicious food, I prided myself on my time management and ability to juggle multiple tasks. Those skills had served me well as a personal chef and for my catered events. They would certainly come in handy for the amount of food I needed to prepare for Mr. Carlyle's retirement party. A wave of excitement washed over me. I was in Louis Carlyle's kitchen. My food was going to be served to Atlanta's elite. I packed a stack of business cards to share with Mrs. Carlyle in case any of her guests inquired about the food, and with the menu I had planned, they most definitely would.

I looked up at the sound of approaching footsteps. I had been diligently at work for over four hours before she made an appearance. I was rolling out the dough for the mango cream tartlets when Mrs. Carlyle entered the kitchen. She flowed in like a breeze. Her lilac skirt suit fit her svelte frame to perfection. She smoothed her side-swept bangs, though not a hair was out of place on her tapered cut.

"I don't think my kitchen has ever smelled so divine." She stood on the opposite side of the island and smiled. "You must be Riley."

"Hello, Mrs. Carlyle. I would shake your hand but…" I stopped working my dough and held up my flour-coated digits.

She waved me off. "I wanted to see how things were coming along and make sure you have everything you need."

"Melba was kind enough to get me situated."

"I apologize I was unable to greet you this morning, but I had a sorority meeting that couldn't be missed." She examined the trays filled with hors d'oeuvres, stacked containers of vegetables, and simmering pots on the range. "You seem to have things under control."

"I'll be ready when your guests start to arrive."

"The servers will be here at four. Utilize them as you deem fit."

"I will, thank you."

Although it was my first time meeting Mrs. Carlyle in person, we had communicated numerous times about the event and menu.

"As we discussed, we'll start with the passed hors d'oeuvres at half past six," she said.

"I'll have the servers circulate three hors d'oeuvres at a time beginning with the smoked salmon tartine, olive tapenade brus-chetta and oyster puffs. The next round will include the mini beef wellingtons, shrimp polenta and grilled mandarin pork belly. We'll finish with chilled asparagus soup shots, lemon basil chicken and crispy prosciutto wrapped melon."

She nodded. "Dinner will be served at eight. Since all of the guests returned their menu selection cards, I hope there aren't any last-minute changes."

"I can accommodate additional requests for either of the main courses—the seared saffron salmon, tenderloin steak, French-trimmed stuffed chicken breast or braised short ribs."

"That's good because even though we're expecting fifty, I imagine a few more people that neglected to RSVP may show up."

"It's not a problem."

"We'll have dessert before port and cigars."

"I'm working on the tartlets as we speak. The raspberry mousse is chilling and the chocolate hazelnut torte will be served warm."

"I'm already glad I hired you. You came highly recommended by my soror."

"Thank you, Mrs. Carlyle."

"Please call me Miriam."

"Okay. Miriam. I have everything covered here in the kitchen."

"I can see that." She smiled again. "I just want everything to be perfect tonight for Louis. All the years he's worked and sacrificed can't go unrecognized."

I nodded my comprehension. "I will do my part to make sure his night is special."

"I'll let you get back to work."

"Nice meeting you, Mrs. Carlyle."

"Miriam," she reminded. "I'll check in a bit later."

I watched her leave the kitchen as gracefully as she had entered.

Miriam Carlyle was an elegant-looking woman. It wasn't just her clothing or jewelry; it was the way she carried herself. She had an air about her—and it wasn't pretentiousness. She was confident. And I was confident the Carlyles would be more than happy with my services.

CHAPTER THREE

handed a platter filled with oyster puffs to one of the servers. I sent him, with two other wait staff, out of the kitchen in succession with the first round of hors d'oeuvres. It was six-thirty on the dot and my service was beginning. The servers had been briefed on the food being served for the cocktail hour, instructed to circulate the ballroom and to return immediately when their platters needed to be refilled. There were six servers at my disposal and we were all in for a very busy evening.

The doorbell had been ringing intermittently for the better part of an hour. I was curious who had congregated to celebrate the special occasion. The sounds of mellow jazz music reached the kitchen. It was a welcome sound after working in relative quiet for the majority of the day. The music gave me a lift I wasn't aware I needed. I readied the next group of servers, furnishing them with the second round of hors d'oeuvres, napkins and cocktail picks. As they filed out of the kitchen, Mrs. Carlyle sauntered in. The man of the hour was by her side. I caught myself staring. He was an Atlanta icon, after all.

I wiped my hands on a towel and came from behind the island. I extended my hand to Louis Carlyle. "I'm Riley Ryan. Congratulations on your retirement."

"Thank you." He grinned and firmly grasped my hand. "It's a pleasure to meet you, Ms. Ryan."

"I told Louis that you were cooking the most delectable meal for him," Miriam offered.

"Does everything taste as good as it looks?" he asked.

"Even better."

"I suppose I'll have to break the diet Miriam keeps me on all the time."

I laughed. The physically fit six-foot man in front of me didn't appear to need a diet. If it weren't for the salt-and-pepper hair, I would not have thought he was retirement age. Clean-shaven, chestnut-brown face, with very few discernable wrinkles, Louis Carlyle was quite handsome. I prayed I aged as gracefully. They had apparently coordinated their ensembles. Even with no tie, his black suit and shirt to match exuded class. The plunging neckline on Miriam's long black gown showed more than a peek of her honey skin. She was about three inches shorter than her husband in her four-inch heels. Together they were striking.

"I can certainly tell you the healthier items on tonight's menu," I said.

"I intend to sample everything. In fact, I'll try the smoked salmon now."

"No you don't." Miriam tugged his arm. "You need to go greet your guests."

"By the time I speak to everyone, the hors d'oeuvres will be finished."

"You don't have to worry, Mr. Carlyle. There are plenty. However, I will set aside a platter for you just in case."

"You know, Ms. Ryan, I started my own asset management firm thirty-five years ago. And this is what I have to look forward to in retirement—my wife bossing me around." He laughed. "Thank goodness I'm not completely retiring for another six months."

"That's still up for debate," Miriam countered.

"It took years to build my firm. It will take time for me to be able to fully retire. I have to do it my way, in my own time."

A young man interrupted from the doorway. "Dad, the senator is here."

"Thanks, Preston."

The Carlyles' son looked at me for a beat and then winked. I glanced at his parents and then back to him, in time to see him retreating from the room.

"Truthfully," Mr. Carlyle continued, "there's much to be done before I entrust my company to anyone other than myself to run."

"Louis…your guests," she gently prodded.

He clasped Miriam's hand in his and kissed it. "Ms. Ryan, I may be back."

"Your hors d'oeuvres will be waiting."

They left the kitchen hand in hand engaged in lighthearted banter. I resumed replenishing platters.

Once the hors d'oeuvres had been circulating for some time, I held two servers back to assist with plating the first course. While I put the finishing touches on the brandied lobster bisque, they worked on assembling the spinach and quail egg salads. Before sending out a single bite, I checked to make sure they arranged each and every dish perfectly.

I learned early in my career that a poor presentation was simply unacceptable.

CHAPTER FOUR

ourteen hours. I was finally wrapping up in the Carlyles' kitchen after fourteen long hours. I patted myself on the back because service went off without a hitch. Every single item I sent out of the kitchen was perfection. I knew I was a good chef, but moments like these made me realize I was an *amazing* chef.

The remaining food had been packed in containers. I opened the refrigerator and began to stack them neatly inside. I was running out of space. The last few containers would have to go in the under-counter fridge. I closed the refrigerator door and jumped, my hand instinctively touching my chest.

"Sorry, I didn't mean to scare you."

"Oh," I breathed. "I didn't know you were standing there."

"I'm sorry," he said, with a laugh. "I'm Preston."

"Right. The Carlyles' son."

"I don't usually make it a habit to lurk behind refrigerator doors."

I laughed. "I hope not." I reached for a container from the counter, but Preston grabbed it first, handing it to me. I hesitated, looking up at him. Behind that goatee, he resembled both of his parents. Although I couldn't imagine Louis Carlyle sporting a diamond stud in his ear.

"I enjoyed the food tonight."

I took the container from him, placing it in the fridge. "Thank you."

"Any of your delicious dessert left?"

I peered over my shoulder at him. He leaned against the island. Obviously, he wasn't going away.

I turned, warily eyeballing him. "Which one?"

"Which was your favorite?"

Mrs. Carlyle entered the kitchen as I was about to respond. "Preston, I need you to drive Mrs. Akin home. She's not feeling well."

"Too many drinks?"

"Preston."

"As you wish, Mom." He kissed his mother on the cheek, winked at me again, and left.

She watched him exit, then spun around toward me. "Riley, the food was outstanding!"

"Thank you, Miriam."

"Louis loved it. Our guests loved it. I absolutely loved it." She handed me a check. "Here's the balance of your fee and Louis insisted we give you a little something extra."

"This is extremely generous."

"It's just a token of our appreciation."

I was the one that was appreciative they considered a two thousand-dollar tip a token. I showed Mrs. Carlyle what food was left over from the party and she inquired about reheating instructions for a few of the dishes.

"I'm all done in here. It was a pleasure to cater your event."

"I'll see you out."

"Let me grab my belongings."

Mrs. Carlyle escorted me to the door, chatting as we walked. "I was wondering… Are you accepting any new clients?"

"I wish I could. I'm pretty much booked to capacity."

"What about one meal a week? Sunday dinners only?"

"I'm managing a number of clients Monday through Friday, so I typically reserve weekends for myself or catering special events on occasion."

"Well, please think it over and let me know. I would certainly make it worth your while."

I departed with a promise to mull over her offer even though I knew I couldn't juggle any more clients.

CHAPTER FIVE

turned my key in the lock and was happy to be home. I closed the door behind me and listened. Complete silence. I kicked off my shoes at the door and slowly walked through the darkened foyer and hallway to the family room. I turned on the lamp and let my bag drop to the floor. I eased down on the sofa with an exhausted sigh. I had undoubtedly worked hard for my money. The client was satisfied and that was all I wanted. The tip was my confirmation—and the fact that Mrs. Carlyle wanted to hire me on a weekly basis.

I reached over and pulled my planner from my bag. I flipped through several weeks to determine if there was a way I could accommodate Mrs. Carlyle's request to take her on as a client. I scanned a couple more weeks. The schedule I was currently managing was ideal. I had just enough clients where I felt I was maximizing my earning potential. Adding any more could push me to the side of having too many. Although, she did also inquire about providing services for Sunday dinners only. I tossed my planner on the coffee table. The thought of working every Sunday, leaving me with only Saturdays to myself, wasn't appealing. I didn't doubt that she could pay handsomely, but my weekends were my own. Unfortunately, I was unable to accept the offer.

I was blessed that I was in a place that I could turn down business. I had built up my clientele over the years and my services didn't come cheap. I prided myself on providing elite personal chef services. I had established a great rapport with my clients. They welcomed me into their homes. I knew their culinary likes and dislikes. I fed their families. Over time, it became more than just the food. You learned about people while casually conversing during meal preparation. You got to know and care about them. Those were some of the things that I loved most about being a personal chef.

My love for the culinary arts was immensely deeper. As a child, I would tinker around the kitchen, creating concoctions that were far from edible. But, as I got older, my skills matured. When I made the decision in high school to attend Johnson & Wales for college, my mother tried to dissuade me. She felt I should go to school to study law or medicine. I told her that wasn't what I wanted to do with my life. I reminded her that before my father died, he said to me that my dreams were my own and it was my duty to make them a reality. He knew I wanted to be a chef. He would ask me to bake him treats or surprise him with something tasty when he came home from work. That was our special connection. I loved to cook for my daddy. I decided to become a chef because to do anything else would have been to deny my calling.

After spending all day on my feet, my body melted into the sofa. I willed myself to get up to go shower. I crept upstairs to my bedroom. A stream of light slipped through the slightly ajar door. I pushed it open. The muted television cast shadows across the room. Tyler lay sleeping in the middle of the bed. I silently watched him from the doorway. I had sort of hoped that he went to his own house after I left. I told him I wouldn't be home until the wee hours. That should have been his clue not to wait around for me. I shook my head. I undressed in my walk-in closet and then crept into the bathroom.

Freshly showered and wearing an oversized T-shirt, I slid beneath the covers. Tyler rolled over and draped an arm over me. I lay awake, as he slept soundly, wanting nothing more than to be able to stretch out alone.

CHAPTER SIX

was functioning with barely four hours of sleep. The crisp morning air was helping to revitalize me, but a fresh beet, strawberry and lemon juice would really do the trick. I left my house early to meet my best friend, Aja, at the outdoor farmers market. Every Sunday local growers set up booths at the open-air market. I perused the fresh produce in search of fruits and vegetables to incorporate into the meals I was preparing for my clients that upcoming week. My reusable shopping tote containing a half-dozen pears and a few eggplants was slung over my shoulder. I picked up a bunch of basil and sniffed.

Aja was staring at me. "Do you have to smell everything?"

I laughed. "It's the chef in me."

"Can you explain why the chef in you always seems to drag the non-chef in me to the farmers market early on Sundays?"

"It's best to get here early."

"That doesn't explain why I need to be here."

"We've both been really busy lately and we get to catch up."

"Uh huh."

I nudged her with my elbow. "Seriously. I really need to vent."

"Why, what's up?"

"Tyler."

Aja put down the bok choy she was holding. "What happened?"

"Nothing happened. That's the point. He's content with doing absolutely nothing. We don't go anywhere. We don't do anything. He's good with staying home all of the time. I was gone all day long yesterday. He didn't even bother to go home. He was in my bed asleep when I got back after one in the morning."

"That's not so terrible."

"We've only been dating seven months."

"I know."

"That's a little soon for him to be so settled. I could understand if we had some years under our belt. Maybe it would be okay. But seven months?"

"When was the last time you addressed this with him?"

"When don't I? I'm starting to feel like a nag."

"You've told me yourself that other than the going-out thing, he's a great guy."

"He is. That's why I'm still seeing him, but something has to give."

"Don't give up yet. He may change."

My brow furrowed. "Really, Aja?"

"Okay, he may not change. All I'm saying is keep working on him."

"I shouldn't have to work on him. This is a relatively new situation. If he's not giving me what I need now, why would he start later?"

"It's not impossible. When Maxim and I started dating, he wasn't the perfect package. We've learned each other over the years and he does what he can to make me happy. Some things it took time for him to realize he needed to do. If I had thrown in the towel in the beginning, then what?"

"I hear what you're saying."

"We both know you can be impulsive…"

"Yeah, yeah, yeah."

Aja knew me better than most. Her family lived across the street from mine growing up. We played together, had slumber parties together, bickered with each other, trusted each other, shared secrets, double-dated, supported and advised one another. Aja was a true friend. I never questioned her loyalty or that she wanted the best for me.

"You disagree that you're impulsive?" she asked. "I hope not."

"Do you want me to answer?"

"Not really. That was a rhetorical question. Just in case you're going to try to debate me…a month ago you quit your dream job after only a week."

"Let's be clear. Being a personal chef is my dream job."

"So was the executive chef position at Eden2."

I paid for my basil and put it in my bag. "I left because it wasn't going to work out. It had nothing to do with impulsiveness."

"Do you regret leaving?" Her tone had softened and she touched my arm.

"I'm disappointed and I wonder what could have been. Ultimately, it was for the best."

"If you say so."

"I do."

"Well, I think you're doing big things with or without the restaurant gig. I still don't know how you can deal with those persnickety clients and their crazy requests."

"They really aren't bad. I know what they do and don't like and I create the menus. I have a great relationship with my clients. They love me."

"I do too. If I didn't, I wouldn't be meeting your tail at eight in morning when I could be snuggled up with my man." She wrapped an arm around my shoulders.

"Thank you for meeting me, Aja," I said with feigned reluctance.

"You're welcome."

"Let's stop at the fresh juice stand up ahead," I said. "I need a pick-me-up."

"You do seem a little sluggish."

"I worked for about fourteen hours yesterday."

"How was it?"

"I'm not exaggerating when I say it was perfection. First of all, their home was magnificent. It's enormous. The little I saw of it, the décor, was gorgeous. The kitchen was like something out of a magazine. It had every single appliance I could ever want and need. I don't have to tell you the food was amazing."

"Did you meet Louis Carlyle?"

"I sure did."

"What was he like?"

"I only spoke with him briefly, but he was cordial. Get this. His wife gave me a two thousand-dollar tip."

Aja stopped in her tracks. "Are you serious?"

"I told you the food was amazing. So much so, she wants to hire me as a personal chef for one meal a week. Sunday dinners. I can't do it, though."

"Why not?" she asked, her voice raising an octave.

"I have enough clients right now and I need my weekends."

"It's one meal. You're not going there to prepare a week's worth of food."

"It's still my Sunday."

"It's not the worst thing in the world. I have to work some Sundays."

"Well, you're a nurse. You're saving lives so it's worth it."

"It's worth it for you to take on the type of client that gave you a two thousand-dollar tip."

"I don't know."

"I think you're crazy. You better make that money!"

CHAPTER SEVEN

A morning at the farmers market quickly turned into an afternoon of shopping. Aja and I dropped our produce at her house and then went to Atlantic Station. It was my intention to do a bit of window shopping, until I saw a leather peplum jacket that would be perfect when the fall weather rolled in. I had to have it. I scooped up a pair of gloves and ankle boots to match. I could admit I wasn't the best window shopper. I always ended up buying something. We parted ways with Aja teasing me about blowing through my bonus. The tip was icing on the cake for my extremely hefty fee. After the hours and work I put in for the Carlyles, I deserved to splurge.

I came through the door balancing bags on my arms. Tyler was headed toward me, hands outstretched, to relieve me of my packages.

He kissed me on the cheek. "I was wondering when you'd return."

"Aja and I went to Atlantic Station after the market." We headed into the kitchen together.

He started to unpack the produce. "What did you get?"

"Chard, bok choy, eggplant…a few other vegetables."

"Are you cooking this for dinner tonight?"

"No." I cut my eyes at him. "I didn't plan on cooking, but you can take me out to dinner."

"Tonight?"

"Yes, tonight. I would like to get dressed and go somewhere nice to eat."

"I wanted to stay in tonight. I have to be at work at five tomorrow morning. All I want to do is chill at home with you tonight."

I placed the pears on the counter. "Where did you get the impression that I wanted to be home all the time? I know it couldn't have been from me because I'm always saying 'let's go out.'"

"Yeah, you say that a lot and sometimes we do."

"Most of the time we don't. Since we've been dating, I can count the number of times we've actually gone out."

"Come on, Riley, we went out all the time in the beginning."

"How long have we been together, Tyler?"

He squinted, pondering my question. "Eight months."

"Seven."

"Okay, seven…"

"This is still the beginning."

We stared at each other. Clearly we had a difference of opinion. Tyler had been in long-term relationships in the past. He had to know that seven months in was still the honeymoon phase.

"Which means we'll have plenty of opportunities to go out in the future," he rebutted.

I walked away and left him standing in the kitchen. He followed me into the family room. The television was on. A bowl of chips and a bottle of beer were on the coffee table.

"So this is your idea of a fun evening? We should sit around watching TV and eating chips all night? It would kill you to go out to dinner?"

"We can go another night. I'm settled in."

I felt a flash of anger. "You're too damn 'settled in.' I've been out all weekend. Why are you even at my house? If you wanted to stay home all damn weekend and do nothing, you could do that at your own house. You don't need to be here."

"I didn't think my being here was a problem."

"You're missing the point. You know what, Tyler. If we're not going to dinner, maybe you should just go home."

"I should go home," he repeated.

"I don't want to spend the rest of the evening arguing with you. And, since you have to go to work early, you can go home and get a good night's sleep."

He frowned and then nodded. "I'll do that." Tyler went up to my bedroom to collect his overnight bag.

I was standing at the bottom of the stairs when he came back down. "Your car keys are on the entry table by the front door."

"Thanks." He wouldn't look at me.

I trailed behind him as he headed to the door. "Get home safely."

"Yup," he muttered, snatching up his keys.

He left the house without so much as a glance back. I closed the door before he even reached his car. He wanted to chill at home; he could do it at his own house. Not mine. I went into the family room, straightened up and then carried his chips and soda into the kitchen to discard. I finished putting away my produce and realized I still needed to eat something.

I went upstairs to get dressed. I was going out to dinner alone.

CHAPTER EIGHT

*T*he waitress placed a cappuccino in front of me and inquired if I would like anything else. I thought about having a slice of cheesecake but decided against it. The pasta dish I had eaten didn't leave much room for dessert. I sipped my after-dinner beverage and scanned the dining room. Almost every table was filled. I had been to the restaurant once before while on a date. I liked the style and ambiance of the place. Hints of violet lighting mingled with the dark furnishings gave the restaurant a sexy vibe.

It was my first time ever going out, in a little black dress no less, to dine by myself. I thought I would be self-conscious sitting alone to eat in a trendy restaurant, but it was quite the opposite. I felt empowered. I enjoyed a fine meal with a glass of wine and I didn't need Tyler to do it. I smiled to myself. I was lost in my thoughts and only partially aware that someone walked by my table. That is until he double backed and I glanced up.

"You have a beautiful smile."

"Thank you." I sipped my cappuccino.

"I would love to know what you had to eat that put such an expression on your face. Are you dining alone?"

I nodded. "I am."

He motioned to the empty chair across from me. "May I?"

"You aren't here with someone?"

"A couple of my buddies. They won't miss me."

I gave my consent with a wave of the hand.

"I'm Gerald," he said, sitting down.

"Riley."

"Not to sound cliché, but I have to ask. What's a beautiful woman doing eating all alone?"

"We have to eat too, don't we?"

"Lucky for me you don't have a companion."

"So you reserve crashing dinners for the companionless?"

"Honestly, this is a first. I don't usually invite myself to sit down while someone is having dinner. There was something in your smile that made me throw all decorum out the window."

I regarded him for an instant and then chuckled. "It just so happens I believe there's a first time for everything."

"If you don't mind sharing, what were you smiling about?"

"Nothing really," I coyly replied.

"C'mon, tell me."

"Okay. I was thinking to myself how liberating it felt to put on a sexy dress, a pair of high-heels and go out to dinner even though my man didn't want to join me."

"Ahhh. You were having an independent woman moment."

I laughed. "I guess you can say that."

"If I were your man, I wouldn't let you dine alone."

"That's the good thing about being an independent woman. He doesn't let me do things."

"That's not what I meant, but I'll rephrase my comment so that I'm clear. If you wanted to put on a sexy dress and a pair of high-heels to go to dinner, I'd make sure I was with you. Especially with you looking so fine."

"I knew what you meant the first time and thanks for the compliment."

"I see. A brother sits down uninvited and a few licks come along with it."

"That's a risk you take when you let a smile motivate your actions."

We shared a laugh and I assured Gerald I was only kidding.

"I'm sorry I didn't get here earlier. Maybe I could've had dinner with you."

"What about your friends?"

"Dinner with you or them… I'm sure they'd understand."

"What makes you think I'd say yes to dining with a complete stranger?"

"I'm sitting across from you now."

"While I finish my cappuccino. That's not sharing an entire meal. I'm practically on my way out the door."

"I like to think positive. But it's all moot, isn't it? You said you have a man and I'm going to respect that."

"I appreciate it."

"Can you recommend something for me to order? I can think about you while I eat."

I held back laughter. "You can't go wrong with the sea bass in beurre blanc sauce or the grilled prawns served over Bloody Mary risotto."

"I like how that rolled off your tongue. Beurre blanc. What is that?"

"It's French. Simply put, it's a butter sauce. It's made with white wine, vinegar, shallots and cream."

"Sounds like you studied the menu."

"I'm a chef."

"Ugh." He shook his head. "You just get more appealing."

My waitress came over and placed a check holder on the table. I reached for it at the same time as Gerald. "What are you doing?" I asked.

"You let me to interrupt your dinner. At least allow me to pick up your tab."

"I can't let you do that," I said, still reaching for the check.

"Let me?"

Again, we laughed.

"Okay, let me clarify. You don't have to do that."

"I know I don't have to. I want to. Besides, your man should be here with you. Since he isn't, I would be honored to treat you to dinner." He took out his wallet and placed the money in the holder.

"Thank you, Gerald. That's awfully nice of you."

"You're welcome. I enjoyed our brief time together."

"So did I."

"I don't suppose you'd give me your phone number."

I slowly shook my head. "I can't."

"I understand." He reached across the table, took my hand in his, and gave a gentle squeeze. "If you change your mind, my last name is Sang. I own Sang Construction. Just look me up."

"I certainly will." I extracted my hand from his grasp and picked up my purse. "It was nice meeting you. Enjoy your dinner."

We got up at the same time. Gerald went to join his friends and I strolled to the exit. I reflected on how nice my evening had turned out as I waited for the valet to bring my car. I was proud of myself. I didn't let Tyler prevent me from doing what I wanted to do. Getting treated to dinner by a nice man was an added bonus. I enjoyed my night out. I doubted Tyler could say the same.

CHAPTER NINE

*T*he garlic, olive oil and lemon juice were pureeing in the food processor. I added the fresh herbs into the feed tube. I was preparing meals for my second client of the day—a surgeon that spent more hours at the hospital than he did at home. I had keys to a few of my clients' homes, so I could do my job even if they weren't there. I had been working for this particular client for three years and he was one of my favorites. There weren't many things that he did not eat. He didn't make specific requests and allowed me to be as creative as I wanted with the menu.

My cell phone vibrated on the kitchen table. It was the third call I had received in an hour. I let it go to voicemail. I had a sense it was Tyler and I wasn't in the mood to speak with him. I didn't tell him I went to dinner alone and neglected to call him when I returned home. What was the point? He wanted a quiet evening at home and that's exactly what I facilitated.

I had been extremely patient with Tyler. I vocalized on many occasions that I needed more from him. He just didn't seem to get it. I worked just as hard as him and put in long hours. I wanted to spend my time off enjoying life, not sitting at home. That didn't mean I thought we should always spend our time going out, but there had to be a balance. What more could I say to make him understand? One thing was apparent. I was growing weary of grousing about the same thing. It was at that moment I decided I was done complaining. I was finished with mentioning the same things over and over. I told Aja I wouldn't give up on him yet and I meant it. However, Tyler needed to demonstrate that he was willing to put in more effort.

When situations arose with men in my life, I wished my father was still alive. I wanted them to know that I had a father who cared and wanted the best for me. A dad that would protect me and offer sage advice. A father who was keen on vetting anyone that thought they had a chance with his daughter. I liked to think I knew what he would want for me in a partner—a smart and caring man with whom he'd be comfortable entrusting his daughter's well-being. I longed for my daddy and missed him in so many ways. He was gone, but I had to believe that he was looking down on me.

I placed the last baking dish filled with chermoula spiced chicken in the refrigerator. I jotted down reheating instructions for all of the meals on an index card and left them beneath a refrigerator magnet. If the doctor had any questions, he could call. I didn't anticipate he would. He never did. I untied my apron and packed it into my tote. I went over to the table to retrieve my phone. I didn't recognize the number of the missed calls. I checked my voice-mail. There were two messages, both from Miriam Carlyle. She wanted me to call her as soon as possible. I sat down and dialed her number.

Miriam answered on the first ring. "Hello, Riley."

"Miriam, hi."

"I apologize for the multiple calls. I was eager to connect with you."

"Oh, it's fine."

"I wanted to tell you again how wonderful everything was on Saturday."

"Thank you. I'm glad I was able to provide my services."

"That's why I was reaching out to you. I wondered if you had an opportunity to consider what we discussed. It would only be for one meal a week."

"I did give it some thought. However, Sundays are my—"

"Before you decide, I realize I didn't provide you with any of the particulars. Dinner is every Sunday at my home at five p.m. On most Sundays, there will be nine of us. Louis and myself, our four sons, one daughter-in-law and two grandchildren. The menu would be entirely within your discretion. I may have specific requests on occasion, but I would really prefer to defer to your expertise. I was thinking a main course and dessert would be fine, but it might be nice to have a light first course—either a soup or salad or appetizer of sorts. I know it's only one meal per week, but it is two or three courses for nine people. Most importantly, I realize it's your Sunday. Whatever your fee, we're willing to pay it."

Aja's words echoed in my head and I heard myself say, "I think I can do it."

"You'll do it?" she asked excitedly.

"I will be your personal chef on Sundays."

"Louis will be pleased."

"I'll pull together a few menus for your approval with and without a first course."

"Let's do the first course."

"Okay. I'll prepare a first, main and dessert course every week. You can provide as little or as much input as you'd like." I discussed my fee with Miriam and as expected, there were no objections.

"I would love if you could start this weekend."

I wanted to be able to tell her I had plans for the upcoming weekend and couldn't do it, but that was far from the truth. "This Sunday will be fine."

"Can you email me a suggested menu by Wednesday?"

"Absolutely."

"What time will you arrive?"

"I'll be there at three p.m."

"I appreciate you accommodating us."

"I'm looking forward to it and I'll see you Sunday."

I ended the call and sighed. I had committed myself to a six-day work week. It wasn't an ideal schedule, but at the rate I quoted Miriam, I wasn't upset at all.

CHAPTER TEN

The front door opened before I had a chance to ring the bell. I was expecting to see Melba, but Mr. Carlyle welcomed me inside. He was casually dressed in a polo shirt and slacks. I walked with him to the kitchen, reflecting on how I never would've anticipated being back at their home. It suddenly hit me that I would have been foolish to turn down the opportunity. A wealthy, well-respected member of Atlanta society wanted me to provide my personal chef services on a regular basis. The potential for referrals alone made it worth accepting the job.

"Miriam hasn't returned from church yet. They were having a special program today, but she should be back soon." We entered the kitchen. "I have been instructed to tell you that everything you ordered should be in the refrigerator or the pantry."

"Thank you. I know where to look." I washed my hands in the sink.

I opened the refrigerator door. Mr. Carlyle sat in one of the chairs at the island. I glanced back out the corner of my eye.

"I have to commend you on that meal last week. It was outstanding."

I removed the herbs and vegetables I needed and placed them on the island. "Was it worth breaking your diet?"

"Every single bite."

"That's what chefs love to hear."

"How long have you been a chef?"

"I've been a professional chef for eight years, but I've been cooking for as long as I can remember."

"Do you work for an agency?"

"No, I've been a sole proprietor for four years."

"That's good. More of us need to strive toward business owner-ship. I know better than to ask a woman her age—"

"I don't mind. I'm twenty-eight."

"And you've already been in business four years." He nodded his approval. "I was thirty when I started my firm. However, I got my start in the finance industry at J.P. Morgan right out of college. After my first day, I knew I had to run my own business. It took me nine years to branch off. Miriam and I had been married for two years and she was pregnant with our eldest son, Granderson. She thought my leaving J.P. Morgan could not have been more poorly timed. She was going on maternity leave in a matter of weeks and was worried about our finances. I assured her that with our savings, the experience I had under my belt, the contacts I had made and the fire in my belly, she had nothing to be worried about.

"I had always been driven to succeed in life. After about a year at J.P. Morgan, I realized I needed to get my MBA. I would work all day and go to school at night. I received my degree and moved up the ladder. I worked in a variety of divisions and knew the intricacies of institutional and private investing. I was a VP of institutional asset management when I made the decision to leave. I understood my wife's fear; I had concerns of my own. But, I wasn't built to let my concerns overrule what I knew to be my truth. I was meant to have my own company. That company was going to be successful. And, I was going to make a lot of money along the way. There was no room for fear. I forged ahead and I haven't looked back since."

I had started to prepare dinner while Mr. Carlyle was talking. I felt as if I was in a private master class. "It must be bittersweet to be retiring."

"My wife has been encouraging me for the past five years to start winding down. I'm not ready to retire, but after thirty-five years…" He paused. "I finally agreed, but on my own terms. I'm not handing the firm over just yet."

"What do you have planned when you do?"

"We'll travel. And I can always stand to improve my golf game."

"Certainly something to look forward to."

"Maybe I'll start a new business venture."

"That sounds exciting." I returned to the fridge for additional ingredients.

"I'd have to convince my wife to let me do that."

"What are you convincing me?" Miriam asked, sauntering into the kitchen. She stopped beside her husband and draped an arm around his shoulder. "It's good to see you, Riley."

"You too."

"You were saying, Louis?" She peered at him curiously.

"I was just telling Riley about some of my retirement plans."

"Something that needs my seal of approval?"

He laughed. "It might."

"Then let me say no now."

"Well, Riley, I guess that's the end of that." He got up. "The boss has spoken."

"That's right. Why don't you go call and make sure the boys are on their way."

"I'm on it."

Mr. Carlyle left the room still chuckling. I was putting a baking sheet of quartered parsnips and potatoes, tossed in olive oil, garlic and rosemary, in the oven. Miriam took her husband's vacated seat.

"It wasn't too much of an inconvenience to change the dessert from coconut cream pie to the mini chocolate soufflés, was it?"

"Not at all."

"I remembered one of my sons doesn't care for coconut."

"Coconut can be tricky. I find that my clients either love it or hate it. There's no in between."

"I want everyone to be able to enjoy dessert. I've been trying to get the entire family together for regular Sunday dinners for a long time. I had to use my husband's retirement as a catalyst to get the boys to agree. I also pointed out that we're not getting any younger."

I was surprised that approach worked. They looked damned good and one would think they had many years ahead of them. "I think it's wonderful when families come together to share a meal."

"It's tough for a mother to have a full house one day and an almost empty nest the next. The boys grew up so fast. They're living their own lives and I feel as if I don't see them enough. Two of my sons work at the firm with Louis, so he sees the boys regularly. It was important for me to have my family underneath one roof at least once a week. I wanted it to be special—memorable— with great food and conversation. I want to thank you, again, for agreeing to be our chef."

"You're welcome."

"I just had a great idea." Her eyes brightened. "Would it be an imposition to have you present each course to the family?"

My head slightly cocked to the side. "Do you mean serve each course?"

"Not exactly. I have staff to serve the meal. I mean would you be willing to describe what the dish is, whether it comes from a certain region or culture, perhaps some of the ingredients, how you prepared it… "

It was an unusual request, but considering what I was getting paid, I could indulge her idiosyncrasies. We discussed what she had in mind and it wasn't a big deal. I enjoyed discussing food and what made my dishes special. If she felt it would help to create the memorable experiences she was in search of, I could oblige.

It truly was beautiful that she wanted her family together. Sunday dinners were a thing of the past in my family. After my father passed, my family's dynamic shifted significantly. The head of our household was gone and my mother couldn't fill his shoes. She took care of us and was a strong matriarch, but she couldn't possibly be the patriarch of the family. He was the foundation, our rock. His absence changed our entire life. It was as if my mother couldn't bear to do certain things that reminded her too much of how our lives used to be. The empty seat at the table was a blaring reminder that her family would never be the same. The family trips, barbecues, picnics, and even decorating the Christmas tree were abandoned activities. What I wouldn't give to be able to have Sunday dinner with my family again.

"I don't mind presenting the courses," I acquiesced.

"You're a godsend." Thrilled that I had agreed, she went to ensure her husband corralled their sons.

With the Carlyles out of the kitchen, I fell into a rhythm. An hour later, there was sauce in a double boiler, soup simmering, vegetables sautéing and meat marinating. I went over to the oven and removed the roasted parsnips and potatoes. I placed the tray on a cooling rack.

"Are we set for tomorrow morning?"

My eyes darted toward the voice. I promptly realized that the interrupter of my solitude was talking on the phone.

"What else do you need from me?" he continued, gazing in my direction. "I sent the signed documents on Friday. You should have a copy."

I transferred the roasted vegetables from the tray to the food processor, glancing periodically at him. Each time I looked up, he was watching me intently.

"That's unacceptable. I need it by noon. All right, work on it this evening. I'll see you in the morning." He ended his call and assessed me. "I'm Hutton."

"Riley."

"I've heard. You catered the retirement party, right?"

"Yes."

"Your food was mentioned as a selling point when I was summoned for dinner. Had I known you were in the kitchen, I would have agreed the first time my mother asked me to be here."

I went to the refrigerator for cream and when I turned around, he was lifting the lid on one of the pots. I reached over and pushed the lid down. "Please don't do that."

He looked in another. "Is this hollandaise sauce?"

"It's béarnaise. Hollandaise is the mother sauce from which it's derived."

"I enjoy haute cuisine." He replaced the lid. "I was recently at Cezoi having dinner with a couple of my clients who play for the Hawks. Have you been there?"

"No, I haven't."

"You have to make a reservation at least six months in advance. Well, most people do. I called the same evening and was able to secure a table. The chef made us an appetizer of tuna tartare with hollandaise. It wasn't on the menu, but it was spectacular."

"Well, if you're a fan of hollandaise, you should enjoy the béarnaise."

"Not all cooks are familiar with mother sauces."

"I'm a chef. Professionally trained."

"Last month I spent a couple of weeks in St. Barts. I'm thinking about buying a house on the island. Every day it was champagne, fresh seafood and French cuisine."

I couldn't get a read on whether he was trying to impress me or annoy me. "You're fond of French food?"

"*Oui.*"

"*Parlez-vous français?*" I asked.

"*Un peu, et vous?*"

"Actually, I do. I studied French in high school and lived in Paris while attending Le Cordon Bleu." I answered him in English since he only spoke a little French.

"I guess you really appreciate fine cuisine," he said.

"Create and appreciate."

"I'd like to take you someplace special."

"How did you come to that conclusion?"

"Well, for one thing, you're beautiful."

I bowed my head to conceal that he made me blush. "Thank you."

"We obviously have something in common."

"I see." I added salt, pepper and cream to the roasted vegetables in the food processor.

He stood on the opposite side of the island, plucked an apple slice from the cutting board and took a bite. "If there's anything you'd like me to taste," his eyes narrowed, "I'm available."

I observed him while he chewed the apple. He was nice to look at with his full lips, cocoa-brown face and Caesar haircut. However, removing lids on pots and taking food while I was cooking made me not want to look at him at all. There was an air of arrogance surrounding Hutton. To assume I didn't know about mother sauces or secondary sauces when I'm a chef was presumptuous of him. I was surprised he knew as a non-chef.

"I think I can handle the taste testing," I replied.

"If you change your mind…" Hutton grabbed a second slice of apple and departed with a self-assured stride and a smirk on his face.

I brooded over our exchange for a moment. It left me feeling as if I had something to prove to him.

CHAPTER ELEVEN

A member of the Carlyles' staff wheeled the serving cart into the dining room. I approached the table, conducting a cursory examination of the talkative group assembled. Mr. Carlyle was seated at one end of the long rectangular table and Miriam at the other. The chatting ceased when I came to a standstill at the corner of the table closest to her.

Miriam pivoted in her seat. "Everyone, I'd like to introduce our amazing chef, Riley. Riley, this is my family that I finally managed to pull together for Sunday dinner. Seated next to Louis on his right is our oldest son, Granderson, or as we call him, Grand. The little one next to Grand is his son Jayce."

"I'm not a little one, Grandma. I'm seven and almost a man."

"Grandma's sorry, baby."

"Next to the little man is his little brother, Caleb."

"Caleb's three," Jayce piped up again.

"Grand's wife, Jayla, is next to Caleb. Seated on Louis's left is Hutton, our second-born. That's Preston, our youngest, seated across from Caleb."

"We met last week at the retirement party," Preston commented.

"And next to me is Dutton, our third child. Although, he's only six minutes behind Hutton."

"Twins?" I asked.

"Fraternal," Hutton offered.

"Nice to meet you all," I said.

"Riley is going to tell us what we're having this evening."

"For the first course we actually have two dishes." The server began to set the course in front of the family. "A delicate spinach and apple bisque with a golden goat cheese crouton. Also, a crisp spinach and apple salad with a maple goat cheese drizzle. I'm featuring the spinach-apple pairing two ways to showcase and elevate the flavor and textures of the fresh ingredients. The dishes share the same ingredients with a few variations in spices."

Louis began eating while I was still talking. Grand's wife was assisting her three-year-old with the soup. Miriam had insisted that the children would eat the same meal as the adults.

"They both sound delicious," Miriam said.

"I hope you enjoy." I retreated to the kitchen to put the final touches on the main course.

Miriam seemed elated. Whether her family shared her sentiment remained to be seen. I noticed Grand barely acknowledged my presence and Dutton merely offered a head nod when introduced. Jayla smiled briefly at me before her eyes flitted in her husband's direction. Little Man Jayce might have been the cutest member of the family.

I sliced the stuffed veal roast and began plating the main course. I was inexplicably looking forward to presenting what was next to the Carlyles, if only to gauge their reception.

CHAPTER TWELVE

*T*he dessert course had been served and I could start to wrap up in the kitchen. I was washing the remaining bowls and utensils used to make the individual soufflés. I wanted to be finished and on my way out within the next twenty minutes.

"Chocolate soufflés?"

I turned off the water. "I didn't hear you," I said, drying my hands on a dish towel. "What did you ask about the soufflés?"

"Did you say there were nuts in the chocolate soufflés?" Dutton repeated.

"Yes, ground macadamia nuts."

"I thought so. I have to confess I was partially paying attention. Which probably wasn't too smart since I'm allergic to nuts."

"I'm sorry," I alarmedly replied. "Your mother didn't mention any nut allergies."

"It's something I've developed later in life—within the past year. I thought I told my mother, but it's possible I neglected it."

"Are you feeling okay?"

"I'm fine. I came to inquire with you before taking a bite."

"Thank goodness." Relief washed over me. The last thing I wanted was for someone to have an allergic reaction as a result of something I prepared. "Would you like me to whip up something else for you?"

"You've already made dessert for everyone."

"It's no problem."

"I don't want to inconvenience you."

"You're not. Do you like strawberries?"

"I love them."

"I can make you a strawberry shortcake in no time."

"If you really don't mind…"

I was already gathering the ingredients to make the biscuit crust. "If I did, I wouldn't have offered."

"Thanks," he softly answered.

I carried everything over to the island. He hesitantly moved closer, sitting down in front of me. I sifted flour, salt, sugar and baking powder in a bowl. He watched quietly. I smiled at him and he fidgeted with his eyeglasses.

"Did you enjoy the meal?" I inquired, breaking the silence.

"It was delicious."

"What did you like most?"

"If I had to choose, I'd say the veal and the bisque. However, it's not really a fair question because the entire dinner was great. I'm just sorry I couldn't have the chocolate soufflé."

"Don't worry. You'll enjoy the shortcake. I flambé the strawberries with brandy."

"That does sound good." He watched while I made his dessert. "What made you want to become a chef?"

"I was the kid that always wanted the toy ovens and tea sets. I loved to pretend I was cooking food for my friends. I emulated what I saw my mother doing and when she wasn't looking, I would make a mess in her kitchen. When I finally did learn how to cook, I knew there was nothing else I'd rather do."

"In most ancient civilizations cooking was the predominant role of women. As cultures advanced, those responsible for cooking played a major role in the maintaining of culture and traditions."

"That's an interesting piece of information…" I tried for a neutral expression rather than one of bafflement.

He shook his head from side to side. "You have to forgive me. Sometimes I forget not everyone is as engrossed in culture and human history as much as I am. I'm an anthropologist. I teach at Emory."

"You're a professor?"

"An associate professor of anthropology."

I observed Dutton. He was honey-complected like his mother. His close-shaven beard connected to neatly trimmed sideburns. He reminded me of a Clark Kent type—inconspicuously attractive. "You must know a lot about different cultures."

"I study cultures and societies and our roles as humans in them. I have a particular interest in African and South American cultures. They have such rich histories and we're still learning and discovering things all the time about humankind." He stroked his beard. "There I go again."

I snickered. "You're clearly passionate about your work."

"I usually reserve my commentary on the exciting world of anthropology for my colleagues. I definitely don't want to bore you with it."

"I don't find it boring at all. I was watching a documentary about ancient Egypt last week. It's unbelievable how advanced their society was during that period."

"I teach a course on the cultural origins of ancient Egypt."

"I think that's fascinating." He looked at me and started to say something, but instead cleared his throat. I rolled out the dough. He watched wordlessly as I cut out generous rounds, placed them on a baking sheet and into the oven. "If you like, I can bring the shortcake out to you when it's done."

"I wouldn't be able to see you in action from the dining room."

"Is it my turn to bore you?"

"I'm intrigued by what you do. You essentially made bread using techniques that have been employed since ancient times. I can imagine an ancient Egyptian woman making dough in a similar manner. Although, their flour sometimes had grains of sand in it and thankfully, we don't have that problem. They didn't have the capability to sift out the— I'm rambling."

He made me laugh. I apparently made him nervous. "I've always wanted to visit Egypt."

"I've been three times. Primarily for research. I wrote my dissertation on the dichotomy of gender roles in ancient and modern Egypt and the impact on socioeconomic development."

"You have your doctorate. So I'm speaking with an expert."

"I wouldn't call myself an expert."

"Well, you certainly sound like you know what you're talking about."

He went quiet again. I hulled and sliced the strawberries. I added them to a sauté pan with butter and sugar. While the sugar dissolved, I whisked heavy cream with confectioners' sugar in a bowl until peaks formed.

"Whipped cream," he murmured.

"Uh-huh."

"I had no idea it was that simple to make."

"It's literally whipped cream. I guess we've both learned some things today."

"I think I may be benefiting the most from our discourse."

"You're just saying that because I let you see my quick and easy dessert secrets."

"There's also that."

I waited for him to say more, but he remained true to his behavior and didn't. I removed the shortcakes from the oven and set them aside. I doused brandy into the sauté pan and ignited it. Blue flames consumed the pan, flambéing the strawberries. The flame dissipated and I began to assemble the dessert.

"So this is where you've been." Hutton strode into the kitchen looking at Dutton.

I placed the shortcake piled high with brandied strawberries and the light and sweet whipped cream in front of Dutton. "Taste it and let me know what you think."

"Has my twin been in here droning on all this time?" Hutton scoffed.

Dutton pushed the plate back toward me. "Thank you, Riley. I apologize for putting you through the trouble, but I have to get going."

I looked at him, puzzled, and then at Hutton. "Do you want to take it with you?"

Dutton left the kitchen without a response.

"I'll take it." Hutton scooped up the plate and walked out with it.

I was left standing in the kitchen, mouth agape, trying to make sense of what had transpired.

CHAPTER THIRTEEN

I called my sister when I left the Carlyles and decided to stop by on my way home. We were in her living room conversing while she polished her toes the shade of cotton candy pink. Sierra liked to refer to me as her baby sister even though she was only ten months older. My mother said that Sierra treated me like I was one of her doll babies. She doted on, looked out for and took care of me growing up. She had always been a nurturer and extremely protective. It was cute and I was thankful for my sister.

"Why are you watching this?" I asked, turning my head away from the television.

"It's a great show."

"Zombies eating people? This is disgusting."

"But it's not just about zombies. The main focus is what happens to humanity when civilization breaks down."

"Dutton would probably love this show."

"Who's Dutton?"

"One of the Carlyles' sons. I was talking to him tonight about society and humankind."

"Stimulating dinner conversation, huh?"

I snickered. "He's an anthropologist. I had to make him a separate dessert and he chose to stay in the kitchen with me instead of finishing Sunday dinner with his family."

"That's strange."

"I thought so, too. His mother made such a big deal about getting her four sons together."

"Four boys?"

"You heard me. I actually met the entire family. Nine in total. Including the two grandkids."

"What?" she asked, chuckling.

"That was only one strange thing about the evening." I recounted to Sierra how Miriam asked me to present the courses to her family.

"Do you usually do that for your clients?"

"No, they know in advance what I'm preparing for them. Technically, she could have relayed to her family what they'd be eating."

"Lifestyles of the rich and famous."

"I humored her because she was trying to create a special experience."

"That's why your clients love you."

"It was a little awkward, though. I felt like I was intruding on their family time. Grand, their oldest, acted like he didn't see or hear me whenever I entered the dining room."

"Maybe he wasn't into all the pomp and circumstance."

"I guess not." I paused. "Seeing the Carlyles gathered around the table made me miss Daddy."

Sierra glanced over at me. "That's understandable."

"I was preparing their dinner and thinking about us. I felt like I should've been cooking for our family."

"Unfortunately, Dad is no longer with us. Thankfully, we have our memories. They'll have to be enough. And, one day you'll have a family of your own to cook Sunday dinners."

"Not at the rate I'm going."

"Why would you say that? You and Tyler seem to be getting close."

I rolled my eyes. "Tyler is getting on my nerves."

"What did he do?"

"He didn't do anything. It's more about what he isn't doing."

"Riley, you know you can be tough on men."

"Is it wrong for me to want certain things in a relationship?"

"It depends on what you think is missing."

"Don't get me wrong. Tyler is a nice guy. My main problem with him is that he acts like we're an old couple."

"I'm not sure I even know what that means. Is he trying to drag you to Friday night bingo at the senior center?"

"You're trying to be funny, but that would actually be a vast improvement on his part."

"If you want to spend your time playing bingo with your man, maybe the problem is with you."

"That's not what I'm saying. Do you know how Daddy always seemed like he was wooing Mom? He did things for Mom to make her feel special. They had date nights. He took her to restaurants and concerts and plays. I don't have any of that with Tyler and we haven't been together a year."

"You can't compare every man to Daddy."

"Why not? He set an example for us. I want to be wooed, too. Wine and dine me every once in a while."

"You have a problem with a good man because he doesn't take you out?"

"We're still young, Sierra. Sitting at home all the time is not what I want. If Tyler and I start off this way, do you really think it will change down the road?"

"I can't say. All I know is a good man is hard to find. You need to figure out how to make it work."

"You're full of advice. What's going on in your love life?"

"Not a thing. That's why you need to listen to me. There are a lot of women out there looking for a man, myself included."

"So because you're looking for one, you'd settle for anything?"

"Not settle, compromise. There's a difference," she said.

"They both sound the same to me. In both situations, you're not getting something you want."

"That's not true. Compromise means you and your partner consider one another's feelings and work together to find a way you'll both be happy."

My sister had a tendency to be idealistic. It was easy to say what you should do in a relationship when you weren't in one.

"What are you willing to compromise?" I challenged.

"Anything that's not important."

"Could you be any more vague?"

"I wouldn't make a big deal about going out. If I had a good man, I would appreciate our time spent at home."

"You chose the low-hanging fruit. What about sex? Let's say you have this wonderful guy, but his sex drive doesn't match your own. Is that something you'd compromise on?"

She replaced the nail brush into the bottle. "That's tough."

"I'll make it tougher for you. He's attentive to your every need, you're compatible in every way and he wants a future with you."

"How often are we having sex?"

"Once every three to four months."

"Oh, hell no!"

We laughed.

"Exactly! So much for your theory of compromising for a good man."

"You can't compare sex to what you're going through. In my opinion sex is a critical component for a healthy relationship. I don't have to have it every night, but definitely more than once every few months."

"All right. What about size? Let's say he's penile challenged?"

Sierra burst out laughing. "Where do you come up with this nonsense? Penile challenged…really, Riley?"

"He's a great guy, like you said, but he has a small dick."

"How small?"

It didn't take much to rope my sister into my crazy. "Three inches erect."

She shook her head. "I don't know."

"Answer the question."

"Does he tell me that he's penile challenged or do I find out after we've been dating for a while."

"I'll make it easy. He tells you on your second date because it's been an issue for him in past relationships."

"I couldn't do it. Sex is too important."

"Yeah, I thought so."

I wasn't playing fair. There was no comparison between a small penis and what I was dealing with in my relationship with Tyler. The point I was trying to make to my sister was that it sounds great to say you'd compromise for a good man, but it all depends on what really matters to you. I want what my parents shared. I want a good man that understands that you have to keep the fire burning in a relationship. I had made Tyler aware of my feelings on more than one occasion. The fact that I repeatedly had to address it was becoming a major problem for me.

"Sex among other things is important," Sierra continued.

"You haven't been in a relationship in a long time. What are you looking for these days?"

"A good man with a good heart."

"Is that all? Sounds rather vague."

"That's because I don't want a laundry list of criteria that no man would be able to live up to."

"Is that a dig at me?"

"Everything is not always about you, little sister. You asked me what I'm looking for and I told you."

"You can be so frustrating sometimes."

"Ditto." She sighed. "Okay. A good man is one that I'm comfortable with, attracted to and can see the possibility of a future. He knows how to treat me and others around him."

"What about a job?"

"That's a given, Riley. I'm not going to say what type of career he must have because I'm open. If he's a hard worker, understands the value of a dollar and the importance of saving money, then that's all I need."

"Well, you seem to know what you want."

"And, he has to love kids."

"Spoken like a true kindergarten teacher."

"The key word is 'teacher.' I can teach you a thing or two."

I admired my sister and those like her—women that didn't feel compelled to compile every single quality they were looking for in a man. Women that trusted that fate or a higher power would just send the right man their way. Unfortunately, that approach did not work for me. I wanted specific things and needed to take control of getting them.

"We aren't getting any younger, Sierra. Wasting time on the wrong guy is unacceptable."

She propped her legs across my lap. "If you took my advice, you wouldn't be wasting time."

I stared at the television and watched a man battle a horde of zombies to protect his wife. He was willing to fight against all odds for the woman he loved. I smiled and added another item to my list.

CHAPTER FOURTEEN

I turned my head to the right and gazed at Tyler as he crunched on popcorn. He read the movie trivia on the screen in a hoarse whisper and waited for me to answer the question. After a few rounds, I sipped my soda and let him do all of the guessing. He truly was a good-looking brother—sandy complexion with a strong jaw and the thickest eyebrows. I peered at his profile until he caught my eye. He smiled and tilted his bucket of popcorn toward me. I shook my head.

"Isn't this nice?" he asked.

I nodded. When I pulled into my driveway earlier in the evening, Tyler drove up behind me. We didn't have plans and I was surprised to see him, unexpectedly in the middle of the week. After a bit of convincing, I got in his car. I was tired from a long day of work, but he was adamant that he wanted us to spend some time together. I didn't know where he was taking me, but I figured he was making an effort and the least I could do was oblige. Had I known I would end up in a movie theater waiting for a random action flick to start, I would've stayed home.

I leaned toward him. "Who did you say was in this movie?"

"I'm not sure you know him. He used to be a professional wrestler."

I scanned the theater. It was full of males, young and old. "And, you think I'll enjoy this?"

"It got three stars and I loved the first one."

"You mean to tell me this is a sequel?"

"A long-awaited one."

"Why would you pick this movie when I haven't seen the first one?"

He glimpsed at me and I could see it was dawning on him where the conversation was headed.

"I don't know," he mumbled. "I heard it was a good movie and thought it would be a cool evening out."

"Oh, I get it. You don't mind leaving the house when it's something you want to do."

The theater darkened and I directed my attention to the screen. As the movie began, I could see Tyler out the corner of my eye stealing glances at me. My expression remained neutral and I intended to stay that way throughout the entire movie. He could wonder whether I was enjoying it or not.

The night Tyler and I met, he sang to me in a room full of people. I was at an after-hours lounge with Aja on karaoke night. This wasn't your average karaoke. People took their performances seriously. If you couldn't hold a note, you'd better not set foot on the stage. I had seen a couple of people get booed by the audience and the host shut down their performance. I didn't have any singing skills, so I went to be entertained. However, Aja had a beautiful voice and was a regular participant.

I had seen Tyler sitting a few tables over from mine, and every time I looked in his direction, he was watching me. He was the last performer of the night. He took the stage and sang a classic by Tyrese. A sexy man with an amazing voice, serenading me for all to see. As he stared at me while crooning about being his lady for a lifetime, my heart raced. I couldn't refrain from blushing. At the end of the song, he walked from the stage and directly over to my table. He sat next to me, introduced himself and we chatted until the place closed. We talked to each other on our cell phones all the way home. He wouldn't let me hang up until I was safely inside. Right before he said good night, he asked me to have dinner with him the next night. I would have never thought seven months later, this same man would be inattentive to my needs. Tyler grasped my hand and pressed his lips against the back of it. My eyes never left the screen. He let go of my hand and all I felt was buttery residue from his popcorn. I sighed and tried to concentrate on the movie instead of my thoughts.

We silently exited the theater. I eavesdropped on the chatter of those around me. Overall, the guys enjoyed the action. I was glad it was over.

Tyler wrapped an arm around my shoulders. "It's still early. Do you want to go inside the mall for a while?"

"Not really. I'm a little tired." Typical. After dragging me to a testosterone-filled flick, he thought shopping would appeal to me.

"How about a bite to eat?"

"I just want to go home and relax."

"Okay, I messed up." He stopped walking and faced me. "I probably should have planned a different evening for us."

"I agree. I thought you were doing something spontaneous, yet you bring me to a movie that I have absolutely no interest in. I could've stayed home."

"I get it. I wasn't thinking. You're always telling me you want to go out and I figured—"

"Please don't. You're making it worse."

"I'm only trying to explain."

"Please just take me home."

He grabbed my hand and continued toward the car. "Am I staying with you tonight?"

"I have an early morning."

"I'm in the doghouse…"

I hesitated. "Tyler, maybe we need to take a break."

"What?" He knitted his brow in confusion and let go of my hand. "Over a movie?"

I leaned against his car and shook my head. "I think you know it's not about that."

"I like what we have going, Riley. I don't want to take a break."

"It seems like we need to take a bit a time to see if this is what we want."

"Don't say *we*. Those are your feelings. I know what I want."

"Okay, then." I reached for his hand. "I need a little time to see what I want."

"I'll take you home." He inhaled, started to say something else, and then shook his head. Tyler opened my car door, ushered me in and drove me home without another word.

CHAPTER FIFTEEN

*T*he cutting board almost dropped to the floor as two little ones ambushed me in the kitchen. I quickly shuttled the shaved Brussels sprouts over to the island as the kids ran circles around it, jostling me in the process. One minute I was preparing the Carlyles' dinner in quiet calm, and the next, giggling, scurrying children were overtaking my workspace. They were cute, but the kitchen was no place for them to be playing.

A little hand grabbed the hem of my chef jacket and used it to bound faster down the length of the island. Just as they were about to round the corner for the third lap, their father entered the kitchen.

"Jayce! Caleb!" Grand shouted. The boys instantly stopped running, the younger one bumping into his older brother. "You're not outside. Jayce, take your brother and go find your coloring books. And no running."

The kids shuffled out of the room. I stifled a smile.

"I apologize if they got in your way. They can be rambunctious at times," he offered.

"I wish I had half of their energy."

"They spent the weekend here with their grandparents. I'm sure my mother was overly lenient with them."

"I've heard it's the grandparents' role to undermine the authority of the parents."

He sat down at the island. "That may be true, but when they get home, I'll get them back in line. Again, I'm sorry if they disturbed you."

"It's fine. They were only here a split-second before you arrived."

"I certainly don't want them distracting you from your task. Dinner was remarkable last week."

"Thank you." Just when I thought he wasn't impressed.

"My mother mentioned she hired a chef for the occasion, but you elevated my expectations for Sunday dinner. She didn't need to convince me to be here this week."

I glanced up from my cutting board. "That should make your mother quite happy."

A husky laugh flowed from him. "What's on the menu for this evening?"

"Butterflied Cornish hens, pumpkin gratin, warm Brussels sprouts slaw, and a cranberry sage wild rice."

"Mmm. I'm not sure I can wait until dinner. I may need a sample."

I laughed and continued with my preparations.

"Is that a no?" he asked.

"You're serious?"

"Would it make me seem less impatient if I say I skipped lunch?"

"I thought you were kidding."

"Does this look like the face of a man that would joke about food?"

I studied his face. He tried to remove all hints of teasing from his visage. I noticed that he looked most like his father out of all the sons. What really stood out were his chestnut-colored eyes. Deep and intense.

"I suppose you can try something." I went over to the stove and removed the lid from the pot of steaming rice. The earthy scent of sage wafted in the air. Dipping a spoon into the pot, I scooped out a bit of the savory blend and handed it to Grand.

"Now that's good," he said, chewing. "Your husband must love you."

"I'm not married." I resumed working on the slaw.

"Stunning, single, and you can cook… You're a triple threat. It's hard to believe no one has given you their last name."

"I guess it's a good thing I already have one."

He chuckled. "And you have a sense of humor."

"Does that make me a quadruple threat?"

"I'm going to surmise that the reason you're not married is not due to a lack of offers. I think they haven't come from the right offeree."

"That's a bold assertion."

"No, it isn't. There's a certain type of woman where only a certain type of man will do," he pointedly replied.

"You think I'm one of those women?"

"I know you are."

"I'm sorry to refute your theory, but I don't subscribe to types."

"I doubt that. Whether he's powerful, wealthy, famous, intelligent, sensitive, well-endowed…there's a type."

I didn't bother to rebut. I had the Carlyles' dinner to finish and I wasn't going to let the conversation with Grand distract me. I whisked a stream of extra virgin olive oil into a bowl with fresh blood orange juice and herbs.

"My wife, Jayla," he continued, "is a perfect example of a woman with a precise type. She wanted the best and she got it."

I stopped whisking and waited for some sort of indication that he was kidding. He nonchalantly shrugged his shoulders.

"Wow, okay," I said.

"I'm just saying my wife has no complaints. I make sure she wants for nothing. In fact, she's out of town right now at a spa in Arizona."

"Sounds wonderful."

"That's why the boys stayed here for the weekend. The kids

keep her busy. I understand she needs time for herself every once in a while."

"We all do."

I couldn't remember the last vacation I had taken. It was tough for me to leave my clients without services for any length of time. I could probably manage a week; two would be difficult. I had hinted to Tyler on more than one occasion that I wanted us to take a trip together. No plans were ever made, so I had to assume that he just wasn't interested. Yet another reason a break was justified.

"With Jayla out of town and the boys here with my parents, I had two days of peace and quiet at home. Just me…in my big bed… all alone."

Something in the tone of his voice made me not want to look up at him.

"What do we have here?" Hutton strolled in with a smirk on his face.

"You're early," Grand said to his brother.

"So are you," Hutton replied.

"My sons have been with their grandparents all weekend. I came early to relieve them."

Hutton took up a position at the end of the island. "That's convenient."

"I'm surprised you're here two weeks in a row. You're usually preoccupied with all sorts of diversions on the weekend."

"Diversions?" Hutton chuckled. "My weekends are an extension of my work week. Dinner with high-profile clients, exclusive events, decorating my new house."

"Precisely. Sounds like a hell of a lot of socializing."

"Our firm's success with high net-worth individuals and growth of the division is a result of my socializing. Sometimes my business takes me to where the action's at."

"You do love a party. We know why Dad entrusted the institutional investors to me."

Hutton scowled. "Yeah, we know why. The institutional investors are more comfortable with the stuffy type. "

"They're comfortable with me because I'll be Dad's successor," Grand retorted.

"That hasn't been decided."

"Not yet, but it's only a matter of time before Dad makes it official."

I looked from one brother to the next, unsure of why their discussion was transpiring in front of me. I cleared my throat and interjected. "Perhaps I should put both of you to work since you're in the kitchen with me."

Hutton stopped glaring at Grand and directed his attention toward me for the first time since he entered the room. "You don't want us tampering with your food."

"Speak for yourself. I'm an excellent cook," Grand chimed in.

"Is that what your wife tells you?" Hutton asked.

It became clear that it didn't take much to get the two of them going.

"I don't need her to tell me. It's a fact. You, on the other hand, need that type of validation from the women in your life."

"Get outta here," Hutton said, with a dismissive wave of the hand.

"It's true. You've been that way since we were kids."

"I don't need any woman to validate anything I do. I know I'm successful. I know I drive nice cars, expensive cars. I have a house and a condo. And, a few more toys that I won't even mention."

"What's your point, Hutton? We both have nice things."

"My point is I validate myself with what I've accomplished and what I have."

"Flaunt is more accurate," Grand replied cynically.

"You think I flaunt what I have?"

"It's all a part of your persona. But let me give you some advice, little brother. Any woman worth her salt won't be impressed or swayed by your flossing. Isn't that right, Riley?"

I wanted to continue to shred the smoked gouda cheese for the pumpkin gratin and pretend like I didn't hear the question. However, there was no way I could act as if I hadn't been listening to the entire discussion. "You want to know if I'm impressed by material things?" I asked.

"Let me clarify," Grand said. "Do men that flaunt their wealth impress or appeal to you?"

"Not particularly." I was being honest. That didn't mean that I wouldn't date a wealthy man. It simply meant that the wealth would not be the factor that won me over. There were way too many other qualities that were important to me.

"Since we're soliciting Riley's opinion, I have a question of my own. How do you feel about married men that drive family cars trying to chat up beautiful women?"

I shrugged my shoulders, declining to answer. This was personal, between brothers, and I wasn't going to get involved.

"I drive a family car? Is that what you're implying?"

"I didn't mention you. I asked Riley what she thinks of married men who fit that criteria. If that's not you…"

"Riley, you have to excuse my younger brother. He can be crass at times. I would have posed the question differently. May I?"

"Am I going to regret it if I say yes?" I asked hesitantly.

He shook his head. "No. I'm rephrasing Hutton's question. What type of man do you find attractive?"

Hutton replied before I had a chance. "Are you asking for my benefit? Because I can pose my own questions."

"I felt your original question lacked direction," Grand said.

"My question was extremely direct and specific."

"Grand, I believe we addressed this earlier. You disagreed, but I don't have a type." I reiterated my position hoping to put an end to the awkward posturing. "The man that I find attractive will have unique characteristics that call to me. It's that simple."

"I can respect that," Hutton said.

Jayce bolted into the kitchen, running up to his father. "Daddy, Caleb broke Grandma's statue."

"Her statue?"

"The lady by the front door. He was hiding behind it and it fell over."

"The African statue of the woman holding the basket over her head?"

"Yes!" Jayce shouted excitedly.

Grand stood grabbing Jayce by the hand. "Both of you are begging for a spanking."

"I didn't do it, Daddy!"

"Caleb was hiding from someone, right?"

"Yes," Jayce replied, his voice quivering.

"I better go check the damage," Grand said to Hutton and me.

"Good idea. Go tend to your kids and leave the single people to talk."

Miriam stormed into the kitchen. "Everybody out of the kitchen! Leave Riley alone and let her finish dinner."

I smiled at Mrs. Carlyle and carried the baking dish of pumpkin gratin to the oven. A wave of heat washed over me and I realized it was already quite hot in the kitchen.

CHAPTER SIXTEEN

he Carlyles were peering down at their plates as I described the main course. I explained the preparation for the butter-flied hens, even down to the brining method. I used an aromatic mixture of white wine, lemon, rosemary and thyme. It was probably more detail than Miriam was looking for, however, she asked me to present the dishes and that was what I intended to do. I touched on how the pumpkin gratin included cubed and pureed pumpkin and a blend of cream and two cheeses.

"You may taste a hint of cloves in the warm Brussels sprouts slaw. It's a spiced blood orange vinaigrette. There's also toasted almond slivers in the slaw. Dutton, due to your nut allergy, I didn't add any almonds to your plate."

Dutton sheepishly nodded. I shared with them how I prepared the wild rice and told them to enjoy the meal. I was about to leave the dining room when Grand called my name. I turned back, waiting for his comment.

"Is it okay for the boys to eat the Cornish hen since it was cooked in wine?" Caleb and Jayce had already torn into the food on their plates.

"Absolutely. Although wine was used in the brine, the ratio of wine to the water in the brine was minimal. Also, any alcohol would have cooked off in the roasting process. I did use wine in the herb au jus, but I didn't put any on the children's plates."

Hutton, eyes boring into me, immediately followed up with a question of his own. "How do you determine which flavors to marry together?"

His emphasis on the word "marry" gave me pause. I noticed Grand cut his eyes at Hutton. "Well, as a chef you tend to know what herbs or spices pair well with one another. I'm also a lover of food and I experiment quite a bit with different ingredients. When I'm cooking, I seek to create a harmonious, yet vibrant, balance on the plate and the palate."

"I've never seen my sons take such an interest in food," Miriam said. "Riley, did you use pumpkin puree from the can for the gratin?"

"All the ingredients on your plates are fresh. I pureed the pumpkin myself. Nothing frozen or canned."

"Maybe now Preston understands why I tell him to stop eating so much processed food. Fresh is best," she said.

Louis, who had been quietly eating while his family peppered me with questions, commented to his wife that this was what he called Sunday dinner.

Preston raised his fork as if he needed to be called on. "My compliments to the chef."

"Thank you. Please, enjoy your meal before it gets cold."

I ruminated on what transpired in the dining room as I headed back to the kitchen. The first Sunday dinner I prepared for the Carlyles was met with awkward indifference. Tonight, they were actively engaged. All except Dutton. The quiet one. The twin that seemed to be absorbed in his thoughts.

The tension between Grand and Hutton was palpable. I assumed it was a classic case of sibling rivalry. Maybe it was too much testosterone in one family. I couldn't know for sure. I did observe that Preston appeared to be a free spirit, disengaged from brotherly discord. I was still puzzled that Miriam actually wanted me to be privy to her family's private dinners. I mused that I needed to be rich to understand. Rich folks were accustomed to others providing services for them. It wasn't an imposition to have someone in their home witnessing what happens in their lives. It wasn't a lifestyle I wanted. I relished my privacy. I was keen to let others know only what I wanted them to know and see only what I wanted them to see.

My home was a place of solace. I didn't like strangers in my space and I wasn't big on entertaining, at least not in my house. I was the absolute opposite of my clients. They gave me complete access to their homes, some providing me with keys to allow me to come in to prepare their meals for the week. I knew some personal chefs that let curiosity get the best of them and would explore the homes of their clients. That was not my style. I'd let myself in, go to the kitchen and do my job. That was it. No searching to see what type of people they were, what type of possessions they owned, none of that. I earned my clients' trust by respecting their homes and being a fine chef. In this day and age of technology, I wouldn't dare take the risk of being recorded violating the privacy of a client's home. It wasn't worth my reputation or my money.

The Carlyles had been presented with their dessert and I was packing up my tools of the trade. As I slid my knives into their case, I heard footfalls coming down the hall toward the kitchen. I watched the doorway waiting to see which Carlyle was going to enter with some sort of finicky request.

Preston eased into the room. "Are you getting ready to leave?"

"I'm just about finished in here," I replied.

"I can walk you to your car when you're ready."

"Thanks, but that won't be necessary." I barely looked up from rolling up my knife case. I was sure I could make it to the drive-way without an escort.

"Let me. I can carry your supplies and I want to show you some-thing."

I reluctantly shrugged. "Okay. Can you grab that bag on the chair over there?"

Preston did as I asked and then led me from the kitchen. We didn't walk toward the front door. He headed in the opposite direction. I followed him wondering what the heck he was about to show me. He guided me through a sunroom. Golden rays of late-day sun streamed into the glass-enclosed oasis. I noted the lush white furniture and textured rug, vases filled with bountiful bouquets of white flowers, freestanding art pieces in gold and silver tones, and a floor-to-ceiling bookshelf with tomes filling every inch. This was a room for spending lazy Sundays. I envisioned myself curled up on the chaise lounge, a good book in hand, with a cup of steam-ing café au lait and delicate madeleines on a tray beside me.

Preston opened a sliding glass door and we stepped onto a patio of ornate pavers stones. Sectionals, tables and patio heaters were arranged in cozy clusters. At the edge of the patio, the stones narrowed to a path leading into a garden.

"This way," Preston said, motioning toward the path.

I walked beside him, taking in plants and flowers that looked more tropical than what I was accustomed to seeing in Georgia. "Someone has quite the green thumb," I commented.

"My mother loves her gardens."

"This is beautiful." Plants with large green leaves were on either side of the path, landscaped shrubs and flower beds sprinkled in between.

"We've had the same landscaper for over twenty years. At least that's what I've been told."

"How old are you?" I asked.

"Twenty-four."

"You're the baby of the bunch."

He stopped walking and peered down at me. "I'm the youngest, yes, but far from a baby."

"I stand corrected."

He flashed a smile at me and resumed walking. The stone walkway ended and we ventured onto the manicured grass. "I'm sure you can imagine how often someone calls me the baby. When you have three older brothers, that's not something a man wants to hear from a beautiful woman."

"So I hit a nerve?"

"You could say that. I'm the Carlyle son that everyone is still waiting on."

"What do you mean?"

"Well, Grand and Hutton both work at the firm with my dad. Grand is my father's right-hand man. He's settled with a wife and two kids. Hutton has been instrumental in making connections and growing the business. Even Dutton is successful in his own right. He may not be a part of the family business like the other two, but he's making a name for himself in the academic world. He's published white papers and research, and I believe he's working on his second book."

I recalled my prior conversation with Dutton about his anthropological studies. He hadn't mentioned that he was a published scholar.

"What does the youngest Carlyle do for a living?"

"I'm what you'd call a student of life."

"Student of life?"

"Don't give me that look."

I chuckled. "What look?"

"It basically said you think I'm bullshitting."

"I assure you that's not what I was thinking."

"If you were, you wouldn't be the first. Not everyone can relate to my philosophy. I have a different approach than my brothers."

"I would imagine that's a good thing."

"It is to me. I do things my own way. I just graduated with my bachelor's degree a few months ago. I could've finished in four years. It took me six because I wanted to explore a variety of courses. I studied whatever interested me regardless of whether it was in my major. I graduated summa cum laude from an ivy league institution with a degree in finance and knowledge of so much more."

"Does the finance degree mean you'll be joining the family firm?"

"Is that what my family is expecting? Definitely. Will I do it? I don't know. It's tough for me to envision a future where I'm doing the same thing day in and day out. As a student of life, I want to continually explore what's different and new. I need experiences that will continue to shape the constructs of my world. Following in my father's footsteps may not afford me that lifestyle."

We veered toward rows of trees ahead of us. I interrupted his stream of consciousness. "Your family has its own orchard?" I inquired.

He nodded. "Peaches directly in front of us and apples a little further to the right."

"Amazing."

"I watched you tonight at dinner," he commented reflectively. "When you were explaining what we were eating and how it was prepared, I could see your passion. You love what you do. You took the time to tell Jayce that Cornish hens are just chickens and if he likes chicken, then he'll love hen. I could tell that you know you're doing what you're meant to do in life… I'm still searching. That's why I consider myself a student. I'm going to keep living the life

I want to lead until I'm satisfied I'm doing what I'm meant to do."

I stood beneath the branches of a peach tree. Ripe fruit was hanging from the limbs. I sniffed the air. "I love that smell."

"This was what I wanted to show you."

"Really, why?"

"There's something about you that inspires me. Most definitely your passion, however, you have a creative spirit and I'm drawn to that. If I pick some peaches next week, will you use them to create a dessert?"

"I don't see why not."

Preston reached up and plucked a peach from the tree. "For inspiration," he said, handing it to me.

He walked me to my car as twilight fell over the orchard.

I took my tote bag from him and placed it in the backseat. "Thanks for the impromptu tour."

"Thank you. I can't wait until dinner next week."

CHAPTER SEVENTEEN

Jill Scott blared through the speakers as I pushed the vacuum cleaner across the carpet in the family room. I only had one client in the morning and had the rest of the day to myself. There was nothing I enjoyed more than a single client day in the middle of the week. After I finished up at my client's house, I ran a few errands and then returned home to do a little light cleaning.

My playlist ended. I turned off the vacuum and went to the docking station to select another artist. My telephone rang. I checked the caller ID and I didn't recognize the number.

I answered with an exasperated, "Hello."

"Riley?" a male voice ventured.

"Yes?"

"This is Hutton Carlyle. I hope you don't mind I got your number from my mother."

"Not at all." I propped the phone between my ear and shoulder and sat down on the sofa. "How can I help you?"

He cleared his throat. "We're having a lunch meeting here at the firm in two days. I would like for you to cater the luncheon."

"In two days—"

"I realize it's short notice."

"How many people will be attending the lunch?"

"It's for the staff of one of my divisions. Twenty people maximum."

"What did you have in mind for the menu?"

"I would leave that completely up to you."

"What sort of budget are you working with?"

"Again, that's not an issue for me. Whatever it costs, I'll pay."

It was definitely short notice and I did have clients that I would have to shift in order to accommodate Hutton's request. I wanted to say no based on those factors, however, I knew I could make it happen. Catering a lunch for twenty people was manageable enough.

"I think I can do it. The lunch will have to be buffet style. Is that all right?"

"That's fine."

"I'll create the specific menu, but I think a salad to start, chicken as a main course with two vegetable options, and either a rice or potato side should be sufficient. I'll also provide dessert. Does that sound like what you had in mind?"

"Works for me. I'll have my secretary contact you with the time and location. Once you have the menu finalized, you can provide her with those details."

We ended our call and I propped my feet up on the coffee table. The Carlyles apparently had money to burn. They wanted my services and were willing to make it worth my while. I was fine with the arrangement and was going to take full advantage of the opportunities. I had catered a few corporate events in the past. If it made fiscal sense and worked with my schedule, I wasn't opposed to accepting an occasional catering gig.

I wasn't expecting a call from Hutton with the last-minute offer. It would make sense that they already had a company that typically provided them with catering services. With the short notice, perhaps they were unavailable. Was it conceivable that he reached out to me because my services were just that impressive? I wasn't certain, but I would ensure that the luncheon was a scrumptious success. I mulled over the menu and had a relatively good idea of what to prepare. I realized I needed to reserve a kitchen to prepare the food for the lunch. I usually rented a kitchen share to prep and cook food when catering events. It's a professional kitchen space, with commercial restaurant equipment from stoves, grills, refrigerators, and counter space that some caterers don't have in their home kitchens. As personal chef that catered events once in a while, it was perfect for me.

I booked the space for the morning of the luncheon and started working on my shopping list. This was what it was all about. I basked in the freedom of running my own business, setting my own hours and calling my own shots. I could remember when I first decided to work for myself. I was nervous and scared. I wondered if I would be able to make a decent living. My biggest fear was that I wouldn't be able to pay my bills. My dad always taught my sister and I how important it was to be able to provide for yourself and not need any handouts. I was frightened that even though he was no longer here with us, that I would disappoint him in some way. That he would be looking down on me and see his baby girl struggling to make a living. Thankfully, that was not my path. I worked hard, established excellent contacts and built my business from the ground up. I was proud of what I had done all on my own. It was time for me to begin thinking about growth. I had been accepting more catering jobs as of late. I needed to seriously consider starting a catering company. I could get a commercial space, hire some employees and build my brand. I was aware there were advantages and disadvantages that would come along with running a business and being the boss of a team of people. I just had to figure out if the pros outweighed the cons.

In that moment, I declared to myself that I would officially make an important life decision in the coming weeks.

CHAPTER EIGHTEEN

*T*he executive dining room at Loucar Asset Management had already been set when I arrived. Hutton's secretary sent a team of staffers to assist me with carrying the food trays inside. The tables were draped with crisp white linens with the place settings atop. Bottles of sparkling water were in the center of each table, along with pitchers of iced tea. While finalizing the details for the lunch, Hutton's secretary had informed me that the firm had plates, flatware, stemware, chafing dishes, serving platters and bowls. I told her what I would need, and she had all of the items ready for me on the buffet table. I transferred the chicken paillard, risotto, asparagus and haricot vert from the trays to the chafing dishes. I was placing the rolls in a cloth napkin-lined basket when Hutton strode into the room.

"Good afternoon, Ms. Ryan."

"Riley is fine, Hutton. Or should I call you Mr. Carlyle since we're at your place of business?" I laughed lightheartedly.

"I like hearing you say my name too much to make you call me Mr. Carlyle."

"I would think you'd want to be sure I'm speaking to you and not your father."

"That too." He grinned at me as he approached the buffet table.

I rolled the top back on the chafing dishes and ran down each item. "I kept the menu fairly light and simple."

"It all looks delicious, especially you without your chef coat."

I turned and faced him. In my four-inch pumps I was a couple of inches shy of what appeared to be his six feet two inches. "Occasionally, we chefs do take off the coat." I was in a tailored blazer and skirt, a professional chic ensemble that ended just above the knee.

He raised his hands in a conciliatory gesture. "Don't take that to mean you're not striking in your chef's attire—"

"I get it," I said, cutting him off. "Thank you."

Hutton's team began spilling into the room and taking their seats at the rounds. He went to the front of the room to kick off the meeting. While he reviewed future projections and past results, I tended to the food, stirring where necessary, placing serving utensils in front of each dish, salad dressing in the decanters, and plated the mini Bundt cakes for dessert.

I listened to Hutton motivate his team and encourage them to take a more proactive approach with their client relations. He wanted each of them to schedule meetings with their clients to review their portfolios and see what additional investment opportunities existed. He focused on strategies for growth and mentioned more than one time that he didn't accept the word "no" for an answer, and it should not be a part of his team's vocabulary. While the meeting was meant to charge and inspire, the underlying message was loud and clear. Falling short of the team goal was not an option. Hutton wrapped up the presentation portion of the meeting and told everyone to enjoy lunch. They descended on the buffet filling their plates, some multiple times. He moved from table to table, chatting with his team as they dined.

An hour later, after his team filed out of the room, he grabbed a plate and came over to the buffet. I took it from him, added a little of everything to the plate, and handed it back.

He sat at one of the tables. "Join me?"

I took two of the Bundt cakes, one for him and the other for me, and sat in the chair next to him. "Good meeting?"

"Time will tell. In about a month I'll circle back on their progress."

"And my services…did they meet your requirements?"

"Exceeded."

I smiled. "I was wondering why you called me to cater this lunch. Don't you have a caterer to handle these affairs for you?"

"We do."

"Were they unavailable?"

"I didn't check."

"Was my rate comparable to what you're accustomed to paying your regular caterer?"

"I didn't check that either."

"You don't know how much you're paying for this lunch?"

"I don't care. It exceeded my expectations and I got to see you."

I shook my head. "Tell me something. How does someone that's expected to be fiscally responsible pay for a luncheon without knowing the cost?"

"I'm an expert at making sound investments. I would consider hiring you to be a great one."

"How so?"

"For one reason, you've provided the food for my father's retirement party and you're cooking for my family every week. Why wouldn't I want to have you cater events at the firm? Thus far every meal has been superb, including this one. I'd call that a great investment."

"I see your point."

"Another reason is that I'm convinced going out with you on Saturday night would be an excellent investment of my time."

"Is that your way of asking me out on a date?"

"If you have to ask, then I need to rephrase that. Riley, if you're available, I would like to take you out on Saturday evening. I guarantee you'll have a great time."

I had to admit Hutton's second attempt was better than the first. That still didn't change the fact that it probably wasn't a good idea. I had a business relationship with his family that I was not willing to jeopardize over his guarantee. "I appreciate the invitation, but I don't date my clients."

"My parents and Loucar Asset Management are your clients. I haven't hired you personally."

"I suppose you have me on a technicality."

"No, it's factuality. Let me show you a nice evening."

I forced myself to meet the intense stare of a man that doesn't accept no for an answer. "All right, I'll go out with you."

I could see the victory in his eyes.

"I'll pick you up at eight. Wear something sexy." He ate a forkful of cake and pushed back from the table, standing up to leave. "Delicious. Just as I expected."

"I'm glad you're pleased."

"My assistant will take care of clearing away the food. Enjoy the rest of your day." Hutton was making his way out of the dining room as Grand entered. "See you on Saturday," he called over his shoulder.

Grand stopped in his tracks and watched his brother leave. I got up from the table and began to collect my personal effects.

"I heard there was a luncheon in the dining room," he said. "What I didn't know was that you were catering it."

"Apparently my catering services are in demand," I replied, with a nonchalant shrug and a hint of whimsicality in my voice.

"Am I too late?"

"There's plenty. Help yourself."

"I plan to." Grand smiled and went for the food.

I wished him a good day and left to enjoy the rest of mine.

CHAPTER NINETEEN

My eagle pose needed work. I was unsteady. Aja was unwavering. She was a regular. I wasn't. I liked taking a yoga class every once in a while. She took classes a few times a week. It definitely showed. The instructor lauded her. She loathed me. Well, maybe not loathed, but I could tell she wished I wasn't taking up space in her class. My extended triangle was much better. Both feet had contact with the ground and required much less concentration on my part.

I whispered to Aja, "I have a date tonight."

The surprise on her face matched her tone. "What? With who?"

The instructor shushed us and told us to lie down for the final pose of the class, the corpse pose. I stayed quiet until the end. As soon as the instructor uttered Namaste, Aja sprung up crossing her legs on her mat. "Who do you have a date with?" she repeated.

"I'm going out with Hutton Carlyle."

"Now which one is that again?"

"One of the twins."

"Tell me more…"

"I don't even know if I should be going out with him."

"It's a little late for that."

"I don't have much to share. He's kind of arrogant. During our first conversation, it was as if he wanted to prove that he knew as much about food as I did. Which, of course, he doesn't. He may be a little entitled, but I'm not sure about that yet."

"And you agreed to go out with this guy?"

"He's handsome as hell, though. Six-two with cocoa-brown skin. Close haircut. There's something beneath all of that arrogance. I think I like that he's so self-assured. He's just so different than... never mind."

"You can say it."

"He's nothing like Tyler. It was almost like he demanded I go out with him and knew I would say yes."

"You're right that doesn't sound like Tyler."

"Please. Tyler could not care less if we went anywhere."

"Where is Hutton Carlyle taking you?"

"He didn't say. Maybe this new restaurant he mentioned to me when we met. The only thing he told me was the time he was coming to get me and for me to dress sexy."

"I guess you better look hot." Aja dramatically fanned herself.

"Am I crazy to go out with my client's son?"

"After all the complaints I heard about Tyler not ever taking you anywhere, do you really think I would discourage you from going out with a very rich, very fine, very rich man? I think you should go, have a great time, and not think about whether or not you're being crazy."

"You realize you said rich twice?"

"Rich, rich, rich! Now I said it three times. No, make that five." Aja laughed.

"I'm not going out with Hutton because he's rich."

"I know, Riley. Please don't let my jokes discourage you from having a good time. It's just a date. Something you obviously need in your life right now."

Maybe it was that simple. I had been craving a normal dating life. A handsome man asked me out and I said yes. I didn't have to make a big deal about it or start dissecting why I was going or whether I should be going. Hutton and I were going out for an evening of guaranteed fun, according to him, and that's what I wanted. Aja was right. I had been complaining for some time about Tyler not meeting my needs. It wouldn't make sense to complain about finally getting to do what I wanted to do. I was still young. I did not want to live my life sitting on the sidelines. Not when there is so much to do and so much life to live. We only get one life. I wasn't planning to live mine with regret. Hutton and I were adults and he was correct; I did work for Miriam and Louis, not him. It would be up to me to set boundaries and maintain a certain level of professionalism in my interactions with him. In my mind, tonight would be all about having a good time. I wasn't looking for anything serious and I would venture to say, neither was Hutton. His assertiveness made me change my mind. I'd leave it to him to convince me that I'd made the right decision by accepting his invite. A small current of excitement passed through me. I was going on a date with someone new. I didn't know where I was going or what we were doing and that bit of mystery was exciting.

I started to roll up my mat. "Do you think I should buy something new for tonight? I want to make sure that no matter where he takes me, I stun."

"I'm positive you have plenty of options in your closet. You may not have been going out much, but you shopped like you were. Didn't you buy a few new dresses about a month ago?"

"I did, but I don't think they're appropriate for tonight. It couldn't hurt for us to go to Phipps Plaza…"

"You don't have to twist my arm to go shopping. Let's go find you something sexy to wear."

CHAPTER TWENTY

I was having second thoughts about letting Hutton pick me up from my home. I heard the growl of an engine emanating from my driveway and peered out of the window. Hutton was climbing out of a flashy, white sports car. I waited for the doorbell to ring and then grabbed my clutch bag. There was no backing out now.

I opened the door and stepped outside. He grinned, checking out my white backless, draped mini dress. I followed his instructions and was giving him not only sexy, but fierce with my scarlet lips. I had no idea I'd be matching what I could now see was his Ferrari. He placed a firm hand on my bare back and led me to the car. I eased into the supple leather seat and then watched his stride as he walked to the driver side. I may have matched the exterior. but his camel-colored ensemble matched the interior. The slim fit suit and shirt with no tie look was working for him. It showcased his well-defined musculature without being too tight.

Hutton unbuttoned his jacket and got into the car. His cologne, a mix of woody and citrusy notes, laced the air when he closed the door. It was a fitting scent for the man sitting behind the wheel of a powerful car. We regarded one another—his eyes traveling the length of my legs, mine, watching him explore them.

"You didn't disappoint," he said.

"I never do."

He smirked at me and revved the engine. "Neither do I." We backed out of my driveway and sped down the street.

"That was a stop sign," I commented, as he blew past the corner.

"Four-way."

I checked that my seat belt was firmly secure. "Where are you speeding us to this evening?"

"A private rooftop party in Buckhead."

"It would be nice to get there in one piece."

"Rest assured that beautiful body will arrive without a single scratch."

I kept my eyes on the road despite his so-called reassurance. "I thought you might have been taking me to Cezoi since you spoke so highly of the place."

"You would enjoy dinner at Cezoi, but I guaranteed you a great time. A few of the Falcons are hosting tonight's event. There'll be plenty of fine food, drinks, music and people."

"The football players hosting the party, are they clients of yours?"

"Yes."

"Is it customary for you to spend time socially with clients?"

"Are you trying to ask me if I always party with my clients?"

I laughed at his frankness. "I guess so."

"People have to be able to trust and relate to you in order for them to part with the amount of money I get them to invest. So, yes, I develop those relationships on and off the clock. You and I don't share the same views on client boundaries."

"My boundaries involve dating clients," I said.

"I recall."

"I assume you don't see anything wrong with it."

"I'll say this. If you were my client," he glanced in my direction, "I'd be available to you around the clock."

I matched his roguish smile with a mischievous one of my own. "To take care of my money, of course?"

"I can take care of all your assets."

"I'll keep that in mind."

Hutton rocketed across lanes on Interstate 85 toward the GA-400 exit ramp to Buckhead. I gripped my clutch as the car accelerated. He drove his Ferrari like a man unconcerned with the speed limit or the risk of being stopped by the police.

We pulled up to a soaring high-rise hotel. A valet was approaching the car before we came to a complete stop. He opened my door and offered me his hand. Hutton left the car idling and told him to park where he could leave an empty space on both sides. I thought he was kidding, but his stern expression told me otherwise. He pressed a bill in the valet's hand and walked to me. Again, I felt the warmth and strength of his touch on my skin. We entered the hotel lobby. I subtly took it all in. It was a grandiose sight to behold. Marble floors, elaborate lighting and sharply dressed staff at the ready, presented quite an image. I caught a glimpse of our reflection in a smoked mirror on the wall as we proceeded to the elevator. I did a double-take. Damn, we looked good together. His energy vibrated through me. We stepped onto the elevator, his hand leaving my back as he pressed the button for the rooftop. The door closed and he turned to me.

"You're gorgeous. I knew you would be but, that dress…"

"Thank you."

"I'll have to keep you close tonight."

The elevator door opened up to the rooftop. I captured glimpses of the action as we made our way through the assemblage. There were clusters of people chatting and laughing, others drinking, some dancing to the pumping music, and very few off to themselves watching everyone else. It looked like a scene from a music video—women in their shortest dresses and highest heels—men in a range of styles from jeans and blazers, to suits and ties. Hutton and I received a number of stares as we moved through the event.

I tucked one side of my bob behind my ear and made sure my gait was runway worthy. If they wanted to watch, I'd give them a show.

Hutton advanced on a group of women seated on a circular sectional. In the midst of them was a solitary man. He was talking and they seemed to cling to every word. There was more grinning, hair tossing and leg crossing and uncrossing than should be permitted at one time. He spotted Hutton and extracted himself from his band of admirers.

The two men clasped hands and brought it in for a brotherly greeting. Hutton introduced his client and host as a star running back for the Falcons. He rattled off some of his stats as if I knew what he was talking about. I wasn't a huge football fan and didn't know much about the game or its players. His client asked the women he was just entertaining to clear out of his VIP section and go mingle. Some happily obeyed; others shot not-so-friendly glances in my direction as they stalked away. He motioned for us to sit on the vacated sectional. Hutton and his client fell into an easy discussion about the football season and where he thought the team was headed. I took in my surroundings. The number of women by far outweighed the men. I determined which men were probably athletes by the amount of ladies hovering around them vying for attention. These were gorgeous women. I wondered if they were looking for a meal ticket or if they had something to bring to the table. How many of them had successful careers of their own and did it even matter to the athletes they were pursuing? I wasn't judging. I was curious.

Hutton squeezed my leg. I was so lost in my thoughts I hadn't heard his client ask if I'd like some champagne. He was off to mix it up with his guests, but said he would have a bottle sent over.

"This is nice," I commented.

"You haven't seen anything yet. It's just getting started."

"So this is a regular Saturday night for you?"

"There's no such thing as a regular Saturday night."

"You really mean that, don't you?"

"I always say what I mean."

I paused, taking a moment to phrase my next question properly. "A low-key evening isn't a part of your repertoire?"

"I can do low-key, my version of it."

"For example?"

"You and I taking a private jet to New York for a quiet dinner at one of the finest restaurants in Manhattan."

"That's hardly low-key."

"It is for me."

"Dinner at home, followed by dessert and a movie on the couch. That's low-key," I asserted.

He swept a strand of hair from my face. "If you're the dessert on the couch in that scenario, I'm sold."

"I'm not."

"That's a shame. I would eat every sweet drop."

I met his gaze. Again, his eyes unabashedly traveled the length of my body. I didn't know what it was about him, but he made something inside of me stir. I found myself eyeing his lips, waiting for him to say something else. I became acutely aware of the intoxicating bassline thumping from the speakers. It was rhythmic, almost tribal. It made me want to move…with him. A server arrived with a bucket of champagne and a tray of flutes. As she poured, Hutton kept his eyes on me. I laughed quietly and shook my head. His arrogance clung to him like a badge. I handed him a glass, tapped mine against his and took a sip. He drank his champagne and poured another glass. "I can do the same to you," he said.

"What's that?" I asked.

"I can drink you down."

"Is that so?" I toyed with my flute.

"Yeah, it is."

"Maybe you should stick to the champagne."

A deep rumble of laughter emanated from Hutton. "I will…for now."

A few more people trickled into our section. We discontinued our private discussion and exchanged pleasantries with the new arrivals. As customary in Atlanta, we ran down our resumes—who we were and what we did for a living. We were an eclectic bunch. An attorney, choreographer, money manager, chef, and a publicist, all gathered around cocktails, with good food circulating, and the perfect soundtrack to accompany our conversation. Somehow we began a dialogue on the plight of the black professional. We compared stories of what it takes to be successful in our industries, some of the struggles and our accomplishments. I took note that whereas Hutton had many successes, he didn't mention one single roadblock.

At some point during the evening, the choreographer was out of her seat showing us routines she had choreographed for some of the hottest performers on the scene. When she started twerking, the lawyer made it rain. The music had gotten louder and the drinks were flowing faster. The party had taken on a different energy. Hutton and I were sitting close to each other, his hand on my thigh. He leaned over and kissed my shoulder. A subtle smile graced my face.

He whispered in my ear. "I could really put a smile on your face."

I pressed my cheek against his so I could whisper back to him. "How do you intend to do that?"

"Let me kiss you where it counts."

"Tell me, where does it count?"

"Let me show you." He discreetly inched his hand to my upper thigh, stopping at the hem of my dress. "I have a suite here at the hotel. We can go down to my suite and I'll show you."

"I don't think so."

"Why not?"

"I just—"

"You don't want to feel these lips," he kissed my shoulder again, "on your pussy?"

I moved my head so I could look at him. There wasn't a trace of jocularity in his expression. "You're serious?"

"I told you I always say what I mean. You're beautiful, sexy as hell in that dress, and it's been driving me crazy all night. I want to taste you." He kissed my neck. "Let me lick you." His tongue flicked my earlobe. "I'll suck your clit and make you come."

My honeypot tingled. I took a deep breath and willed her to behave. "We can't."

Hutton stood and held out his hand. I sat watching him as if in slow motion, wondering what I was going to do. Watching him as if someone other than me had a decision to make. He looked a question at me.

I took his hand and let him coax me from the couch. "I'm not sleeping with you," I stated.

"You don't have to."

Hand in hand, we returned to the elevator, taking it one floor down. We walked a long corridor to a corner suite. Hutton took a door key from his wallet, inserted it in the slot and punched in an access code. He led me inside a grand foyer. I immediately realized calling this space a suite was an understatement. It ran the length of the corridor we had just traveled and further still in a perpendicular direction. There were two steps leading down to a well-appointed living room. The night sky glittered through the crystalline floor-to-ceiling windows.

"Make yourself comfortable," he said, heading down the stairs.

I removed my heels in the foyer and followed Hutton, my feet sinking into the plush carpeting in the living room. I sat on an overstuffed sofa facing the largest flat-screen television I had ever seen. He picked up a remote and pointed it toward a sound system in the wall. Soft music filled the room. He grabbed another remote and a panel of heavy drapes opened, exposing more windows. He moved about the space like he knew it well. He must have been one of those people that requested the same suite when staying at a hotel. I had to ask.

"You must stay here quite a bit. How many times have you requested the same suite?"

He seemed momentarily puzzled. "I think you misunderstood me. When I said I have a suite here, I didn't mean a reservation. I meant own."

"Oh…"

"Full disclosure. My family owns this hotel and this is our suite. Technically, it's more of an apartment, but we call it a suite."

"I see," I said, taking in my surroundings and the décor with new eyes. Now it made sense why he felt comfortable telling the valet exactly how to park his car.

"Can I get you something to drink?"

"What are you having?"

"Scotch."

"I'll stick with champagne."

"Coming right up."

I went over to the windows and looked down. The shine of headlights and red glow of tail lights illuminated the road. Hutton approached from behind, reaching around my body to hand me the glass. His chest ever so slightly brushed against my back. I brought the glass of nectar to my lips, drinking half of its contents. I could see him remove his jacket and toss it aside in the window reflection. I felt the gentle press of full lips on my neck. My head intuitively craned to the side. He palmed my stomach and snatched me to him. The firmness of his body molded against my own sent a shiver down my spine. His hand traveled downward. My mind raced. What was happening? What was I about to do? As he reached beneath my dress, my head lolled back, resting in the crook of his neck. The scent of his cologne wrapped around me like an intoxicating elixir. I breathed him in. He stroked me through my little black panties and my body responded.

"Is that a yes?" he asked.

"What's the question?" I exhaled.

"It hasn't changed."

"You want to taste me."

"Your panties are wet. You want me to taste you. Tell me what I want to hear."

"Yes…" I whispered.

He stuck a finger through the lace of my panties and yanked, ripping until they fell from my hips. I shuddered from the bruteness. He moved from behind and stood in between me and the window. He stared and I met the look.

"Can you get my drink from the bar?" he asked.

I looked over my shoulder and saw his tumbler set on the bar top across the room. I hesitated, feeling slightly self-conscious that my underwear were lying on the carpet and I wasn't in them. I smoothed my dress down as best I could with my champagne-free hand and went to retrieve the Scotch. I turned around to find Hutton sitting on the carpet with his back leaned against the window, legs outstretched. "Can I get you anything else?" I teased, trying to chase away my nerves.

"Put on your heels."

I backtracked to the foyer to slip into my shoes. I took a deep breath and crossed the room, handing him the Scotch. He took a drink and then set the glass on the floor next to him. "Come closer," he said, placing a hand on my calf. "Stand over me."

I stepped one leg over both of his, careful not to catch them with my heels. I looked down at him as I stood with my legs open, heels on either side of his upper thighs. He reached up and pushed my dress higher, exposing my honeypot. He reclined his head back against the window and swigged his Scotch. I was on display. With trembling hands, I tipped my glass and finished my drink. He removed it from my grasp and placed it on the floor, never diverting his gaze from me.

A moment passed. He leaned forward slightly and kissed the small strip of my Brazilian. Once. Twice. A third time. He gripped the backs of my thighs and worked his way down to my lips, turning his head to the side. His full lips planted exploratory kisses on mine, each one increasing in intensity. He pulled me closer, his tongue simultaneously breaching my folds. I heard myself draw a sharp breath. The very tip of his tongue glided along my most intimate place. Tasting, no, sampling my honey. He licked and it was with the full force of his oral utensil, firm and sure. His tongue covered me, enveloped me, and warmed my honey. He sucked me into his mouth, sucking as if savoring a favorite piece of candy. My breathing quickened. His tongue flicked across my clit. I tensed. Again, a rapid flit, and then another. He toyed with my sensitivity. My right leg shook. I reached out and steadied myself with one hand on the window. His tongue thrust upward. I jerked, caught off guard by the suddenness of him entering me. I looked down at him and his eyes were on me. Hutton's tongue twirled, drilling deeper into me. My honey started to drip. He lapped at my sweetness with fervor. I was holding back a murmur, fearful if I let even one escape, I wouldn't be able to stop more from coming.

Hutton moved his face away from my honeypot. "Turn around, Riley."

"Turn around?" My voice sounded husky, not like my own. The champagne and his oral skills had my head buzzing.

"Yes. Turn around, bend over and hold your ankles."

I did what he said. My hair swung forward as I peered at him through my spread legs. He took a gulp of his Scotch, spread my pussy with his fingers and plunged his tongue inside. Over and over he penetrated, his momentum building with each thrust. A moan escaped my throat. The sensation was too intense to stifle my pleasure. He echoed me. My eyes closed and my sense of balance wavered. I quickly let go of my ankles and caught myself, digging my fingertips into the carpet. He didn't stop his undulating exploration. Hutton twisted, probed, jabbed and sucked me until my juices dripped and I proclaimed I couldn't take any more.

Between the V of my legs, I saw a self-satisfied smile decorate his face as he licked his fingers. I slowly righted myself on unsteady legs. My head pounded slightly from being in a semi-upside-down position. I tugged on my dress, covering up what had already been explicitly seen.

Hutton chuckled into his glass. "You can't be feeling modest."

"Well…"

"You should be feeling audacious…exhilarated…definitely satiated. I know I delivered. Tell me I'm wrong."

I could tell him no such thing. He was damn right. My honeypot was throbbing. "I'm satisfied." I could have offered more, but I wouldn't allow myself to feed his arrogance.

He scoffed and drank the last of his Scotch. "You don't have to say another word. Your still-wet-pussy told me everything you're not saying."

I didn't want to engage him, but I refused to let Hutton have the upper hand. "Sometimes things are better left unsaid. You ate my pussy because I let you. Yes, you ate it well, but only because I allowed you to do what you kept asking to do. You got what you wanted. You should be the one feeling audacious, exhilarated and satiated."

An eyebrow raised. "Touché. Are you staying the night or am I taking you home?"

I retrieved my discarded panties. "I'm going to freshen up and you can take me home."

"One question. Are you glad you came?"

I smiled. "Touché."

CHAPTER TWENTY-ONE

My tote was slung over my shoulder and I was carrying my chef coat. Mrs. Carlyle was walking with me to the kitchen. She mentioned Melba had the day off and if I needed anything to ask her. She had just come home to meet me moments before I arrived. Mr. Carlyle was out golfing and would most likely be ravenous when he returned. I had nodded the entire distance from the front door to the kitchen. She was certainly chatty.

"I finally told my sorority sisters that I was done with the meeting. It wasn't over, but it was done for me because I needed to meet you. I was thinking about giving you a key, but that's probably unnecessary. Between Louis and the boys, I can make arrangements for someone to always be here when you arrive."

"Isn't Melba usually here?" I set my bag on a chair in the corner.

"Not always on the weekends. Melba has been with us a long time. She never married and doesn't have any children, but she's like family to us. Her mother is advancing in age and she tries to spend as much time with her as possible. I believe they're seeing a play today."

I carried my knives over to the island. A large bowl filled with peaches was sitting on the countertop. I picked one up, sniffed it and tested its firmness. "These are perfectly ripe."

Miriam reached for the bowl, turning it and looking at the peaches. "I didn't leave these here."

I saw the confused expression on her face and spoke up. "It must have been Preston. Last Sunday he showed me your orchard."

"That's not like Preston to pick fruit from the trees out back. In fact, he leaves that for anyone else but himself."

I returned the peach to the bowl. "He asked if he picked some, would I use them for dessert."

"Did he now?"

"I said I would—if that's okay with you."

She waved me off. "That's fine. I wish I used them more. Don't worry; we don't let them go to waste. We take them to the food pantry at my church."

"That's very generous of you."

"There are a lot of hungry people in the world. Heck, right in our own backyards. That fruit has been growing in my orchard for years. We eat very little of it. If it can help provide healthy options to the hungry, free of charge, it's the least we can do."

I admired that. There were too many families starving and in need of a good meal. I respected that the Carlyles didn't just bask in the beauty of having an orchard, but they were using it for good. How easy it would have been to let the fruit fall to the ground, uneaten, to go to waste. No, they were harvesting and sharing. Something that was so simple, but surely made a huge difference to many.

"I was thinking about making a cobbler with the peaches, topped with peach schnapps whipped cream. Regular whipped cream for the children, of course."

"Peach cobbler is one of Louis's favorites."

"Perfect." I started to gather the ingredients for the dinner menu from the fridge.

"You really are quite an amazing chef."

"Thank you, Mrs.—Miriam."

She smiled that I caught myself. "We all have talents in life. Mine, unfortunately, are not in the kitchen."

"No?" I asked, surprised.

"I mean, I can cook. My mama made sure of that, but, I know I'm not the best cook. When Louis and I were dating, he told me the woman he marries has to know her way around a kitchen. I told him that's fine as long as he knew his way around it, too."

I laughed. Miriam had spunk. "Can Mr. Carlyle cook?"

"He thinks he can. I wouldn't eat it."

There was a sparkle in her eyes when she mentioned him. I recognized love when I saw it. He told me they had been married for two years when he started his own business at thirty years old. They're now retirement age. That's a lot of years together. Even more amazing is that she still has a twinkle in her eye.

"Is his cooking really that bad?" I asked.

"Oh yeah."

"Inedible bad?"

"He either over-seasons or under-seasons. There's no in-between and no reason for him to set foot in the kitchen."

"That's not good."

"Thankfully, we have you. At least on Sundays." She pushed the bowl of peaches off to the side. "I'll leave you to your prep. Let me know if you need anything."

I thanked her and got down to business chopping, slicing and mincing. I was a little surprised at how talkative and open she had been. I enjoyed our chat. It seemed that although the Carlyles were extremely well off, Miriam and Louis were quite grounded. Sure I was making my determination based on a few interactions, but my impressions thus far had been positive. Immediately, my mind wandered to Hutton and the impression he'd made on our date the night before. I had put it out of my mind, convinced that was the best way to get through Sunday dinner. I was having second thoughts about the evening's events. Not so much the party, but most definitely what had taken place after we left.

We didn't talk much on the drive to my place. If he hadn't been driving like a madman on the way to the party, I would have thought he raced me home so quickly to get rid of me. When we got to my house, he opened my car door for me, walked me to my front door and thanked me for a great evening. No hug, no kiss, just a good night. Wait a minute, I thought. We hadn't kissed at all. Well, he kissed plenty, but we didn't share a kiss. Funny how I hadn't realized it until that moment while preparing dinner.

I sat on one of the chairs at the island. Again, I began to question whether I'd made a mistake by agreeing to go out with Hutton. When I'd accepted his invitation, it was merely to go out with him. I could have never anticipated the rest. No, accepting the date wasn't my concern. I was questioning my decision to let him pleasure me. What was I thinking? I wasn't. And, instead of preparing dinner, I was sitting down brooding. One moment I was rationalizing that I was grown and did what I wanted to do, and the next, I was beating myself up for knowing better. My mother liked to say, if you know better, you do better. I laughed out loud. I had to regroup. The evening happened, I couldn't take it back, and I enjoyed it. Hutton said he'd show me a great time. I had no idea it would involve him playing in my honeypot. That was last night and this was today. I had work to do and was on the clock. He spent last evening with Riley. Chef Ryan was on the premises today.

The chicken fricassee was simmering on the stove. I was serving it with a crisp potato galette, which was baking in the oven, and pureed kale. The kale was similar to creamed spinach and I hoped the children would eat it. If not, I could make them spring peas or broccoli. I turned my attention to the cobbler. I gathered flour, sugar and salt for the crust from the pantry. I made peach cobbler with a double pie crust—top and bottom—flaky, buttery and perfect for the sweet, syrupy peaches.

In my periphery, I realized I had company. I looked up from cutting butter into my dry ingredients to see Dutton tentatively approaching. There was a book tucked beneath his arm. He smiled and it disappeared nearly as quick as it had appeared.

"Hey, Dutton."

"I hope I'm not disturbing you. I know you're busy at work."

"Not in the least."

He stood on the opposite side of the island from me, looking curiously into the bowl. I turned the dough out onto the floured surface in front of me and began to knead. I gave him an expectant look, waiting for him to say something.

"Oh, I have something for you."

"Really, what's that?"

He held the book out for me to take. I shrugged and put my flour-covered hands up.

"Right, sorry," he said. He seemed embarrassed.

"Can you hold it up for me to see?"

"It's a cookbook. I'm sure you have plenty…"

I read the title aloud. *"The Ancient Egyptian Kitchen."*

"It's a book of recipes from Ancient Egypt." He adjusted his eyeglasses. "Of course you figured that out from the title."

I snickered. "There's that. And, you telling me it's a cookbook."

He laughed and seemed to relax a bit. "I came across it at a conference I attended this past week. I thought you might like it."

"Thank you. That was very thoughtful."

"I flipped through some of the recipes. I'm not much of a cook so I can't say whether they're any good."

"Well, I look forward to checking them out."

"I'll put this over on the table for you."

"Thanks."

He placed the book on the table and then made himself comfortable at the island. "Do you mind?"

I shook my head. How could I mind? It was his parents' house. He watched silently while I rolled out the dough, shaped it into discs, wrapped it in plastic and carried it to the refrigerator. I struck up a conversation while I peeled the peaches; apparently, he wasn't going to.

"Where was the conference you attended?"

"It was local. Hosted by the University of Georgia. The author of the cookbook was on one of the panels. I asked her to sign the book for you."

"Did you?" I said, surprise in my voice.

"Well, she was signing copies so…"

"Again, thank you."

He smiled. "You're welcome."

"Maybe there's a recipe in the book your family would enjoy for next Sunday."

"I don't believe they would be receptive to substituting your delicious meal with one from ancient times."

"You never know. Let me take a look at them. Maybe there's something similar to what we eat today. If not, I'm positive I can put an updated spin on something. That is, if you would like me to try."

"I would like that."

"I'll see what I can do." I sliced a peach and tasted it for sweetness. I offered Dutton a slice.

"Are these from the orchard out back?"

"Yes, and it's delicious."

"I don't think I've eaten a peach from that tree, or any tree for that matter, in fifteen years." He took the slice from my hand and placed it in his mouth.

"That's a long time. Is there a reason why?"

He looked away. "When someone decides it's a good idea to throw hard, unripe peaches as a form of amusement, you sort of lose your taste for them."

I wondered who would do that, yet refused to ask. If he wanted to say more, then he would have. I was inclined to believe it was one of his siblings, but who knew for sure. It could have been a friend or another family member, maybe a cousin.

"Well, how did your first peach in fifteen years taste?"

"Very sweet."

I smiled and handed him another slice.

"There's an exhibition in downtown Atlanta on Wednesday evening featuring Ancient Egyptian antiquities. I was planning to attend. Would you be interested in joining me?" he asked. "I understand if it's not your thing."

"I believe I mentioned the last time we were chatting that I find that time period extremely interesting. I'd love to go to the exhibit."

"I attended a similar exhibit a month ago and I marveled at the collection. I think you'll enjoy it. "

"I'm looking forward to it." I cut the last peach. "One more?" I asked, holding a slice out to him. "This one is really sweet."

We were interrupted before he had a chance to respond.

"I bet you taste just as sweet as those peaches." Hutton held my gaze, a smirk on his face.

Dutton frowned at his twin brother. "Have some class."

Hutton laughed, leaving the kitchen without another word. I let go of the breath I hadn't realized I was holding.

"I apologize for my brother's comment, Riley."

"It's okay."

"No, it's not. Hutton's always been kind of a wild card. Growing up, people always thought we would be more alike. They didn't seem to get that we're fraternal twins. Like night and day. He was always into something. Somehow he managed not to get caught. If something was amiss, I knew who was to blame. My mother would not be happy he came in here being disrespectful."

"It's fine, Dutton. No harm, no foul." I wanted to put an end to any discussion surrounding Hutton's comment. I had experienced firsthand a taste of how wild he could get.

He stood up to leave. "I look forward to dinner."

"I'm looking forward to the exhibition."

CHAPTER TWENTY-TWO

_l_ast course. Warm cobbler with peach whipped cream was in front of the family. I had assured Jayla that the kids had cinnamon whipped cream without the liqueur. She asked twice. I chalked it up to her being a doting mother. Miriam chimed in for her to taste it if she wanted to be safe. She did exactly that, dipped her spoon in both Jayce's and Caleb's dessert. I wrapped up my presentation and was ready to make my final exit from Sunday Dining Room Theatre.

"Riley, this cobbler is sweet and delicious," Hutton said.

I shot him a warning glance and he winked. "I'm glad you're enjoying it," I replied.

"You all should be thanking me. I'm the one that asked her to make something with the peaches from our orchard." Preston clearly wanted his credit.

I seized the opportunity and capitalized on Preston's levity. "He picked them and everything."

The Carlyles laughed. All except one. Grand's beautiful wife just eyed me with an undecipherable expression. She was beautiful. I didn't want to make assumptions because I knew nothing about her, but my initial thoughts registered trophy wife. Her kids were gobbling up the cobbler and not paying attention to any of our discussion. However, Grand, Hutton, Dutton and Preston were all engrossed. I reiterated that I was glad they all enjoyed the meal and I would see them the next Sunday. I made a swift exit from the dining room and back to the kitchen.

I didn't have much to clean up. As always, I had packed the remaining dinner and placed it in the refrigerator. Those boys, men rather, were a trip. Preston made sure everyone knew he had a hand in the dessert menu. It didn't seem to matter how old siblings were, there was always an element of childhood folly in their interactions. That damn Hutton liked to push the limits. The way he said the cobbler was so sweet and delicious made the hair on the back of my neck stand at attention. It didn't appear anyone took notice of his insinuations, but it was an unnecessary comment. We knew what transpired between us; no one else needed to know.

Mr. Carlyle came into the kitchen with great exaltation, rubbing his stomach. "That was delicious."

"Thank you, Mr. Carlyle."

"My mother used to make the best peach cobbler. Yours is right up there with hers."

"What a nice compliment."

"You know, Riley. I wasn't sure about this Sunday dinner idea my wife hatched. Growing up, my mother made dinner for our family every night. I grew up in the South and although we didn't have much, my mother turned out hearty meals for her family. My father worked hard at a menial job in a textile mill. He was handy, though, and worked as a carpenter on the side. He did what he had to do to feed his wife, five kids and two dogs." He laughed when he mentioned the dogs. "He expected everyone to do their part. We kids needed to go to school and make our grades, as he would say. He wanted all of us to have a college education. My mother was home to take care of the family. She cooked, cleaned, sewed, and helped with homework when she could. In fact, I think she learned some things along with us. She cherished her role in our household. At least from my perspective, that's how it seemed.

"I'm not saying I expected the same from Miriam; it's a different time, but Sunday dinner was the meal I always presumed she'd personally have on the table. As the boys got older and started going their own way, we stopped gathering for dinner—unless it was a holiday or special occasion. So, you could imagine when Miriam told me that she wanted you to make Sunday dinner for us, I kind of balked at the idea. I felt if she wanted to bring the family back together, then she should do the cooking. I don't know; maybe I'm old school. I've enjoyed your food ever since the retirement party, but tonight you struck a chord. You inadvertently took me for a trip down memory lane with your peach cobbler. You made me realize how far I've come. My parents never could have afforded to have anyone come in and prepare meals for their family. Yet, here I sit in this house—that far exceeds anything I set foot in as a child—and dine with my own family. I'm fortunate enough to have you come in and prepare these decadent meals, and I'm grateful enough to appreciate it."

I was touched. "I appreciate you sharing that with me."

"Just tell me there's some cobbler left."

"There is. I'll tuck it behind the chicken on second shelf in the fridge."

"I like the way you operate," he said, beaming. "See you next week."

I watched him leave the kitchen with a smile on my face. I had officially developed a rapport with my newest clients.

CHAPTER TWENTY-THREE

parked my car and hurried through the lot. I was about ten minutes late, thanks to the traffic on I-85. I approached the entrance to the gallery. Dutton was inside the vestibule waiting on me. He looked intellectually dapper in a houndstooth blazer and slacks. He smiled when he saw me.

"You made it," he said.

"I'm sorry I kept you waiting. There was a bit of congestion on the roads."

"I hit some myself on the way in."

He led me inside the gallery. Soft lighting illuminated the various works of art positioned throughout the spacious room. Thirty or so people milled about, their paces on the glossy hardwood floors echoing hollowly. They were stopping at a piece, chatting quietly for a minute or two and then moving on to the next. There was a rhythm to it all and we fell right in.

We stopped at a display case filled with amulets of varying sizes. Dutton explained they were amulets of different deities and that Ancient Egyptians were polytheistic. Another case was filled with engraved scarab amulets.

"These amulets were likely buried with the Ancient Egyptians. They believed they would grant them safe passage into the after-world."

"Some of them are really quite beautiful."

"They were sacred to the Egyptians. Scarabs were the equivalent of what the Christian cross is in our times."

We moved on to a statue. Overall, it was well-preserved, though the nose was chipped and one of the arms broken off. The plaque stated the subject was unknown. "I look at this art and I'm in awe that this was made thousands of years ago."

"We're getting a glimpse into history. A mere snapshot of a time that was so advanced, we can't even imagine how they accomplished many of the things they did…the structures, agriculture, medicine."

I looked over at him. "You really love this, don't you?"

"Ever since I was a kid."

"And now you've made it your work."

"I suppose I did."

"What do you do for fun or are you all work and no play?"

"Actually, I find events like this enjoyable. You won't find me at a bar on Friday night or a club on Saturday. I don't socialize much."

"Where would someone find you on a Friday or Saturday?"

"A bookstore, perhaps a lecture, or maybe a movie. Traveling on a whim."

"Sounds very educational," I said.

"I suppose it does." He laughed. "Where would I find you?"

"Lately, at home. Though I'm working on changing that."

"I'm finding that hard to believe."

"It's true, but I'm turning over a new leaf." I wasn't in the mood to explain I was in a relationship with a couch potato. I didn't want to bring Tyler up at all.

"I'm glad you were able to join me tonight."

"I appreciate the invite."

We continued through the room and into the next gallery. Dutton elaborated on the information provided on the works displayed, offering nuggets of fascinating detail. We stood in front of the last piece, a bust of Anubis. I stared at the canine head as Dutton rattled off his history as a protector of the dead. I was only partially listening. I glanced in his direction. He stroked his close-shaven beard as he spoke. It must have been an unconscious action. I wondered if it was something he did while teaching his classes. If he taught his students with the enthusiasm he had this evening, they were lucky to have such a professor.

"There's a reception upstairs being hosted by my anthropology department. Would you like to attend?"

"Yes, I'd like that."

We went up to the reception in a loft area of the gallery. There was a bar set up in the corner and platters of cheese and crackers arranged on highboy cocktail tables throughout the room.

"Would you like a drink?" he asked.

"A glass of merlot would be nice."

Dutton cupped my elbow as we took our wine across the room and joined a group of his colleagues in a discussion about the preservation of antiquities. It certainly wasn't my expertise, but they made me feel welcome and solicited my opinion all the same. Their spirited discussion was engaging, informative and academically stimulating. I inquired where their travels had taken them. It ranged from Cairo, Prague, China, Bahrain, Iceland and Paraguay. They were a well-traveled bunch. Dutton placed a gentle hand on my lower back and shared with the group that I was a chef. They began to regale me with stories of the strangest foods they had eaten during their travels.

"Thank goodness there's only cheese and crackers on the menu this evening," I remarked.

Laughter erupted among the group. Someone commented that I should provide the cuisine at the next reception as they were dissatisfied with the meager offerings. Dutton and I had another glass of merlot with his colleagues before bidding them adieu.

We walked down the stairs side by side, his hand rematerializing on my back as we descended. "Thank you for making my evening," he spoke quietly.

"I had a nice time."

He walked me to my car. An awkward silence fell over us. "Thanks again for an educational and entertaining evening," I said.

"You're welcome." He started to lean toward me, stopped and then advanced again, clumsily brushing his lips against my cheek.

I disarmed my car alarm and got inside. "Well, good night."

"Drive safely." He pushed my door closed and waved as I pulled off.

An interesting end to the evening but, in my opinion, it was a Wednesday night well spent.

CHAPTER TWENTY-FOUR

looked down at my cell phone again to check the time. Still no Aja. Mamie's Kitchen Biscuits closed at two and it was quickly approaching half past one. Mamie's was a small, homely spot, but the food was so good. I was just about to go order when she came through the door.

"Don't give me that look," she said.

"I didn't give you a look."

"You have me driving from Roswell to Lithonia in the middle of the day, after I just worked a thirteen-hour shift at the hospital, just so you can stuff your face with a chicken biscuit from Mamie's."

"That's why you're my best friend."

"What's wrong with Chick-fil-A and don't you have clients?" She exasperatedly plopped into the seat across from me.

"Chick-fil-A can't touch Mamie's and I'm finished with clients for the day. One of the perks of being self-employed."

"Next time you and your perks can eat alone."

"Oh, come on, Aja. You sit here and relax and I'll go to the counter for the food. What do you want?"

"Everything."

"Okay, I got you."

I went to the counter and ordered a chicken biscuit and sweet tea for myself and eggs, bacon, sausage, grits, biscuits and peach cobbler for Aja. She laughed when I returned to the table with the tray of food.

"Really, Riley?"

"You said everything."

"You're a mess."

"Now eat fast before they throw us out of here."

One of the ladies behind the counter overheard me. "You're okay, baby. Take your time and eat your food."

"Thank you," I said. Aja was already digging in to her plate.

"I couldn't help notice I haven't heard from you since your date last Saturday."

"Today is only Thursday."

She twisted her lips. "Yeah, five days after your date I've heard nothing about. Of course I'm wondering why not?"

"I was going to tell you about it."

"When you got around to it, right?"

"There's not much to tell."

"Remind me which one you went out with?" she said.

"Hutton, the twin."

"Right. Where did he end up taking you?"

"We went to a rooftop party in Buckhead. A lot of football players, entertainment industry folks, model types."

"And…"

"I had a nice time."

Aja put her fork down. "Okay, now I know you're leaving something out. You are being painfully vague."

I laughed. "You're right. It was a crazy night."

"I knew it! What happened?"

"So the evening started off well enough. He picked me up in his Ferrari."

"Are you serious?"

"Dead. But you know material things don't impress me."

"I know," she said matter-of-factly. "You're ridiculous."

"He picks me up, looking fine as hell, smelling good and acting all manly."

"Oooh, this is what I wanted to hear."

"Are you going to keep chiming in?"

"Nope." She mimicked zipping her lips.

"My dress was smoking hot and he was in a fitted suit with the top buttons on his shirt undone. We looked so good together," I gushed. "Anyway, we get to the party at the hotel—which his family happens to own—and spend the evening talking, drinking and flirting a little. He was the one doing most of the flirting. I knew he loved the dress because he kept hinting at how sexy I looked. Remember how the dress draped?"

"Yes."

"He couldn't keep his hands off of my back and, eventually, my thigh."

"I'm waiting…"

"Okay, okay." I giggled. "At some point in the evening he started to ask if he could taste me."

Her eyes widened. "You mean taste you taste you?"

"That's exactly what I mean."

"What did you say?"

"At first, I didn't think he was serious, but he kept asking."

"So, what did you say?"

"I got tasted."

Aja's mouth formed a giant "O."

"Close your mouth," I said.

"I can't let you go anywhere," she teased.

"I knoooow. I said no at first, but he has this energy." I shivered at the thought. "I don't know. I wanted to let him taste me. He said he wanted to suck my clit and make me come."

"And did he? Did you?"

"Girl, yes to both!"

"Good for you," she said, returning to her food.

"Really, Aja? I feel some kind of way about it."

"Why? You're grown."

"Because of the client thing."

"You're on that again?"

I told her that I was feeling a little uncomfortable especially after the comments he'd made at Sunday dinner. The last thing I wanted was to appear unprofessional in front of the Carlyles. Mixing business with pleasure typically wasn't a good idea.

"I thought we established Hutton isn't your client."

"Isn't that a matter of semantics?"

"Not to me. Every Sunday you go to the home of Miriam and Louis Carlyle. Am I correct?"

"You're right."

"That's all there is to it. Miriam and Louis are the clients. So, did you have sex with him?"

"No, it didn't go that far. He asked to taste me, he did and that was it. We didn't even kiss."

"Now that's strange."

"I'm thinking that's just Hutton. He's arrogant. He wanted what he wanted."

"Apparently, so did you."

"He made it a good first date." We laughed. I wondered if men knew just how much of their business we told our girlfriends. Aja knew all of my secrets. I kept none from her. I could confide in her without fear of judgment or exposure. "I almost forgot," I continued. "I went to an exhibit with his twin, Dutton, last night."

Her brow furrowed. "What?"

"Dutton's the professor. I was telling him how interesting I found ancient Egypt. There was an exhibition last night and he invited me to go."

"You went out with two brothers, twins no less?"

"It wasn't like that. Hutton and I went on a date. Dutton invited me to attend an event on a subject he knows I enjoy."

"That sounds like semantics."

"It really isn't. Trust me. It wasn't a date."

"I believe you believe that."

I swatted her hand. "That's because it's true!" My phone vibrated on the table. I picked it up and shook my head. "It's Tyler texting me."

"How's he doing?"

"Fine, I guess."

"What did he say?"

"'*Hope you're doing well.*' I texted back, '*same to you.*'"

"You don't miss him?"

"Not yet. It's only been a couple of weeks."

"I was just checking."

"I'm fine."

"I bet you are, going on dates with twins."

"Aja! I only had one date!"

"I'm teasing."

"They're an interesting family. Not quite what I expected."

"Nothing ever is."

CHAPTER TWENTY-FIVE

My client and I met in her driveway. She was loading her children into their SUV as I was pulling up. I said hello to the kids, reconfirmed the menu with her and headed inside as she jetted off. She was a divorcée with three kids and a high-powered job as a federal judge. I completely understood why she was in need of my services. She'd told me on quite a few occasions that she did not have time to cook. It was perfect for me because she was one of my best clients. I prepared six meals for her family each week.

I went to the kitchen and got right to work. Her children had finicky palates and it took a while for us to perfect her menus. There would always be food from the previous week in the refrigerator when I arrived. Once we finally found the right combination of foods that all three of her kids would eat, the leftovers problem was resolved. I honestly felt a part of the issue was that she was allowing the kids to dictate what they weren't willing to consume. Growing up, that wasn't an option in my home. You ate what was cooked. Since the judge wasn't doing the cooking, she was overly indulgent to the whims of the young. If you asked me, there were far too few vegetables on her menu. The amount of vegetables on the menu wasn't my decision. I was the chef, not the mother.

There were times when I'd suggested adding vegetables here or there to the menu, but she declined. She said after a long day in court, she didn't want to come home to fight with her kids to eat their vegetables. Eventually, she did agree to let me hide some in sauces or casseroles. I made a lasagna for the kids with four different veggies hidden in the cheese and sauce. They had no idea and gobbled it up each time I made it. She was thankful that I could find creative ways to disguise them. It was the responsibility of the mother to make sure her children were receiving nutritious meals, but I was happy to do my part.

I was heartened that Louis Carlyle thought my peach cobbler was close to his mother's. He looked back fondly on the meals she prepared and what she did for her family. I wondered if that would matter to the judge's kids when they got older. Would they care that their mother didn't cook? I was sure she did other things for them that they could look back on one day with fondness. I just hoped she didn't pay for someone else to do all the important things in life, the little things that counted.

I thought about Miriam saying she wasn't the best cook. I could only imagine it didn't make a difference to her family that the meals weren't spectacular, as long as their mother prepared it. Ironically, she knew her meals weren't going to lure anyone to the dinner table on Sundays. According to Hutton, she used me as a selling point to get them there. I felt a pang of guilt. I had a mother and sister that I could be having dinner with every Sunday, yet I was concerned with the Carlyles. Maybe I would call my mother to discuss having family dinners again. Maybe.

I was at home on the couch with my tablet in my lap working on menus for my clients. I'd create specialized menus for each one and email their proposed options for the upcoming week. They could make changes or suggestions at their leisure. My process was designed to be collaborative; however, it was rare that they'd make any changes.

Creativity was one of my favorite things about being a chef. I could use my knowledge to create something that others would love, crave and request. There was no higher compliment than a client asking for a signature dish that I created because they just had to have it. It was flattering when they'd tell me they were thinking about or pining for it. Although my stint as an executive chef was brief, I had an inkling the type of connectivity I shared with my clients would have been limited in a restaurant setting. How much of a rapport could I really build while in the kitchen, possibly passing through the dining room occasionally? A future as executive chef in a restaurant wasn't off the table; it just wasn't in the cards for now. The hand I was holding showed a catering business. That was where I'd be directing my attention in the very near future.

CHAPTER TWENTY-SIX

arrived at the Carlyle estate at my usual time. I wasn't expecting to see Grand and his family arriving at the same time. I parked and got out of the car. Jayce and Caleb ran up, surprising me with hugs. They shot off toward the house before I had a chance to ask how they were doing. Boys, I thought. They were full of unbridled energy. Grand followed behind them. Jayla lingered by their car. I grabbed my bag from the trunk and headed in her direction.

"Hello, Riley," she said. Her hair was caught by the breeze, blowing across her face. She tried to sweep it to side and away from her eyes.

"How are you, Jayla?"

"Wishing I pinned my hair up like you."

My hair was in a top knot. "It is a bit blustery today."

She started to stroll alongside me to the house. "It feels sort of tropical. It reminds me of when Grand and I were in Bora Bora six months ago. It was so humid and the ocean breeze was unrelenting. Have you been?"

"No, I haven't had a chance."

"It's a beautiful island. I wouldn't mind returning for a visit, maybe with the boys next time."

I felt like she should have linked her arm through mine. She was chatting as if we were old friends or even like we'd had a single conversation in the past. "I'm sure it was lovely."

"Are you originally from Georgia?" she asked.

"Yes, born and raised."

"I'm from Boston. I came to Georgia for college and never left."

I thought once we were inside, she would go find her family. Instead, she tailed me to the kitchen, seating herself at the island. I felt obliged to continue the conversation. "Where did you go to college?"

"Spelman. And you?"

"Johnson & Wales and Le Cordon Bleu in Paris."

"I love Paris. The shopping is amazing."

"It is a magnificent city." I washed my hands and slipped into my chef jacket.

"Are you also a chef in a restaurant?"

"No, I'm a personal chef. I provide culinary services to people in their homes. I also cater occasionally."

"Yes, you catered my father-in-law's retirement party."

"I sure did." I wasn't clear why the sudden interest in me. If she hadn't already, she could have asked Miriam all of these questions.

"As a personal chef, do you have to work seven days a week?"

"I'm self-employed so I set my own schedule." I wasn't going to be the only one answering questions. "What do you do for a living?"

"I work for a foundation. Well, volunteer, actually. I was a public relations executive before I had my sons. I stopped working after I had Jayce seven years ago. I've been volunteering at the foundation for about a year. I started when Caleb turned two. We had just placed him in daycare and I needed something to keep myself occupied. I do PR for the foundation two days a week for a few hours each day."

I was surprised. I thought she was most definitely going to say she was a lady of leisure. It was nice to hear that she was doing something productive, and giving freely of her time. I realized that

I was judging and I wasn't sure why. "I think that's wonderful," I heard myself say.

"Eventually, I'll return to corporate America when the boys get a little older. It was never my plan to leave, but Grand thought it would be good for our family. It took a bit of convincing, but I relented. We've been married for ten years and he says that it took just as long for me to get into agreement with him."

I smiled, not really having a response.

"Grand knows I was in agreement with him from the moment we met. His mother and my mother are sorority sisters. They claim they didn't arrange for us to meet, but we found it oddly peculiar that they both insisted we attend a charity auction their sorority was hosting. They seated us next to one another at the table, encouraging us to chat all evening. That was the beginning of us. We dated for a year before we got married. If you listen to Grand, he jokes that he had an arranged marriage." Jayla smiled, but it appeared slightly melancholic. "I have to ask, what are you making tonight?"

"Fresh pappardelle pasta with a lamb and mushroom ragout."

"Maybe you can share some of these recipes that seem to have my husband raving about your cooking."

I politely laughed. "Where would I be if I gave you all of my secrets?" I made it a joke but wasn't sharing my recipes with anyone, certainly not a client's daughter-in-law.

"I consider myself to be a pretty good cook. Your Sunday dinners seem to be all the rage in this family."

"That means I'm doing my job." I glanced up from chopping herbs and added a smile.

"Jayce loves your desserts. On the drive over, he kept asking can he have seconds. I told him he doesn't even know what we're having. Do you know what he said?"

"What did he say?" I asked, mirroring her tone.

"He said he didn't care because he knew it would be delicious."

"That means a lot. Children can be the harshest of critics."

"Do you have any children?"

"No, I don't."

"I don't see a ring. Though, I suppose a chef might not wear one while working."

"I'm not married."

"A beautiful, single, smart, professional woman in the Carlyle den every week…"

"The Carlyle den?"

"It's how I refer to their home full of men. It's like a lodge or a fraternity. Full of brotherly love and comradery."

"Think of me as the lodge cook."

Caleb came tearing into the kitchen calling for his mother. "What is it, Caleb?"

"Jayce won't give me my robot," he bellowed.

"Where is your father?"

"Talkin' to Gran'pa."

"Go tell your father."

He ran from the kitchen in search of his father. She smiled after him, looking in his direction after he was long gone. She turned back to me. "With those two energetic munchkins on our hands, can you believe we want another one?"

"Really?"

"Yes, a little girl. In this family full of boys we could use some pink. Miriam has been hinting ever since Caleb turned one. My husband wants to keep trying until we have a girl. I'm willing to try one more time and that's it."

"I wish you luck." I didn't know what else to say. This was our first conversation and she was taking oversharing to a new level. I was ready for her to leave me alone in the kitchen. I had spinach and bean soup to make, the pappardelle noodles to start, and lemon basil cannoli for dessert. Thankfully, I put the lamb in the pressure cooker while she was chatting.

I didn't usually mind company while I was cooking, but I was trying to figure out Jayla's angle. I didn't want to do that much analysis while supposedly having casual conversation. I needed my thoughts to be on making creative dishes, not deciphering innuendo. One thing was clear: she was curious about my relationship status and she wanted me to be clear about hers.

I hoped she had collected enough information and disseminated enough to be on her way. A moment after the thought crossed my mind, Caleb returned in tears.

"Excuse me, Riley. I need to take care of my family."

I said a silent prayer of thanks. "No problem." And, message received.

CHAPTER TWENTY-SEVEN

*D*inner and dessert felt like it lasted an eternity. It could have been my time with Jayla—distracting and exhausting. I was held captive to her musings since I couldn't put her out of the kitchen. Other than the rough start, dinner went off without a hitch. Unlike the first Sunday dinner where no one was talking when I'd enter the room, now the family seemed to be a little more conversational. I had to interrupt Miriam's convivial chatter when I came in to present the main course and dessert. I kept my presentations brief as not to impede on their family time. I was wrapping up in the kitchen and planned to be headed home within the next fifteen minutes.

"You're still here."

I turned my head to see Jayla's other half entering the kitchen. "Just finishing up."

"My compliments to the chef."

"Thank you," I said, tucking my knives into their case. "Did the kids like the pasta?"

"They did. I was surprised they ate the mushrooms."

"I was positive Jayce would be in here asking for more dessert. Your wife told me what he said."

"I sent them home already. I needed to stay for a meeting with my father. Jayla drove the boys home to get them ready for bed."

"Caleb looked like he was ready to drop when I brought the dessert in."

"He goes out like a light around this time. Especially if he didn't take a nap. Thanks to you, the boys' bellies are full, and they'll be sound asleep in no time."

"I plan to do the same when I get home."

"All alone?" His voice had dropped an octave.

I waited a beat before responding. "That's the plan."

"That doesn't seem right. Someone should be there to hold you tight while you sleep."

"Well, not tonight."

"Maybe another night?"

"That sounded like an offer."

"Did it?"

"It did, but I must be mistaken since you're married." I looked Grand directly in the eyes when I said that.

"I am married."

"And trying to have a baby with your wife."

"I do want a daughter." He held my gaze. "I bet you would give me a beautiful one."

"Excuse me?" I couldn't hide the surprise on my face.

"I said I think you would make a beautiful daughter."

"I'm sure I will one day...with my husband."

"What was it you told me the other week? Oh, right. You have to find a man that calls to you."

"That's right."

"What's your number?"

I laughed and so did he. "That's not what I meant."

"You're not the only one with a sense of humor."

"Are you flirting with me, Grand?"

"I'm a married man." He twisted his wedding band on his finger.

"Yes, I know."

"Married men flirt."

"They also talk in circles," I said.

"There's nothing wrong with flirting. Marriage does not mean an end to acknowledging what's beautiful. It doesn't mean that the laws of attraction no longer exist. In fact, sometimes it's enhanced. Sometimes, when you can't have what you see, you want it more."

"I can positively say that when I do get married, I don't want my husband out flirting on a whim."

"Maybe you'll be fortunate enough not to marry a flirtatious man. My wife married one."

"She accepts it?"

"We've been together eleven years. It would be romantic to say my wife is the only woman I see, but how realistic would it be? I see lots of women. I see one standing in front of me right now. I see your cinnamon complexion, lips that are full and natural, a nose with cutest, slightest upturned tip, a long graceful neck… I see you. Am I supposed to pretend I don't because I'm married?"

"Appreciating an attractive woman is different than flirting with one."

"Jayla and I got married young. I was only twenty-five."

"It's not that young."

"It was for me. But that was the decision I made. I think back and can acknowledge that I probably had some more living to do before settling down."

"You must have thought you were ready if you made the decision to tie the knot."

"There were other factors influencing my decision."

I didn't respond. I realized I was making assumptions about a situation in which I had zero knowledge. I had started my evening with one half of this duo and the other half was closing out the night. I was beginning to feel like a bartender, listening to the chronicles of the patrons. The island had become my bar. It was close enough to one—a countertop with chairs on the other side—albeit way more expensive.

"When you're the firstborn son of a finance titan, there are expectations. There's a legacy to uphold. I was aware of what those expectations were and my duty as a Carlyle. I didn't have the luxury of being the baby of the family or taking an egocentric approach to life. I followed the path set for me. That included marriage and children."

"Where does love factor into all of that?"

"I love my family. More than life itself."

"I get that. I meant how did love factor into your decision to marry."

"It was an important factor, just not the only one. Remember, at the end of the day, marriage is a contract. You are agreeing to love, honor and cherish…in sickness and in health…until death. In order to live up to what's specified in that contract, it takes a lot of work. In contractual agreements, sometimes one or both of the parties evade their responsibility or default altogether. If I'm going to fulfill the part of the contract that states until death do us part, I'm going to live a life that will allow me to do that."

"The flirting…"

He shrugged.

"You know," I said, "a lot of married women would consider flirting a form of cheating."

"Cheating is a part of marriage. That's just the way it is."

My brow wrinkled. "Does that mean you're fine with your wife having an affair?"

"I didn't say that. But, the reality is, I can't control her any more than she can control me. Control is not in the vows."

"As you mentioned, love, honor and cherish are."

"If you ask my wife, she will tell you emphatically that I do all three. I'm working on the til death part by trying to get my wife to be open and receptive."

I could imagine they were on two different pages with that. She was in the same seat earlier delivering veiled messages about how in love they were. I wasn't sure to what extent he wanted her to be open, a threesome maybe, but judging by the behavior she displayed to me, she wasn't going for it.

Grand got up and came around to my side of the island, standing painfully close to me. I picked up the containers of leftovers and carried them to the refrigerator, putting some distance between us. While I was making room on the shelves, he approached from behind and leaned in, the front of his body touching the back of mine.

I spun around and squeezed by him. "Grand," I cautioned, making my way back to the protection of the island.

He started to follow, but stopped in his tracks. I looked to see what caught his attention. Preston ambled in, heading for the refrigerator.

"Hey, I thought you left already," Preston said.

Grand and I answered simultaneously—me stating I was about to leave and him sharing that he had a meeting with their father.

Preston laughed and shook his head. "I was talking to Riley."

"Oh," Grand replied.

"I was just leaving," I reiterated.

"I'll help you with your bags."

"Thanks, Preston." I gathered my belongings.

"Good night, Riley, see you next week," Grand said.

I glanced at Grand before walking out of the kitchen and responded with a quick wave.

Preston and I headed to the front door. I was grateful for the reprieve. Grand may have been a married man, but he flirted like a single one. It was apparent Jayla knew what she was dealing with when it came to her husband. My conversation with Grand actually shed more light on my discussion with her. She wanted to know my status, probably concerned her husband would do exactly what he just did, make a pass at me. I pushed Grand and Jayla from my thoughts.

"I appreciate your help, Preston, but I can take it from here," I said.

"Let me do what I offered to do."

"Fine."

"I wanted to thank you for making the cobbler last week. I wasn't sure you would actually use the peaches when I left them in the kitchen for you."

"I said I would and it was no trouble."

"Maybe I'll make a special request every week."

"I wouldn't go that far." I laughed at Miriam's youngest child. We approached my car and I popped the trunk.

Preston put my bag inside. "Hey, are you in hurry?" he asked.

"Well, I'm going home to relax for the evening."

"Do you have a few minutes? I want to show you something."

"This is becoming a habit."

"What's that?"

"You wanting to show me something."

"Do you mind?"

I sighed. "Sure, what is it?"

"It's at my place."

"Your place? I don't think so, Preston. I just want to get home. I don't want to drive out of my way."

He shook his head. "I live here—in the guest house."

"Oh." I hadn't realized that.

"It's a short walk on the other side of the orchard."

I looked back toward the house. "Should I leave my car here in the driveway?"

"We can park behind the guest house. No one will know you're still here."

He must have read my thoughts. I was done providing my services and had left the Carlyle home. I didn't necessarily want them to see my vehicle sitting abandoned in their driveway, wondering where I was on their property. He walked toward my passenger side. "Come on, get in," he said.

We jumped in the car and he directed me down a back road on the estate. Again, I marveled at the property. We passed a monument of sorts, a fountain trickling in the center of a garden. At the end of the road, nestled in a cul-de-sac, sat a two-story residence.

"Follow the lane around the guest house. You can park in the back."

I pulled around and there was a paved parking area, definitely off the beaten path. I pulled beside his car and cut off the engine. "Okay, let's see what you want to show me."

CHAPTER TWENTY-EIGHT

*P*reston flipped on lights as we entered the guest house. My initial thought was his guest house was an extension of the main house. Photographs adorned the walls in different sized frames, expensive flooring and lighting that enhanced the ambiance of the space. He led me into a den. A massive leather sofa and two loveseats flanked a stone fireplace. An oak coffee table was centered in the midst of the seating, portfolios strewn on top.

"Have a seat," he said.

I went over to the sofa and sat down. A couple of cashmere throws were fashionably draped over the back extending onto the cushions. Preston sat next to me and reached for one of the portfolios. He opened the case, situating it across our laps. An image of the setting sun, streaming through the orchard, was on the first page. Golden light and shadows entangled on the print. It captured the essence of what I had admired when Preston first showed me the orchard.

"Did you take this?"

He nodded and turned to the next photo. "I wanted to share one of my passions with you."

I stared at an image of a single peach hanging from a branch, orbs of light highlighting the fuzz on the fruit. "Impressive."

"I took these pictures after I showed you the orchard. In a way you were my inspiration."

"Me?"

"As we walked through the gardens and orchard, there was something in your eyes. You were taking in everything in a way I never do, having been around it all my life. I wanted to capture what you saw as if through your lens."

The next set of images was in black and white. The starkness of the colorless images gave them a sense of timelessness, as if he encapsulated a moment in time.

"You have a good eye."

"Photography was one of the side interests I pursued in college."

"The framed photos on the walls—"

"All mine."

"You're talented."

"I appreciate that."

"It's true."

"I recently created a visual media piece of all my images. Thousands of my photos in one artistic medium. I want you to see it."

I refrained from checking my watch. I wanted to be heading home, but I didn't want to be rude. If he wanted to share his creative work with me, I could spare a moment and look at what he developed.

"I'd like to see what you have."

He smiled. "I'll put it on. Would you like a drink?"

"No, thank you."

"I'm going to have one."

Preston left me in the den alone. I gave my surroundings a secondary examination. He basically had his own luxurious house on his family's property. I wondered if Miriam and Louis charged him rent. Though, somehow, I doubted it.

He returned carrying a bottle of spring water and a beer. He placed the water in front of me. "In case you get thirsty." He went over to the entertainment console and slipped a DVD into the player. "I haven't shared this with anyone yet."

"I'm the first to see it?"

He sat next to me. "Yeah."

I smiled and then turned my head toward the television. I wasn't sure if I merited the distinction of being the first person to view his project. However, if he wanted me to see it, I'd watch. I had to admit to having more than a little bit of curiosity about what a student of life did to keep himself preoccupied.

A barrage of images appeared on the screen. Deserts, beaches, bridges...vivid pictures set to a pulsating beat. A honey-toned tenor sax faded in. "The music is a nice touch," I commented.

"That's me playing."

"Seriously?"

"I started playing in college."

"That sounds like someone who's been playing their entire life. In fact, I was going to ask you what jazz saxophonist was playing."

"I'll take that as a compliment."

"You definitely should."

He looked over at me. "Why don't you relax? Take off your shoes and kick back."

"No, that's all right."

"You've been on your feet for hours. You can relax for a little bit while you watch."

I thought about it. I had already agreed to look at his project, so I might as well get comfortable. I removed my shoes and settled into the corner of the couch. "Better?" I asked.

"You're getting there. I'd feel better if you let me get you a drink."

"I'm fine, really."

"You won't hear me dispute you on that."

I cocked my head to the side, not sure I correctly interpreted his comment. "Okay..."

"Put your feet up." Preston patted the cushion.

"I'm fine, Preston."

He reached over, seized me by the ankles, and deposited my legs on the couch. "Now you look comfortable."

I shook my head and directed my attention back to the television. Time-lapsed photos showed the changing of the seasons. Sunny spring days morphed into gloomy winter evenings. The video reminded me of something you would see in a museum of modern art. Edgy. Bold. Dramatic.

"Your photographs are remarkable."

He reached for my foot. "So are you."

I pulled my leg back, but he held firm, tugging it back toward him. He began to massage my foot.

"What are you doing?"

"Doesn't that feel good? I thought I read somewhere that chefs love a good foot massage."

"I don't know where you heard that, but I can assure you we don't expect people to randomly rub our feet." I tugged again.

Preston continued to knead, applying more pressure. "But, how does it feel?"

I flexed my foot in his hands. It felt damn good if I were being honest. Though, I opted to say something else. "Feels like you shouldn't be massaging my feet."

"Why not?"

"Just…because…"

"That's a non-answer."

"I don't need a foot massage."

"I want to give you one, so let me."

"Don't tell me you have a foot fetish or something."

"No." He chuckled. "I'm accustomed to dealing with older women. I actually prefer them to women my age."

"Wait a minute. I'm not much older than you, Preston."

"I know that."

"Do you? A moment ago you seemed to be grouping me with older women."

"I only meant that in dealing with older women, I've learned how to treat a woman. You may not need a massage, but I'll give you one because no matter what you said, I can tell that it feels good to you."

"I'm glad you cleared that up." I laughed.

"Believe me. I wasn't talking about you when I said older. I'm talking forty and up."

"You're dealing with forty-year-olds? What do you have in common?"

"I'm a mature twenty-four."

"Even so, that's a sixteen-year gap."

"I actually said 'and up.' I've dealt with women in their fifties, even sixties."

"Let me preface this by saying, I'm not trying to be disrespectful. I'm sure that cleft chin and bald head works to your advantage, but what would a sixty-year-old woman want with a twenty-something-year-old man?"

"Don't go for the obvious. It's not just sex. It depends on the woman."

"What could you possibly want with a sixty-year-old woman?"

"There are women in their fifties and sixties that don't look a day over thirty-five. And when you factor in they're living good and taking care of themselves—there's nothing sexier. I've spent time talking to older women, gone out with them, made love to them… There's plenty to want from an older woman."

"I guess I stand corrected."

"If my mother ever has you cater one of her sorority events, take a look around the room. You won't be able to guess the ages of most of the women."

My mouth opened. "You didn't?"

"A few," he nonchalantly replied.

"You slept with your mother's friends?"

"I said a few."

"What if she finds out?"

"She won't. We're discreet. They don't want her knowing any more than I want her to know."

"I could imagine. Seems like a scandal waiting to happen."

"Maybe it is." He switched and started to massage my other foot. "I still have love for women my age. I know I should probably focus my attention on them."

"That might not be a bad idea."

"Possibly someone slightly older." He grinned. "Know anyone?"

"I can't say that I do."

"Your hair looks nice like that."

"It's nothing special, just a bun on top."

"The first night I saw you at my father's retirement party, you caught my attention."

"I was really busy that evening."

"I winked at you. Twice. You didn't notice?"

"I vaguely remember something like that."

Preston hung his head and laughed. "Oh, man."

"Your older women didn't teach you that trick, did they?"

"I deserve that. I know a wink doesn't convey anything of substance. It definitely didn't tell you that all evening I wanted to come and talk to you. I thought about excusing myself from the party to learn more about you."

"It must've been the student in you."

"No, it's the man in me. You're appealing. I couldn't ignore that."

I quickly turned my face back toward the television. "Where was that photo taken?"

"Dubai."

A light sensation caressed my foot. Preston was leaned over it.

"Were the men aware that you were photographing them?" I asked.

"Yes."

His lips softly touched the top of my foot again.

"What about this picture? What country is it?"

"This one."

His kiss drifted to my ankle.

"Which state?"

He didn't look up. "Right here," he mumbled.

"Georgia?"

He gazed at me. "You know what I love about photography? The journey it takes me on." Preston's hands roamed up my calf. "I see amazing sights." His hand slowly slid up my thigh. "Capture rare moments." He shifted on the couch and crept toward my end, his body hovering over mine. "And, I appreciate the beauty of what's in front of me."

He bowed his head and kissed me on the lips. Both of our eyes were open. He drew back. I searched his face. Preston's expression questioned if I was receptive. If he could read mine, he saw ambivalence. He approached again. This time his eyes closed as he dotted my mouth with small, successive kisses. I returned the gesture. Through shut eyes, I could feel him prodding me to match his level of intensity with the increasing tempo of his kiss. His tongue tangled with mine. He led, I followed. I guided, he shadowed. He pulled me beneath him and covered me with the weight of his body. I immediately felt his excitement pressing into my leg. I pulled away from his kiss and gently nudged his shoulders. He peered at me for an instant as it registered that I was putting on the brakes. Preston nodded, extricating himself from me. He sat up and adjusted himself in his jeans.

"I'm sorry if I got carried away," he said. "I didn't mean to overstep my bounds."

"No, you're fine."

"Are you sure?"

"I'm positive. Don't worry about it. I think I should be going, though."

"I understand. You sure we're okay?"

"Yes, we're good. So, stop asking."

"All right." He sighed. "Thanks for coming to check out my passion."

"I appreciate you sharing it with me." I slipped back into my shoes and grabbed my car keys. "You're extremely talented."

"If only you knew."

I was aware I put a hasty halt to our make-out session. I was supposed to be there to view his photography, not to partake in what had just transpired. It was innocent enough—at least until I felt his erection. When innocence shifts to corruption, it's time to recuse oneself. I bade Preston a good night and headed home like I should've done in the first place.

CHAPTER TWENTY-NINE

could not believe what I was seeing. I pulled up next to Tyler's car in my driveway. All I wanted was to spend the rest of my evening at home, alone. His unexpected visit would undoubtedly prevent that from happening. I checked my face in the rearview mirror and stepped from my car smoothing my hair. Tyler's door opened. He approached me carrying a gift bag.

I continued to my front door, him trailing closely behind.

"How long have you been waiting in my driveway?"

"About an hour."

I looked over my shoulder at him and sighed. "You should've called first."

"I didn't mind waiting."

We walked inside the house. I punched in my code to disarm the alarm.

"Where are you coming from?" he asked. "It's almost ten o'clock."

"I was working."

"You had an event?"

"No, a client. What are you doing here?" Impatience seeped out of my question.

"I wanted to talk to you." He held up the gift bag. "I brought you something, too."

"Can you give me a minute? I need to take a quick shower."

"I'll be in the family room."

I turned and started up the stairs.

Tyler lingered. "I miss you, Riley."

"I'll be back." I went into my bedroom and closed the door behind me. I was surprised to see Tyler. If he wanted to talk, he could have called. His dropping by was indicative of what he thought. In his mind he assumed I would be home. It probably never occurred to him that I could be out on a Sunday night.

I peeled off my clothes and tossed them in the hamper. I went into the bathroom, covered my hair with a cap and stepped inside the shower. Warm water rained down on me while I stood directly beneath the showerhead. Tyler showing up was not ideal. I had a long day and finally made it home to relax.

I did wonder what was in the gift bag, though I probably shouldn't accept it. The look on his face was one of hope. I just wasn't there. I needed time. It wasn't that I didn't miss him at all. I simply viewed our break differently than he did. The break wasn't meant to be a bad thing. For me, it was to help me get to a better space. I understood it probably had the opposite effect for Tyler. He was a good man and we got along nicely. I missed him a little, too. I just didn't know if I missed our relationship. I was looking for something that wasn't there. A wave of guilt hit me. Tyler and I were taking a break so I could make some decisions about the future of our relationship. I hadn't given it much consideration since the day at the movie theater. If he asked me what I thought about reconciling, I wouldn't be able to answer.

I couldn't answer a few things lately. Specifically, what I was doing with the Carlyle brothers. My interlude with Preston didn't make sense. One moment we were talking about his photography, and the next, he's massaging and kissing my feet. I let Hutton kiss even more, exposed my honeypot to him. I didn't know why it happened, but one thing was for sure. It couldn't happen again.

I finished in the shower, dried off and slipped on my robe. I came out of the bathroom and went downstairs to the family room. Tyler was flipping through the channels. I cleared my throat and he turned off the television. That was a first. I sat across from him. "What did you want to talk about?"

"I need you to know that I heard you."

"What does that mean?"

"It means I wasn't doing what I was supposed to be doing—listening to your wants and needs."

"But, I've been saying the same thing for quite some time."

"I know you have. I thought about it and I realized that I could try harder."

"Honestly, Tyler, you shouldn't have to try hard to want to spend time together."

"We do spend time together, Riley."

"Outside of the house, Tyler." I wasn't sure how much realizing he had done if he was countering what I said.

"I get it." He slid the gift bag across the coffee table to me. "This is for you."

"You didn't have to bring me anything."

"Open it."

I stared at it, contemplating whether to decline the gift. He got up and sat next to me, grabbing the bag and putting it on my lap. I reached into the tissue paper and pulled out a plastic document folder. I opened it and read the contents.

"You booked a trip to Paris?"

"You said you wanted us to go away together."

I heaved a sigh.

"Not the response I was looking for…" he said.

"Tyler…I appreciate the gesture. I really do. But, I can't go to Paris."

"It's an open ticket. Maybe we can go in the next few weeks."
He inched closer to me on the couch. "I miss you." He kissed the
side of my face. "I don't want this break."

"Tyler, we can't go."

"We can book for whatever dates work best for your schedule."

Never mind that I had lived in Paris and if I was going to travel,
I'd want to visit someplace new. It just wasn't a good idea that
Tyler booked a trip for us when I'd clearly told him I needed time
away from him and our situation. I didn't want to hurt him and I
was fearful of coming across as insensitive. He had to understand
my position. I wasn't in a place in my life where I was willing to
settle. Aja thought maybe Tyler could change. She may have been
right. By him showing up at my house, trip in hand, it demonstrated
he was willing to make an attempt. Whether his attempt was driven
by wanting to make me happy or make himself happy was an entirely
different issue. I wanted to ask did he book the trip as a result of
missing me. I had mentioned it numerous times before, so why
now? I wanted to be able to say yes to the trip, but knew in my heart
that I couldn't go. I didn't want to go with Tyler. It spoke volumes
that he booked a trip to Paris when I had mentioned other destinations of interest. He did just enough to fulfill my request to go
away together, but not enough to ensure it was somewhere I'd
want to go.

I clasped his hand. "I'm sorry, Tyler."

"What can I do to make this right?"

"Give me space."

"That's not what I want."

"I think that's our issue. We want different things." I placed the
travel documents back in the gift back and handed it to him.

He put the bag on the table. "You hold on to these. I'm not giving
up on us yet."

CHAPTER THIRTY

yawned again. I was tired, but if Tyler needed to talk, I would do it so we could be on the same page. I couldn't lie. I loved Tyler. It wasn't as if he was sitting next to me and I felt nothing for him. For the past seven months, we were developing a relationship. We spent countless hours together, discussed almost everything with one another. I was intimate with this man. I didn't make the decision lightly to take a break from him.

"What exactly does this break mean to you?" he asked, for the second time.

"I just need time to figure out what I want to do."

"That's real vague, Riley."

"Maybe it is a little vague. I'm still trying to figure it all out."

"I know you were pissed about the movie, but I'm finding it hard to connect all the dots here. I thought we were heading in the right direction."

"I told you it wasn't about the movie. I thought you said you heard what I've been saying?"

"I guess I don't understand how the things you mentioned warrant a break."

"You're completely content with our relationship?"

"Damn near. What do I have to complain about? I have a good woman, smart, beautiful, funny, great company... Why wouldn't I be content?"

"See, that's interesting. I didn't ask about me, per se. I asked if you were content with the relationship. When you think about a relationship, what are your expectations?"

"I expect to be able to share who I am and what I want in life with this person. I want to communicate and talk about any and everything with this person. I want to be able to envision a future together. I want to have their back and feel that they have mine. We have to be compatible in the bedroom. As far as I'm concerned, we have all of that."

Tyler was right; we had all of those things. Yet, there was one key element missing. I needed the fire and the passion. That spark I saw in him the first night we met had extinguished too soon. I could appreciate sharing and communicating; I needed that, too. What about wanting to spend the rest of our lives together, not just saying you could see a future? Why not feel it has to be exciting in the bedroom, not just a matter of compatibility? Have my back, but fiercely defend me. I didn't know how to convey that to Tyler without making it seem he was doing something wrong.

A part of me felt that maybe I was being too idealistic. Somewhere along the way, I may have romanticized what a real relationship was. My sister told me to stop comparing men to my dad. She thought I set the bar too high. I didn't agree. Why lower the bar when I saw firsthand that the things I want in a relationship are attainable? I couldn't deny Tyler was a good man, but I could question if he was the right man for me.

"I can't disagree with you," I said.

"Then what is this about? You want to see other men?"

I flinched. "It has nothing to do with other men."

"How long is this break supposed to last?"

"I can't answer that."

"You need to tell me something, Riley."

"All I know is that I need time to figure out some things."

"We can figure things out together. We don't need a break to do that."

"Tyler, I'm dealing with my own feelings and emotions. I'm trying to determine what I want for myself in life. I need to be able to do that by myself."

"I get that we haven't been together a year yet, but we've grown close in a short time."

"Yes, we have."

"I don't want to lose that."

"I think because we've only been together seven months, now is the best time to figure out where we stand."

"I know where we stand," he said.

"You can't possibly know that. Not when I don't know where I stand."

"I'm trying to rectify the situation. Why else would I come over here with a booked vacation if I wasn't ready to be everything you need me to be?"

"I know I harped on going out and traveling. That's only a part of why I need to take a break. You have to understand that I'm at a point in my life where I'm reevaluating many things from my career to relationships. This is more about me than it is about you, Tyler."

He frowned. "Am I supposed to just wait around?"

"I'm not going to tell you what to do. That's your decision."

"Just like that?"

"You want me to tell you what to do? I don't think that would be fair to you."

"So, I should assume if you're not expecting me to wait on you, that this break makes you a single woman?"

I looked away and then forced myself to meet his gaze. "We're both single."

"I don't like it and I don't agree with this break."

"I'm sorry."

He kissed me on the forehead and stood to leave. "I hope I hear from you soon."

I nodded. We walked to the front door together. Tyler wrapped me in his embrace, my head resting on his shoulder. He kissed my forehead again and then my lips. With the slightest smile on his face, he walked out.

I headed back to the family room and lay on the couch. My heart was a little heavy. I didn't want to hurt Tyler. I honestly didn't know how long this break would last and what would come out of it. The only thing I was certain of was that it was necessary.

I was definitely taking a risk that he may find someone else to make him happy. I had no control over that. I felt a pang of guilt when he asked if I wanted to see other men. No, that wasn't my intention yet, somehow, I had found myself in unexpected situations with the Carlyles. I could admit I didn't know what I was getting myself into having spent time with Hutton, Dutton and Preston. They were brothers and seemed to have enough issues between them already. They didn't need me to complicate matters more. Moving forward, I would do my job for the Carlyles and nothing more.

CHAPTER THIRTY-ONE

My phone rang through the Bluetooth in my car. It wasn't quite eight in the morning. I was on the way to my first client of the week, and suffering from the Monday morning blues, thanks to my late night with Tyler. Too much talking and too little sleep.

I pressed the ANSWER button on my steering wheel. "Good morning."

"Ms. Ryan?"

"Yes, this is Riley."

"Good morning. I'm Granderson Carlyle's secretary and he asked me to give you a call."

"How can I help you?" I said, peering in my rearview to switch lanes.

"Mr. Carlyle would like to schedule a meeting with you in his office for this morning."

"This morning?"

"Yes, Ms. Ryan."

"What is this regarding?"

"I'm not at liberty to say. He just asked me to arrange the meeting."

"Well, Ms…"

"Washington."

"Ms. Washington, I can't commit to a meeting without knowing the purpose of said meeting. I'm sure you understand."

"Again, I'm not at liberty to discuss it, but I believe it involves catering a private cocktail reception."

"Thank you, that helps."

"Can I put you on Mr. Carlyle's calendar for this morning?"

"Unfortunately, I'm not available at all today. However, I can meet with him on Wednesday at three in the afternoon."

"I'll schedule the meeting and will see you on Wednesday."

I disconnected from the call. I wondered what was with the sudden influx of business from the Carlyle family. I wasn't the only chef in town.

I told my phone to dial Aja. She answered on the first ring. "Hey, bestie." She was sounding rather chipper for so early in the morning.

"Aja, listen to this. I just got a call from the secretary of one of the Carlyle sons. She was calling to schedule a meeting with him and me for this morning. Not later today or tomorrow, but this morning."

"She called pretty early."

"Extremely. I'm trying to figure out what is with all the business they're throwing my way. I mean, I know I'm a great chef, but come on. I'm not the only chef in town."

"Which son is it?"

"The oldest one, Grand. He's the married one."

"Oh, okay. So he wants to meet to discuss your services. What's wrong with that?"

"Technically, nothing. But I happen to know from Hutton that they have a company they use to cater their events. They don't need me."

"Riley, you're great at what you do. People change service providers. You're at their home every week making dinner. It makes sense that they would want to expand your business relationship. You should be happy about that."

"I am."

"But?"

"Uh…"

"Oh, boy. What does that mean."

"Just that I've complicated things a teeny bit."

"Keep talking."

"I told you about Hutton."

"Yes, he ate your box."

I burst out laughing. "Aja!"

"Well, he did. Don't get shy about it now."

"Hush up."

"And then you went on a date with his twin."

"It wasn't a date but, yes, Dutton and I went to the exhibit together."

"So, what's the problem?"

"I kissed the youngest son, Preston."

"What the hell?"

"I know, I know."

"What is going on with you?"

"It's not how it sounds."

"Enlighten me then."

I turned off the main road and into a residential neighborhood. "It's a little hard to explain. I know they're brothers, but my interactions with them couldn't be more different. Does that make sense?"

"Not really. I got caught up on the brothers part."

"They're nothing alike and things just sort of happened with Hutton and Preston."

"Don't you think they talk to one another? What happens when they start exchanging notes?"

"I haven't really done anything for them to discuss."

"Do you hear yourself? Hutton ate your box. You don't think that's discussion worthy?"

"I don't know. I can't say if a grown man is going around telling people that he performed oral sex on a woman."

"Not people, his brothers."

"Fine, his brothers. Either way, it's not going to happen again, so…"

"You need to make sure of that and conduct yourself in a professional manner."

"I always do, Aja."

"I know you do. It just seems like you're wandering into uncharted territory."

"I hear the concern in your voice. Don't worry. I'm on top of the situation and it's not even a situation."

"That's a lot of double-talk, but okay. I hope your meeting goes well on Wednesday and you get some more business. That's what it's all about."

"Right. I'll keep you posted."

We ended our call as I pulled up to my client's house. Did I have a situation? I didn't think so, but I could imagine how it sounded to Aja. It's funny how not long ago she'd encouraged me to go out with Hutton; now I sensed she was dissuading me. I'd take heed because I had the same thoughts myself and I didn't need a situation of any kind in my life.

CHAPTER THIRTY-TWO

*l*egs crossed, portfolio on my lap, I sat patiently in the waiting area. One of the financial channels played on the flatscreen affixed to the wall. The offices of Loucar Asset Management were imposing. Located in downtown Atlanta, the firm occupied three floors of a luxury office building.

A commercial came on and I looked away from the television. The secretary smiled pleasantly at me. In fact, each time I glanced in her direction, she was watching me. An office door opened and Grand exited. He beamed, coming over to where I was seated.

"Sorry to keep you waiting. I had a meeting run over."

I stood. "It's all right."

"Come in to my office."

I followed Grand, reciprocating yet another smile I received from the secretary as I passed her desk. He closed his office door behind us. He led me over to a meeting area with a sofa, two chairs and a low table in the center. I sat on the sofa, adjusting my ivory, asymmetrical neck dress as I got settled. I placed my portfolio on the table.

"Your secretary wouldn't tell me specifically why you wanted to meet, but I brought my menus. I wanted you to see what your options are for a variety of events."

Grand joined me on the sofa. "I appreciate your coming in."

"I'm sorry I couldn't make it Monday. It was short notice and I had a full schedule."

"I should have known. You're a much sought-after chef."

I waved him off. "As long as my clients are satisfied."

"My mother definitely is."

"That's what I love to hear."

"You've made Sundays the highlight of our week."

"That's some compliment."

"It's true. I went home Sunday evening and I couldn't stop thinking about you."

"You mean the dinner?"

"No, I mean you."

I unzipped my portfolio, opening it to the first page. "What type of event are you planning?"

He chuckled. "See, you make me laugh."

"I wasn't trying to be funny. I'm here to discuss business."

"I know and it's endearing."

I pushed the portfolio in front of him on the table. "Grand, do you want to discuss your event or not?"

"If you're giving me the option, I'd much rather talk about how our conversation on Sunday stayed with me. I found myself going back to your comment about being with a man that calls to you."

"I wasn't giving you an option. I'm saying I'm here for business. Let's keep it professional."

"I recall saying to you that for certain women only a certain type of man is acceptable. A certain man that's worthy and could live up to her standards. A certain type of man that could give her what she needs." Grand completely ignored me and took our discussion where he wanted it to go. "I should be the man that calls to you."

I watched him silently. Maybe he'd get a clue that what he was saying had nothing to do with why I was there. I dramatically looked at my watch. "The clock is ticking. Do you want to discuss this event?"

"There is no event, Riley," he matter-of-factly stated. "I just wanted to see you."

I leaned forward, zipped my portfolio closed, grabbed it by the handle and started for the door.

Grand seized me by the arm. "Please, sit down for a minute."

"I don't think so. You get me here under the guise of an event?"

"Let me explain."

"Did your assistant know? No wonder she kept smiling at me."

"Riley, sit down, please."

I stood tense, halfway between the couch and the office door. "No, that's okay."

"Riley, please. Give me a chance to explain myself."

I exhaled, shoulders relaxing. "Fine."

He didn't release my arm until I was reseated on the sofa. "I'm sorry," he said. "I couldn't think of another way to get a chance to see you."

"You see me every week at Sunday dinner."

"I wanted to see you alone."

"My time is valuable too, Grand."

"I know it is. I would plan an event just to see you. Fake guests and all. Do you want me to? We can book it today."

Despite myself, I laughed. "You're not funny."

He bit his bottom lip. "I think you think I am."

"I think I'm pissed. What do you need to talk to me about?"

He gazed at me intently. "I'm not the man calling to you?"

"What makes you think you are?"

"Because you're calling to me."

"You're married, Grand."

"We covered that on Sunday."

"Right, nothing's changed."

"It has for me. I know that I can be that man in your life. I can give you whatever you want, whatever you need."

"You don't even know me."

"You're calling to me, Riley."

I looked into his chestnut-colored eyes. "Are you asking me to have an affair with you?"

"A love affair."

"Is that what you called them in the past?"

"I've never cheated on my wife. I said I flirt, but I've never physically cheated."

"What about emotionally?"

"That's up for debate. I would have to believe that's a form of cheating and I don't know if I do."

"Yet you're proposing that I have an affair with you?"

"I want you."

My eyes narrowed. "Why?"

"You're my type of woman."

"Again with the types? It shouldn't matter what type of woman I am. You. Are. Married."

"You don't have to keep telling me that. No one is more painfully aware of that fact than me."

"Except your wife. She made it clear to me on Sunday that you were in wedded bliss."

"That's not true."

"She made sure to tell me about how you two were paired by your parents, your romantic vacation in Bora Bora, and of course, the baby girl you're working on. It sounds like bliss to me."

"Jayla's a smart woman. She knows my tastes. She wanted to make sure if I did flirt with you, that I wouldn't find a receptive ear. Was she successful?"

"Your marital status prevents me from being receptive."

Grand visibly exhaled. He gazed at me for a moment before nodding. "You asked me why I want you. That's why. I could give you the world and you turn me down."

"I don't need the world."

"I'm not sure my wife ever felt that way. When we met, she knew of my family, our reputation and our money. Her mother was instrumental in getting us together or I should say securing her daughter's future. The version of the story she told you is partially accurate. I won't lie. I love my wife, but I haven't been in love for a long time."

That was information I didn't need to be privy to. It was unsettling to know how a man felt about his wife when she may not have been aware. Some details should stay within the marriage. A husband and wife should respect their bond and maintain a sense of privacy. Jayla overshared with me and Grand was doing the same.

I tried to redirect the tone of the conversation. "You two really have a beautiful family. Jayce and Caleb are the cutest kids ever."

"Thank you. In our family of men, everyone is waiting for the girl. I want a daughter, but lately, I've been thinking if I should bring more children into my marriage. Right now, I'm the only one following in my father's footsteps. My brothers will get around to marriage and children, but when my parents think of grandchildren, and most recently a granddaughter, they look to me. My father always looks to me."

"You all seem to have an interesting relationship with your father."

"We do. All separate and distinct. He's not the same father to all of us. We all know him in very different ways. I'm probably the closest to him and it's a blessing and a curse. If I wanted to live by my own rules, and not the ones set forth by Louis Carlyle, it would be completely unacceptable. I'm the number one son and I live my life as such. Imagine being your own man and at the age of thirty-five, you still have to do everything your father says. And you look at your siblings and they are living their lives however they choose." He stared blankly in front of him. "And, you have a wife at home that some days you think about leaving, but you don't because you have two beautiful sons that you don't want to put through a divorce. So you work hard, do what's expected of you to one day fill your father's shoes, and find your joy where you can." He looked pensively at me. "You get the gist."

"I do."

"I want to apologize for bringing you here under false pretenses."

"Apology accepted." I smiled at him. "You owe me an event."

"I'll make it up to you."

I stood up to leave. "I'm going to hold you to it."

"Can I take you to dinner?"

I shook my head. "Grand, no."

He stood in front of me. "I enjoy talking to you, Riley. It would be nice to take you to a quiet restaurant, with soft music. We could just talk and have dinner."

"I'm sorry, I can't."

He stepped closer, lowering his voice. "We can leave from here. Right now if you want. I can have my driver take us wherever you want to go."

My pulse quickened as his face brushed against mine. I moved back and he stepped forward.

"Wherever you want to go," he whispered. His hands grasped my waist at the same time his lips touched mine. Heat roiled off him as he kissed me deeply. Grand pulled me closer until his body was against mine. The fire inside him swept me up in his quenchless kiss. Our tongues intertwined, stoking the flame. He squeezed me tighter and a moan rumbled from him. My eyes fluttered open. I began to ease myself from his arms and his kiss.

Reluctantly, Grand let go of my waist. The fire was still smoldering in his eyes. I backed away from him and grabbed my portfolio. "I'm sorry. I can't do this," I whispered.

I rushed out of Grand's office aware that I officially had a situation.

CHAPTER THIRTY-THREE

y thoughts kept returning to my conversation with Aja. What the heck was I doing with the Carlyles? I had just told her a couple of days before that it was strictly business with that family. Then, I go to Grand's office and end up sharing a torrid kiss with him. A married man, no less. If Aja knew I had done that, she'd kill me. I didn't even have anything I could say in my defense. I didn't believe it would be sufficient to say he kissed me. Although, he did, I kissed him back of my own volition.

What I wanted to know was why they seemed to be drawn to me. Jayla made a comment about me being in the Carlyle den. Maybe I needed to ask more questions about what exactly that meant. If I had the opportunity to chat with her, I would do just that. Hopefully, she'd be in a talkative mood and not done over-sharing, since her message had already been delivered.

I found each of the Carlyle sons were engaging in their own way. I liked Dutton for his reserved nature and intelligence. He was smart, but he didn't flaunt it. It was merely a part of his make-up. He was passionate about his work and following his own path. I appreciated being around people from whom I could learn something. He most definitely was a wealth of knowledge and eager to share. He had a giving nature. I appreciated that he thought of me at his conference and bought me a cookbook. It was such a thoughtful gesture.

Hutton, on the other hand, was an entirely different story. He was flashy and wanted everyone to know he was the most important person in the room. I did give him credit because he didn't mind sharing the spotlight when I was on his arm. He made me feel like the costar in his own constantly playing movie. Hutton exuded virility. His strength and masculinity were magnetic. They pulled you in like a moth to a flame. He made me want what he wanted and the pleasure was all mine.

Preston was all about pleasure. He wanted to live life in a way that would bring him joy. He was on a mission to find his passion. I couldn't fault him for that. How many people were living lives and working in careers that were unfulfilling? Preston's approach was a constant reminder that I needed to be striving to turn the things I was passionate about into opportunities. There was no reason why I shouldn't be focusing more on building my catering business. He lived with an abandon that was inspiring. I wanted a little of that in my own life.

Grand was the one to watch. He had a fire inside his belly that motivated everything he did. He was ready to own the world or at least his father's business. With Louis grooming him, he would do everything it took to carry their firm into the next generation. He recognized what he was due. Call it a sense of entitlement or even privilege, Grand went after what he felt he deserved. When I considered it, I realized that's not a terrible way to be. I wanted what I deserved; why not go after it?

As I tried to explain to Aja, they were all so different. The time I spent with each of them was primarily harmless. I could acknowledge that for me, someone that doesn't believe in mixing business with pleasure, I had tipped across a few lines. I wasn't accustomed to doing that. I found myself in a situation I had never before experienced. The only thing I could do about it at that point was to not make it any worse. I could limit my contact with the Carlyles. There was no reason that I needed to see or speak to any of them outside of Sunday dinner, with the exception of a catered event at Loucar. I made a silent vow to myself that I would not be drawn in by the Carlyles or into their den, whatever that meant. I may have put myself in a precarious position, but I could also get myself out.

My doorbell rang. I wasn't expecting anyone. I took my time going to answer it. I hoped it wasn't Tyler showing up uninvited again. I went to the front door and looked through the peephole. A delivery man was on my porch, his florist van parked in my driveway. I opened the door and greeted him. He smiled broadly as he passed a large bouquet of pink roses to me. I thanked him and closed the door. I carried the arrangement back to my family room, counting the stems along the way. When I reached thirty-eight, I stopped counting. I was unable to see the entire arrangement and made the assumption there were four dozen. I placed the flowers on the coffee table and reached for the card attached to the vase.

You're calling to me and I'm trying to answer. We shouldn't let the obvious get in the way, when something more beautiful is right in front of us. Searching for joy. Help me find it.

–GC

I read the card again and placed it on the table. Granderson Carlyle. He had to know, just as much as I did, that nothing could happen between us. I had reiterated multiple times that he was married. The kiss we'd shared should not have transpired. If he was unhappy in his marriage, I could not be the conduit to joy. I accepted onus that kissing him in his office had sent a mixed signal. As soon as I had the opportunity, I would rectify the situation. Not only was I hoping for a moment to speak with Jayla, I definitely needed a moment with her husband on Sunday.

CHAPTER THIRTY-FOUR

*S*undays seemed to roll around faster each week. I had officially settled into a groove at the Carlyle home. Creating in that magnificent kitchen had become second nature. The amount of space and top-of-the-line appliances I had at my disposal, allowed for seamless meal preparation. I was proud of the dishes I was turning out of their kitchen.

I thought about how I almost didn't accept the job. One day a week at the rate I was charging, I obviously wasn't thinking clearly. I smiled, pleased with myself that I had changed my mind.

"That's some smile. What are you thinking about?"

I looked up from the cutting board. "Hi, Miriam. I didn't hear you come in."

"You seemed lost in your thoughts."

"I was just thinking about how much I love what I do for a living."

"That's a blessing, you know?"

"Oh, absolutely. I know people who dread going to work each day. I, thankfully, don't have that problem. How could I when I work in surroundings like this?"

"This is some kitchen," Miriam commented in a conspiratorial tone. "It's nice to see that it makes you appreciate what you do."

"Environment matters when you're a chef. This space definitely inspires me."

Miriam perched herself at the island. "You have been a wonder in here."

"Thanks."

"Do you cook for your family?"

"Not as often as I'd like."

"That's surprising. I would think having a chef in the family meant guaranteed gourmet meals."

"I may cook on special occasions, but it's sort of infrequent."

"How old are you, Riley?"

"I'm twenty-eight."

"And you're single?"

"I'm not married."

"I knew you weren't married. I was wondering about a boyfriend or fiancé."

I glanced at Miriam curiously. "Yes, I'm single."

"I know it's difficult for young people to focus on careers and relationships these days."

I remained quiet, acknowledging her statement with a solitary nod.

"When I was younger, we didn't think about choosing between work and marriage. You were expected to find a man and marry him. There wasn't a whole lot of dating around."

"Times have changed on that front," I said.

"They sure have." She watched me prick holes in the yellow skin of two large spaghetti squash. "I'm not sure that's for the better, either," she continued.

"You don't think women should date to find the right man?" I wanted to retract the question as soon as I asked.

"I think young women these days don't take the time to cultivate relationships. They want to jump from one man to the next in search of who knows what."

"I think they're fearful of devoting too much time to a guy that may not be the one."

"How will you know if he's the one if you're just dating, dating, dating—instead of getting to know one man?"

"I think most women know what qualities they want in a man. They move on when they don't see it."

"If you ask me, it's all very counterproductive. You all can stand to learn a thing or two from my generation. Everyone is too free these days. You're single. What are you looking for in a man?"

I opened my mouth to respond just as Dutton came into the kitchen.

"Hey, Mom." He leaned over and kissed Miriam on the cheek. "Hey, Riley."

"My sons seem to arrive earlier and earlier each week." She wrapped an arm around Dutton's waist and squeezed. She looked up at the man standing next to her and smiled. "How are you, son?"

"I can't complain."

"I can. You haven't called all week. This is the first time I'm hearing from you since last Sunday."

"I'm sorry, Mom." He leaned down and kissed her cheek again. "I had a hectic week at work."

"I don't want to hear it," she replied, with feigned anger. "I expect that behavior from your brothers, but not you."

"I promise I'll make it up to you. I'll call you every day this week." He laughed.

She swatted at him. "Don't get cute."

"I can't help it. Everyone says I look like you." He stroked his face. "Without the beard, of course."

I did see a lot of Miriam in Dutton—the complexion, same sharp features and even the eyes partially concealed by his glasses.

"Do you hear this, Riley? My son thinks he's cute. I don't see it, do you?"

I smiled at their exchange. I was beginning to get an idea of which son was Miriam's favorite.

"I will definitely be calling you this week so I don't have to be embarrassed in front of Riley again." He chuckled.

"Don't mind me," I said. "I'm just making dinner."

"One or two calls is fine. I know you're a busy college professor."

"I was a little busier than usual. My students had exams this week. I've also been trying to finish writing my book."

"I understand, honey."

Dutton sat next to his mother at the island. I went to the fridge to grab a few ingredients. I took out a carton of eggs, parmesan cheese, a container of milk and bunch of basil.

Dutton saw me attempting to carry everything at once. He started to get up. "Can I help you with that?"

"No, I have it, thanks. Chefs are experts at juggling a lot of things at one time."

"I'm just sitting here watching you try to balance all of that. I'm no cook, but I could make myself useful."

"Really, that's not necessary. This is what I do. "

Miriam glanced at Dutton and then peered at me.

"Did you have a chance to look at the cookbook I gave you a couple of weeks ago?" Dutton asked.

"Yes, I did. Interesting recipes. I think a few of them can be modified with an updated spin."

"What book is this?"

"I gave Riley a book on Ancient Egyptian cooking."

"I told Dutton that I would be willing to try one of the recipes for Sunday dinner."

"Please run that menu by me first," she said. "This isn't Ancient Egypt."

"Absolutely."

"Think outside of the box, Mom. A lot of what we do in the kitchen can be directly correlated with ancient practices. The skills Riley has acquired, and mastered, originated with people that had no modern conveniences. Yet, they managed to ultimately do the same thing. Provide sustenance and nutrition for their families."

"That's my son, the professor. Always educating and enlightening those that need enlightenment."

"You're giving me too much credit. I basically get carried away sharing information no one wants to hear," he replied.

"I disagree," I said. "You've shared information on things I find very interesting."

Dutton smiled and it looked very close to a blush. His mother watched him curiously. "Well," she said, standing up. "I need to go see what your father is up to. He's probably glued to the television watching golf. Why don't you come see if you can tear him away?"

"No, I think I'll keep Riley company for a while."

Miriam hesitated. "Don't stay in here distracting Riley too long. I'm sure she'll put you out when she grows tired of your sharing, as interesting as it may be."

I was about to tell Miriam that he wasn't distracting me and he could stay, but I held my tongue. A mother was telling her son what to do and it wasn't my place to interfere. Miriam left to find her husband without another word.

Dutton looked over his shoulder in the direction his mother just left. "I hope I didn't cross any lines?"

"Cross any lines?" I repeated.

"I love crossing lines." Hutton's voice filled the kitchen. "It's one of my favorite things to do."

Dutton and I watched him approach the island. The smirk I was getting used to seeing on his face was ever-present. Dutton glared at his brother.

"What's wrong with you?" Hutton asked him. He stared squarely at his brother who had yet to respond, before turning his attention to me. "Ah, I see. Someone is crushing on the chef. I understand, bro. How could you not crush on something so sweet?"

Dutton frowned. "Can you excuse us, Hutton? We're having a conversation."

His eyes widened. "Yeah, okay," he answered stiffly.

Hutton made eye contact with me before retracing his steps out of the kitchen. I was surprised at the way Dutton spoke to his brother and even more surprised that Hutton actually listened. He seemed completely caught off guard by Dutton.

"That felt good," Dutton said. "Now, where were we? Oh, right. Did I cross the line when I kissed you at the museum?"

"The peck on the cheek?" I asked. "Weren't you just saying good night?"

"I was, but when I thought about it later, I realized it was inappropriate."

I fought the urge to giggle. One twin had insisted on kissing my private parts and felt no way about it. The other barely connects with my cheek and thinks he did something wrong. They were nothing alike.

"You didn't cross any lines, Dutton."

"I was concerned about that. Knowing firsthand how my brother can be, I wanted to make sure nothing I did resembled his behavior."

"Believe me. You are in no danger of having done that."

"My colleagues enjoyed meeting you and they were serious about you catering our next event."

"If my schedule permits, I'd be happy to whip something up for your peers. Maybe they'd appreciate the Ancient Egyptian recipes. Your mother doesn't seem too keen on my using them for Sunday dinner."

"I could convince her to try it."

Dutton was definitely the favorite. It was as if Miriam lit up when he arrived and he certainly became more animated. The mother-son relationship was an enigma to me. I'd seen mothers fawn over their sons in ways they didn't do for their daughters. Up until today, I hadn't seen Miriam show an extreme amount of deference to any of her sons. They all appeared to receive the same regard. However she made one comment that stood out. She said she expected her other sons to neglect calling, but not Dutton. That led me to believe their relationship must have been different than the others.

"I'm sure you could," I said. "But, it might be a better idea to save it for a group that can appreciate the context of the meal."

"You're right. That meal might not go over well with the family. I don't want to tarnish your stellar reputation as the Carlyle chef supreme."

I laughed. I'd never seen him so witty. "Oh, you wouldn't. I'd give you complete and total credit for the ancient meal."

"I'd take it because I like having you around."

I paused whisking the eggs. "To make dinner?"

"I enjoy talking to you, Riley." He looked down at the counter and then up again. "I was planning to ask if I can take you out again."

"Really?" I began vigorously whisking.

"I like your company."

"Likewise," I said, not exactly sure how to respond.

I wasn't expecting an invite from Dutton. I had already established that I needed to cease whatever was brewing with the Carlyle men. I was there to make dinner and nothing else. Not talk. Not check out passion projects. Not party. Nothing. I had to stay true to what I knew—that Dutton and I would not be going out. I needed to find a way to let him know that although I had a good time at the exhibit, I would not be going anywhere with him again.

"You've been nothing but nice to me. I realized that I would rather sit in the kitchen with you than at the dinner table with my family."

"You can't mean that."

"I've had plenty of dinners with them. You're intriguing to me. I want to spend more time with you outside of this kitchen. There's a festival in Rome next week. Maybe you'd want to go? We could drive up for the day, take in the scenery and explore the Cherokee culture."

I stalled, looking for the right words to turn him down. "That's awfully nice and I appreciate the invitation. It's just that my schedule is a bit crazy."

"We could drive up on Friday. There would be less people and less traffic."

I didn't want to be hurtful. "Let me give it some thought."

"That's all I can ask." Dutton got up from the island with a smile on his face. "I'd better take heed of what my mother said and not distract you. I'll leave you with your prep and my invitation." Dutton walked from the kitchen with a relaxed stride.

Handling the dinner prep was easy. It was declining the invite that I was having trouble with.

CHAPTER THIRTY-FIVE

iriam and Louis needed to install a revolving door in the kitchen with the amount of traffic it had been receiving as of late. Though I didn't know for sure, I made the assumption that it wasn't typical. Hutton was back and the expression on his face told me that he wasn't pleased. I continued checking on the bacon that was rendering in a Dutch oven on the stove. He stood next to me like he was my sous chef.

"Did my brother ask you out?"

I glanced at him. "Why didn't you ask him?"

"I prefer to find out from you."

I walked away from him and back to the island. "He invited me to a festival."

"What did you say?"

"I told him I'd think about it."

Hutton scoffed. "What could you possibly want with him when I can give you so much more?"

I was perplexed and certain it showed on my face. "How could you talk that way about your twin?"

"I can because he's my twin."

Point taken. It was none of my business how these brothers dealt with one another. The fact that Hutton came to question me, rather than talk to his brother, was very telling. I offered the only response that I had. "I told Dutton I would consider it. I didn't say yes."

"Save yourself the trouble."

"Wow."

"I don't want you to take anything I said the wrong way. I know my brother. He can't handle a woman like you."

"A woman like me?"

"I'll just say that in the past, he's struggled in the woman department. It could be a case of nice guy syndrome, who knows."

"Women like nice guys."

"Not when they can have rich and powerful guys." He eyed me. "Isn't that right?"

"I have no idea."

Hutton leaned against the counter, folding his arms across his chest. "When we were younger, I had a group of friends that I hung out with all of the time. Dutton was a bookworm and didn't go out much."

"I could see that."

"My mother would make me take him along wherever I was going. At first, I really didn't mind, but when it continued throughout junior high and eventually high school, it became a problem. Imagine a group of young men out carousing and having fun. Then visualize the one dude in the group hanging back and lurking. The one dude that makes everyone feel uncomfortable because he's not talking or interacting with anyone. Add pretty girls into the equation. There were only so many introductions I could make. I'd start the conversation for him, stay in the mix for a few minutes and then excuse myself. Minutes later, the young lady I had introduced him to would be walking away. If I asked him what happened, his answer was always the same. He didn't know."

"Why are you telling me this?"

"He's still that same guy."

"You're not in junior high anymore."

"I know my brother. He can't do anything for you. I can." Hutton came around the island and sidled up to me. I kept julienning carrots. He moved closer, standing directly behind me. Hands on the countertop on either side of me, his body molded to mine.

He lowered his head until the familiar touch of his lips made contact with my neck. Delicate caresses on my skin sent a tingle through me. My head tilted to the side.

"What kind of game are you playing?" I asked softly.

"No games here."

A flick of the tongue made me put down my knife. "Then what are you doing?" I breathed.

"My twin and I obviously share the same good taste," he said, in between kisses. "Where we differ…is right here." Hutton pressed harder against me.

"Stop it." My voice came out in a strained murmur.

"I keep thinking about the night you let me taste you."

"Hutton…no…"

"You loved it."

"Stop." I pleaded, surprised at how unconvincing I sounded.

His kisses traveled from one side of my neck to the other. "You tasted so good to me. Let me taste you again."

"I shouldn't have let that happen."

"Why not? We both enjoyed ourselves. I'm enjoying myself now."

Slowing steps pulled my attention away from Hutton. I looked toward the door in time to see Grand come to a standstill. A dour countenance stared at us. Hutton moved his hands from the counter and gradually backed away from me. He watched Grand through narrowed eyes.

Hutton cleared his throat. "Hey, Grand. How's it going?"

Grand didn't answer. He stood feet away from the island, watching me.

"Are the wife and kids with you?" Hutton asked. I turned toward him. The smirk was back.

"Jayla and the boys are at her mother's." He sounded and looked tight.

"Shouldn't you be there too?"

He approached the island. "I'm where I'm supposed to be."

"Yeah, I wouldn't miss all of this, either," Hutton replied. "Sunday dinner, I mean."

I wanted to stomp on his foot.

"What did I just walk in on?"

Hutton shrugged. "Riley making dinner."

"Don't be an ass, Hutton. You know that's not what I'm referring to." Grand glared at me. "What's going on?"

"Nothing that concerns you, big brother."

"Maybe it does."

"I realize since your kids aren't here, you probably need to tell someone what to do. Unfortunately for you, there are no kids in this kitchen. Just two grown adults."

"Watch it, Hutton."

"No, you watch it. You're not running things."

"Not yet, but soon."

I stayed quiet, but inside I was screaming.

"What's the problem, Grand? Did you want something in here?"

The brothers stared at each other. Grand turned and stormed out of the kitchen. Hutton immediately followed. I, on the other hand, was confined to a space that, although it was rather large, felt like it was closing in on me.

CHAPTER THIRTY-SIX

The first course had been placed in front of the family. I stood near the head of the table, waiting for their conversation to subside. Miriam shushed her men. I tried to avoid direct eye contact with Grand, but it was virtually impossible not to meet eyes with everyone at the table. I was talking too fast as I described the chive soufflés. I had never felt more awkward than I was feeling at that moment.

The Carlyle men sat quietly during my presentation. Hutton began eating before I concluded.

His mother shook her head at him. It didn't matter to me. I just wanted to make my exit back to the kitchen.

"Hutton, you couldn't wait until Riley finished?" Miriam inquired.

"I'm excited to get to what's next. I know it's going to be good."

I felt my face flush.

"You're always moving too quickly," Grand said.

"Not anymore. I'm taking time to savor this."

"It is delicious," Preston added. "Riley, how do you keep it erect?"

"Excuse me?" I asked.

"The soufflés? Don't they collapse easily?"

I nodded, swallowing hard. "They do. You have to be really careful when baking and handling them."

"You obviously know how to handle them just right," Hutton commented.

Louis picked up his fork. "If the peanut gallery is finished, I'm going to dig in."

"I'm already digging in."

"We know, Hutton."

The room started to feel warm. I unsnapped the top button on my chef coat. I felt small beads of perspiration forming on my forehead. "Miriam," I interjected. "I'm not feeling well. I'm going to leave early."

She shifted in her seat, surveying me from head to toe. "Do you need to sit down for a minute?"

"No, I think I should just head home. Everything is already prepared. It just needs to be served."

Louis chimed in. "We'll take care of it. You don't look good. Are you well enough to drive?"

"I can take her home," Dutton offered.

"No, that's okay. Stay and finish your family dinner. I can get myself home."

"Dutton, take her," Louis asserted. "You can drive Riley's car and I'll have my service pick you up and bring you back to the house."

I wasn't in any shape to argue the point. I thanked the Carlyles for understanding and went to retrieve my things from the kitchen. Dutton carried my bags out to the car. I started to feel better as I stepped into the fresh air.

Dutton held his hand out. "Keys."

"You really don't need to drive me."

"You heard my father. He, we, won't accept no for an answer."

I reached in my purse and gave him my car keys. Dutton asked where I lived, started the car and drove me away from a dinner with the potential to collapse, like the soufflés I'd served.

CHAPTER THIRTY-SEVEN

*D*utton pulled into my driveway and turned off the engine. I had kept my eyes closed the entire ride, not wanting to have any discussion about the dinner. I wanted to get inside my house, lock the door behind me and regroup. The spectacle of it all was turning my stomach. Hutton's and Grand's comments, and even Preston's unintentional one, were an embarrassment. Their jockeying never should have included me. I never should have become a pawn in their posturing.

I glanced over at him. "Thank you for driving me home."

"I couldn't let you drive yourself. Are you feeling any better?"

"Yes, I think I just needed fresh air. I'm going to go inside, relax and order some takeout. " I opened my car door.

"I'm a bit hungry myself." He peered at me over the top of his glasses. "Seeing as I missed dinner… And, I do have to call and wait for the car service…"

I sighed. "Do you want to come in?" I asked, while getting out.

"That would be great." He hopped out the car and grabbed my bags from the back.

We went inside and I led him into the living room. "You can put my bags on that ottoman in the corner." I opened the blinds to let in the final hours of daylight. "Have a seat."

"You have a nice home."

"Thank you." I turned on the television and handed him the remote. "Can I get you something to drink?"

"I'll have some water."

I went to the kitchen and got two bottles of water from the refrigerator. I was a little parched after my heat spell and drank half of my bottle before leaving the kitchen. I returned to him leaned forward, watching boxing. I handed him the water.

"It's a replay of the fight last night."

"I didn't take you for a boxing fan," I said.

"I love boxing. We used to watch it with my father growing up. Mike Tyson, Evander Holyfield, Riddick Bowe, Oscar De La Hoya, Lennox Lewis, Sugar Shane… My father referred to them as the new jacks. He would always tell us we should've seen the Ali and Frazier fights. That was boxing to him. He doesn't understand the Mayweathers and Pacquiaos of today."

I smiled. "My father used to love boxing, too."

"Used to?"

"Yeah…" I said quietly.

"I'm sorry."

"Thank you. Listen, I'm going to change and I'll be right back."

"Take your time."

I headed upstairs to my room. I really did appreciate Dutton driving me home. I would've made it home with no problem, but it was apparent Louis wasn't having it. I could understand. I was in his home, not feeling well, and he wasn't comfortable with sending me out in that state. I was surprised that Dutton offered to drive me. He had commented earlier that he preferred to stay in the kitchen over the dinner table, but I didn't think he would abandon dinner altogether.

I had seen more of their family dynamic that evening than ever before. The exchange between twins had caught me off guard. I had seen Hutton push his weight around with his twin before, but I hadn't observed Dutton push back. Tonight, he held his own.

Hutton's halo of arrogance dimmed a bit, if only for a moment. It was definitely short-lived. He returned to the kitchen with a vengeance, and hell-bent on making his position known. He was very clear; his brother didn't compare. I could see feeling that way about someone that you didn't care about, but your own family? It wasn't right. If he truly felt that way, it certainly wasn't appropriate to verbalize to me. Yet, half the things Hutton and Grand verbalized at the dinner table weren't appropriate. They were throwing around double entendres with recklessness, at my expense. They weren't concerned in the least if their parents caught on. Well, I cared. I had to care about how I was perceived and my reputation. I had to be all about my business. I sat on the edge of my bed. How many times was I going to keep rehashing what I needed to do? I had to stop thinking about it and be about it.

I washed my face and then slipped into a pair of comfortable sweats and a fitted tee. I went downstairs to retrieve the menus. I entered the living room and handed them to Dutton. He gave me a once-over and read my T-shirt aloud. "*I bring the heat.* That's cute."

"My best friend gave me this shirt. She thought it was fitting, being I'm a chef and all."

"I get it," he said with a smile.

"Of course you do." I sat next to him on the couch. "So, those are your dinner options."

He spread the menus out on the coffee table. "Indian, Chinese, Greek, Italian and Southern. What's your favorite?"

"I can go for any of those places."

"I asked what's your favorite."

"Honestly, the soul food spot. I don't cook or eat too much soul food. And, it's tough to find a place that makes it like, or better than, your mama."

"So this place cooks better than your mama?"

"Don't talk about my mama."

"I'm not." He laughed, handing me the soul food menu. "You order. Whatever you want, I'll eat."

"I hope you have a big appetite." I placed an order for smothered pork chops, black-eyed peas and rice, candied yams, cabbage and macaroni and cheese.

"Can you actually eat all of that?" he asked.

"Watch me."

"I'll be too busy eating my own food to watch you."

I laughed. "How about some wine?"

"That sounds good."

I opened a bottle of chardonnay and poured two glasses. I handed one to Dutton and tapped mine against his. I looked at the TV and noticed the fight was over. "Who won?"

"Not my guy. I owe my colleague fifty dollars."

"You're a betting man?"

"Not really, but he is. I took the bet so he'd stop bugging me about the fight."

"Now he can bug you about the money you owe him."

"I won't give him a chance to do that. I plan to slap the money on his desk first thing tomorrow morning." He picked up the remote and handed it to me. "What do you watch on Sunday evenings?"

"I don't really have weekend shows. I watch a lot of Food Network."

"That's like me. I watch an obscene amount of the National Geographic and Discovery channels."

"Sounds stimulating," I joked.

"Right, like watching someone bake a cake on TV is the most exciting thing ever."

"You'd be surprised."

"Turn it on. Let's see."

I switched the channel to Discovery. "No, let's see what you overdose on." A naked woman trying to build a shelter was on the screen. "Really?"

"May I?" He held out his hand for the remote. I passed it to him. He scrolled until he found the Food Network. Three people ran through the aisles with shopping carts, tossing groceries into them. He looked over at me. "See, don't judge me."

We both laughed. "Give me that." I took the remote and put on a movie channel. "Better?"

"Much." He settled back against the cushions. "Do you mind if I ask you a personal question?"

"Sure, go ahead."

"Is there a special someone in your life?"

I drew my legs up on the couch. "Actually, no. I recently broke up with my boyfriend."

"If you don't mind my asking, how long were you together?"

"About seven months."

"Why'd you break up?"

"Ultimately…" I paused. "I guess I wasn't happy with the relationship."

"Happy is an interesting concept when it comes to matters of the heart."

"How do you mean?"

"Well, it's just that there can be so many components that make up a relationship. Think about it. Relationships can provide us with mental, physical and emotional aspects that can either help or harm us. Is the relationship a benefit or detriment to our well-being? Are we flourishing or languishing with this person? And, then you mentioned not being happy. Well, what's the contrast to happy? Is it sad? So, did the relationship make you sad? That doesn't seem like an accurate measure for assessing the state of a relationship. There's a lot in between happiness and sadness. There's frustration, disappointment, uncertainty, complacency, boredom… You see where I'm going? I'm sure you can add a few of your own."

"I understand what you're saying."

"So why did you break up?" he asked, again.

"I broke up with Tyler because I questioned whether I wanted a future with him. I had doubts about him being the right man for me. He wasn't doing what I expected from the man in my life and I felt unfulfilled."

"Ah, that's much different than not being happy."

I nodded. "You're right. However, all of those things influence happiness."

"They absolutely do. Yet, now I know why you're no longer with him."

"What about you?" I inquired.

"I'm single. I was dating another professor at the university, but it wasn't anything serious. She wasn't looking for anything permanent and neither was I."

"When was your last serious relationship?"

"Five years ago."

"That's a long time."

"I guess it is. Time gets away from you when you know what you want yet you don't find it."

I sipped my wine and considered his comment. "Does that mean you're searching for a specific woman or hoping she'll cross your path?"

"Sometimes I'm looking and other times I'm not."

"Are you on dating sites?"

"I've tried them."

"What are you looking for that's so hard to find?"

"Three things: intelligence, humility and compassion."

"That can't be it."

"Why not?" he challenged.

"Because there are so many other qualities in a person."

"Those three qualities are the foundation to everything else I need in a woman. If she's smart, she has the faculties to make a living, engage and stimulate me intellectually. If she has humility, she's respectful of herself and others, unpretentious. If she has compassion, she's kind-hearted and her actions are borne from that kindheartedness."

At least he knew what he wanted and didn't have a laundry list of requirements, like myself. I felt I needed to be more specific. If I was completely clear on each and every thing I needed, there could be no room for error. Well, there was always room for error, but I could do my best to minimize it. "I would think you could find a woman that possesses three qualities."

"You'd be surprised. Humility and compassion aren't as easy to come by as one would imagine."

"And some of the smartest people lack common sense."

"Now that's one hundred percent true." He clinked his glass against mine. "What are you looking for, Riley?"

"I can't pretend I'm not one of those people with a very long, very specific list of requirements. I don't know whether that list will matter at all at the end of the day. I do know that I need a man that will love me and treat me the way I want to be loved and treated."

I didn't need anyone to tell me that would be no easy feat. I was willing to be patient as long as it wouldn't take forever to find him or for him to find me. I only hoped I never got to the point where I would settle. My sister called it compromise, but that was a nice way to say I'm not getting what I want and I'm okay with it. We could compromise on the small things. Who would wash the dishes after a big meal? Do you want vanilla or chocolate ice cream?

Should we take your car or mine? I wasn't compromising on the important things. Is marriage necessary? Do we want children? Is keeping the spark alive in the relationship important? I knew what I needed and deserved.

The doorbell rang. "That's the food. I'll get it," Dutton said. He got up before I had the chance. I heard him in the foyer laughing with the deliveryman. He closed the door and stood in the entryway to the living room, holding two plastic restaurant totes. "The delivery guy got a kick out of all this food being for two people."

"Two hungry people." I stood up.

"Nope. Sit back down and relax. I'm going to plate this up."

"You don't know where anything is."

"It's a kitchen. I'll figure it out."

That was sweet and unexpected. I picked up the remote and perused through the channels. If he was going to serve the food, the least I could do was find something we could watch while eating. I stopped when I saw a movie about King Tut was on. That was something we both could enjoy.

Dutton returned carrying a tray with my plate, napkin and fork.

"Look at you finding everything, even the serving trays."

"I told you I could handle it." He placed the tray on my lap. "I'll be right back."

He came in carrying his tray. He picked up the bottle of wine I had opened earlier and refreshed our glasses.

"Thank you for paying for dinner and serving it."

"It's nothing."

"I appreciate it all the same."

He settled next to me. "What's this on TV?"

"A movie about the boy king."

"Tut?"

"Yup."

"Good choice."

"I knew you'd approve."

We ate our dinner, commenting on the movie and drinking wine. He, of course, pointed out the inaccuracies of the film from a historical context. I kept reminding him that it was a movie for entertainment, not a documentary.

I turned to him as the closing credits rolled. "You would think for a three-hour movie, they would have done a better job at getting the facts right," he complained.

"Did you enjoy it?"

"Even though they took too many liberties, it was a good movie."

"Then they did their job. You were entertained."

He laughed. "Well, I'd better call the car service."

"If you plan on getting back to your parents' house, that's a good idea."

"I thought maybe you'd drive me back."

"No you didn't." I laughed.

He placed the call and gave them my address. "They should be here in fifteen minutes." He smiled. "I had a nice evening."

"So did I."

"Does that mean you'll go with me to the festival in Rome?"

I cocked my head to the side, considering. "I guess I could clear my schedule on Friday."

He nodded. "It's a date."

CHAPTER THIRTY-EIGHT

My oversized shades were on, his sunroof was open and smooth jazz was coming from the speakers. We were a few minutes into our ninety-minute drive to Rome. Dutton was in a crisp, white polo shirt and dark jeans. His biceps strained against the sleeves of his shirt as he handled the steering wheel. His beard was slightly more than a shadow.

"Has anyone ever told you that you resemble Omari Hardwick?"

"A few of my students. I don't see it."

"The beard is apparent, but it's also the lips and eyes."

He looked over at me. "You think Omari is handsome?"

I smiled. "He's all right."

"What about me?"

"You too."

Dutton laughed. I was amused at his roundabout way of finding out if I thought he was attractive. He was definitely a good-looking man. It wasn't the first thing I'd noticed about him. His quiet preceded him, his intelligence following closely behind. Once I got a glimpse of his personality, I was able to see everything about him. His face, smile, physique and style.

I agreed to go to Rome when he asked the second time because I knew I'd have a good time and he'd be a gentleman. I didn't have to worry that he'd try to come on to me or run lines on me. He had not done any of those things in our previous encounters. The time I had spent with him had been nice. There was no other way to describe it. Dutton was a nice guy and behaved as such. I almost corrected him when he called it a date. I didn't quite see it that way. We were spending the day together. No labels or classifications were necessary.

He tapped the steering wheel to the beat of the song. "This is what I love about traveling," he said. "The open road, sunshine on my face, music playing, and today," he glanced at me, "company."

"You told me you like to travel on a whim. Where else have you been?"

"I'll drive to Florida, the Carolinas, Tennessee, Alabama…"

"You obviously like driving."

"When I'm taking a quick jaunt. My whims take me overseas, as well. Most recently I flew to Dublin for a long weekend. Before that it was London."

"I've always wanted to travel internationally on my own. I haven't gotten up the nerve. What do you do alone in a foreign country?"

"Well, I'm not really alone. There's a country full of people." He chuckled. "But, I know what you mean. It's freeing. I do exactly what I please. I operate on my own schedule. I meet new people, see new places, and something you can appreciate, try new foods. Sometimes it's nice to leave everything and everybody behind. It's just me."

"Do you think it's the anthropologist in you that makes you want to go off and see all these places?"

He pondered my question. "I think that's a part of it. The other part is being raised in a male-dominated family where you have to carve out your own niche. There are times when I choose to create my own place elsewhere. Someplace where I'm not one of the Carlyle men, I'm the *only* Carlyle man."

I could understand what Dutton was saying. Although, I couldn't relate since it was only Sierra and me. There wasn't a clan of Riley women to contend with. It was just us two and we cherished the closeness of our relationship. I would imagine it to be different with men. Especially four men with lots of testosterone between them.

"Is that why you don't work at your father's firm?"

"Not really. I wasn't interested in finance. At one time there was an expectation that I would join the firm. My father put a little a pressure on me while I was in college that I needed to consider what the family business means and my role in it. I almost changed my major. Every time I thought about switching, I got angry. It wasn't what I wanted to do. I came home for Christmas break and my mother told me if I let my father dictate my future, then I was a fool." He nodded at the recollection. "Grand and Hutton can scrap over Loucar and who will run it after my father officially retires. My interests lie elsewhere."

"Like the book you mentioned you're writing. How exciting."

"It's purely academic, published by a university press. Most people won't even hear about it."

"Those in your field will. It's still quite an accomplishment."

"Thanks." A little of his bashfulness returned.

"What is the book about?"

"The cultural ramifications and long-term effects of the slave trade on West Africa."

I lowered the volume of the music. "That's quite a subject to tackle."

"It needs to be tackled more often."

"When will the book be published?"

"A year from now. I have a few more chapters to complete and I'll be submitting my manuscript."

"I look forward to purchasing my copy."

"You'd want to read it?" He sounded surprised.

"Of course. The ripple effects from the slave trade can still be felt today. I'm very interested in reading your perspective on its lasting impact in Africa."

"Okay." Dutton smiled. "When I finalize my manuscript, I'll share it with you. I trust you not to post it online."

I laughed. "I'm not sure I can resist the temptation of sharing it with the world."

"I'm safe there. The world's not interested."

"You're selling yourself short. The world is interested. We just have to be aware that you've written something so important."

"I hope you feel the same after you read it."

"I'm sure I'll be even more emphatic about it."

"I like the way you think."

Dutton parked the car and we began to stroll through the festival. Vendor after vendor was set up with tents, hawking their wares. We stopped every few paces to look at a variety of crafts, jewelry, clothing, leather goods, motorcycle accessories, memorabilia, and of course the food. Dutton and I got into a discussion about the confederate flag which adorned a few of the vendors' products. Was it Southern pride or a symbol of racism? We went back and forth over the issue, him approaching it from an anthropological standpoint. As our discussion transitioned into the power of symbols and began to pick steam, I suggested we table it for later.

"Can we at least agree that we should have some lunch? We can visit the Chieftains Museum after we eat," he said.

"I'm in agreement with that."

Dutton grabbed my hand and led me through the crowd. We were seated on an open-air deck at the restaurant. The sun was directly over us, not a cloud in the sky.

"Do you want to move to a table with an umbrella?" he asked.

"I'm okay. There's a nice breeze blowing. If it's too much sun for you, we can move."

He reached into the plastic bag hanging on the arm of his chair and pulled out a Rome Braves baseball cap he purchased from one of the vendors. He tugged it on his head. "I'm good."

We ordered catfish po'boys and sweet tea. I took in our surroundings. The wooden deck stretched around the entire establishment. In addition to dining tables of varying sizes, there were also lounge-like areas with low tables in the midst of the seating. "This is a nice restaurant," I commented.

"It's pretty good—the food and the service. I've been a couple of times."

"They have an extensive menu."

"It must be interesting for you as a chef to dine out at different restaurants."

"There are times when I'm overly critical. I dissect everything that comes out of the kitchen. When I'm dining with my friends, I try to remind myself that I'm a diner just like everyone else. I try not to ruin their experience by picking apart what's wrong and right with the meal. Unless, of course, it's something harmful like undercooked or spoiled food."

"For the record, I don't mind you telling me your thoughts. How often do I have the chance to dine with a professional chef? Tell me whatever you think I need to know."

I chuckled. "You might regret that."

"Have you ever thought about opening your own restaurant?"

"That's not an endeavor I'm prepared to undertake. I am planning to officially branch out and start a catering business."

"Your delicious meals would be available to the masses."

"I don't know about the masses, but at least to people in the Atlanta area."

"You know you already have a client in my anthropology department."

"And if you need a caterer for your book signing, you know who
to call."

"That's a given."

Our lunch arrived and as far as I could see, there was nothing to
pick apart.

On our way back from Rome, we were caught in a bit of traffic.
It took us an hour longer to reach our destination than it did to
get there. Gone were the days of lulls in our conversation. Dutton
chatted the entire ride back. I asked him about his research for his
book. He told me about his travels, the people he spoke with and
the sites he visited. He was an engaging conversationalist. When he
pulled into my driveway, I was even more ready to read his book.

He told me to stay put as he came around to open my car door.
I stepped out and he grabbed my hand. "I had a great time today,"
he said.

"It was fun."

He leaned in and kissed me on my lips. One sweet, closemouthed
kiss. "Good night, Riley."

"Good night." I walked to my front door and turned to wave at
him before going inside. I closed the door behind me and my
phone began vibrating in my bag. I fished it out and answered.
"Hey, Sierra."

"What's going on, baby sis?"

"I just walked in the door."

"Don't get too settled. I want you to come out with me tonight."

"Tonight?"

"Yes, it is Friday night."

"Ugh, where are we going?"

"Nowhere until you check that 'tude."

"Sierra."

"I have tickets to a charity event. It's some shi-shi affair downtown. Get dressed so you can meet me by nine."

"Make it nine-thirty."

"I'll text you the info."

Just as I thought my Friday was coming to an end, it was only just beginning.

CHAPTER THIRTY-NINE

waited in line to valet park for ten minutes. The charity event must have been the must-attend affair of the night. I got out of my car and straightened my pale gold dress, holding it so the hem wouldn't drag on the ground outside. My hair was styled with a center part, both sides of my bob tucked behind my ears.

I walked inside the country club and was greeted by a bevy of people loitering near the entrance. They were waiting to have their names checked off the guest list. I hoped Sierra made sure my name was on the list. If it wasn't, I'd have no problem going back home to get some rest. I gave the attendant my name and she handed me a black coin. She explained the coin was for a complimentary magnum of champagne. I looked over at the couple checking in next to me to see whether they received a coin. The attendant didn't hand them anything. I immediately wondered where Sierra got the tickets for the event. The attendant pointed me in the direction of the ballroom. All she had to say was follow the music. I proceeded down the corridor to the large double doors. Two doormen pulled open the doors when I approached. Inside, the room was filled with well-dressed men and women, socializing with one another. The buzz in the room was palpable. I scoped out the gathering in search of my sister. With the dim lighting and the crowd, locating Sierra would have been like finding a needle in a haystack. I sent her a text. She replied immediately with her whereabouts.

I found her seated at a table with one other person. I sat next to my sister and kissed her on the cheek. "Hey, this is some event."

"It's a who's who in Atlanta."

"I have a coin for a bottle of champagne."

Sierra opened her palm. "I know. I have one, too."

"Where did you get these tickets?"

"The superintendent of my school district gave them to me."

"Why you?"

"I was on a special task force she created to help ESL students adjust to a new school setting."

"ESL?"

"English as a second language."

"Oh."

"I kind of went above and beyond on the task force. She had these tickets for tonight and couldn't make it. So, she gave them to me."

"Aren't you the golden girl," I teased.

"No, you are in that dress." She laughed. "You look beautiful."

"So do you, sissy. Dusty rose is your color." I pushed the table-cloth to the side. "And, look at you showing off those legs."

"I'm going for short and sassy tonight."

"Mission accomplished."

"We should probably use one of these coins," she said.

"I'd like some champagne." I handed her my coin.

"The waiters will bring it over." Sierra signaled to one of the servers. He came to the table and she handed him the coin.

"I'll be right back with your magnum," he said.

"What are we going to do with two magnums, Sierra? That's the equivalent of four bottles of champagne."

"We can share it with our table."

"I don't think the one lady on the other side will make much of a difference."

"People are still arriving. Don't worry; it won't go to waste."

"We're good for at least half a magnum on our own," I said.

The server returned with our bottle and a tray of glasses.

"See, he knows that the magnum is for an entire table." Sierra asked the other table guest if she wanted a glass. She graciously accepted. The server poured three glasses and jetted off to another table. The ballroom was getting more crowded. I spotted the deejay booth on the side of the room near the dance floor. He was playing good music, a mix of classic and current R&B.

"What's the charity this event benefits?"

"TBI research."

"What's going on with you and these acronyms tonight?"

She chuckled. "Traumatic brain injury research. A lot of soldiers that came home from Iraq and Afghanistan suffer with TBI. It's also becoming an issue in the NFL. Players repeatedly getting hit in the head are showing symptoms too. I believe the Falcons are one of the sponsors of the event."

That explained why I saw so many well-built men in tuxes circulating the room. They were football players. "They should raise a lot of money with all of the people in here."

Sierra nodded and sipped her drink. "Where were you just getting in from when I called?"

"Remember the anthropologist?"

"Yes, the Carlyle."

"I took a ride with him to Rome."

"Took a ride?"

"There was a festival and he invited me to go."

"Was it a date?"

"He referred to it as one. I viewed it as us going to a festival."

Sierra chuckled. "Either it was a date or it wasn't."

"It wasn't for me."

"But it was for him?"

"When I agreed to go with him he said something like 'it's a date.'"

She laughed a little bit more. "You may not want to admit it, but that was a date. Did you kiss him?"

"He pecked me on the lips when he dropped me off."

"Why are you making it sound like you were an unwilling participant? You weren't a hostage. You agreed to go out and you kissed him. Call it what you want, Riley, but that was a date."

"It felt like being out with a good friend. Not a romantic interlude."

"Well, be careful dating your clients' son. If he thinks it's one thing and you another...you don't want it to jeopardize your job with his family."

"We're not dating," I said quietly. I didn't say any more to Sierra. If she was convinced Dutton and I were dating, she wouldn't understand what had transpired with the other Carlyle brothers. I didn't even understand it.

Sierra refilled our glasses. She motioned for the woman on the other side of the table to come closer so she could refresh her glass as well. They struck up a conversation. Once my sister started talking, she could go for hours. I interrupted her long enough to tell her I was going to find a restroom. She nodded and kept chatting.

I meandered through the crowd, inching my way in between people talking and drinking cocktails. I was stopped by a strapping man who insisted on grabbing my hand to lead me on to the dance floor. I halted him with a hand on the chest, telling him I'd be back after I visited the little girls' room. He said he'd be waiting. I hoped not because I wasn't planning to search the crowd for him.

I walked in on women in the lounge primping in the mirror, reapplying makeup and fussing with their hair. There was a longer line for mirror time than for the bathroom. I rushed past the frenzy. I caught a glimpse of myself in the mirror on my way out—hair was still in place and dress smoothed in all the right places.

I scoped out the best path back to my table and started in that direction. A hand grabbed me by the arm. I turned to see who I needed to tell to release me and found myself face to face with Hutton. He was grinning.

"I'm surprised to see you here," he said.

"Likewise."

"You look gorgeous, as usual."

I looked him over. "You're looking handsome."

He stared at me. "Are you here alone?"

"No, I'm with my sister."

"I thought you were going to say you were with my brother. Don't look so surprised. I know how to get information out of my twin. When I saw the pep in his step after he dropped you off, I figured he might actually have something worthy to talk about for a change. How was your date, by the way?"

"I accompanied Dutton to Rome. It wasn't a date."

"I thought I told you he can't do for you what I can."

"I don't need you or your brother to do anything for me."

"I bet he droned on about his anthropological findings. No, I probably wouldn't call that a date, either."

"Are you done?" My impatience was rising.

"No." He grabbed my hand and started walking.

"What are you doing?"

Hutton led me on to the dance floor and started doing a two-step. "Are you just going to stand there?" He came in close and wrapped an arm around my waist, swaying side to side. "I know you can dance. Let me see you move."

He dipped me unexpectedly and a smile crept across my face.

He relished his small victory, drawing even closer. I started moving in sync with his body. His flow was sexy, bumping and touching to the beat. I pulled my hand away and stepped back a couple of paces. If he wanted to see sexy, I'd show him sexy. My hips swayed to the rhythm. I turned around so he could see everything I was working with in my fitted dress. The subtle pop of my ass drew him to me. He closed the gap, rocking with me from behind. His face was next to mine, hand pressed on my hip feeling each shake and pop.

"Work that," he whispered in my ear.

If I pushed, he pushed back. If I rolled, he rolled with me. When I dipped it low, he stood back to watch. The grin on his face told me that I was serving up the dance he wanted. Song after song, we vibed with one another. I took his hand and made him move to my flow. He bit his bottom lip and nodded to the beat. We sang along to the music, prodding each other to work it out. His guard came down and so did mine. We left the dance floor chatting and laughing with one another. I took him over to my table.

Sierra was engrossed in conversation with a few people when we approached. I tapped her on the shoulder.

She looked from me to Hutton. "Where have you been?"

"Sierra, this is Hutton. I ran into him on my way back to the table."

She extended her hand. "Nice to meet you, Hutton."

"You as well," he replied.

Hutton and I sat down.

"His parents are my clients…the Carlyles…"

"Ohhh, okay." The lightbulb in Sierra's head switched on. "You've been gone so long, we're on our second magnum."

"I was enjoying the party."

"Hutton, would you like some champagne?" Sierra asked.

"If you're pouring, I'm drinking." He smiled and held a glass out for Sierra to fill. "Beautiful, thank you."

"Sierra teaches kindergarten in Marietta."

"You're an educator shaping young minds. That's commendable."

"Someone has to do it."

"They didn't have kindergarten teachers like you when I was a kid. I might have paid attention more if they did."

"Sure they did. If you were paying attention, you might have noticed."

He laughed, his smile lingering. I watched him observing my sister. He glanced at me. "You ladies look a lot alike."

"We get that all the time."

"I'm the one with the twin, but you two could pass for twin sisters."

"You have a twin brother?" Sierra asked.

"Fraternal. I'm six minutes older."

"I'm ten months older than Riley. People have confused the two of us many times over the years."

"The Ryan sisters… I would definitely take time to know who's who."

I frowned. "More champagne, Hutton?"

"You know my tastes. I'm drinking if it's you pouring." He winked at me and I actually winked back.

Sierra introduced us to the people she had been chatting with in my absence. Apparently, it didn't take much for Hutton to strike up a conversation. I figured he was ever searching for new clients and sizing people up. There was money in this room and he was after it.

After a few more drinks and a lot more conversation, I noticed Sierra yawning. "Are you all right?" I asked.

"I think I'm going to head out. Are you ready?"

I surreptitiously glanced at Hutton, still engrossed in discussion. "No, I think I'll hang out for a bit."

"Okay, be safe and have a good time. Call me tomorrow?"

I hugged my sister. "I sure will."

Sierra stood up. "Hutton, it was nice to meet you."

He got up and hugged her. "My pleasure."

I watched my sister walk away. Hutton eyed me hungrily. "Can I lure you back on the dance floor?"

I took his outstretched hand and went with him willingly. His hands didn't leave my body as we grooved to the music. He turned me around and hugged me close to him, speaking into my ear. "Do you want to get out of here?"

I nodded.

He grasped my hand and we left together to resume our party.

I had followed Hutton in my car back to the Carlyle suite. We burst through the door, him unzipping my dress, me pulling at his jacket. Our lips met in a feverish collision, licking and sucking as he advanced us down the hallway. We were bumping into walls, tripping over discarded shoes and clothing. I unbuttoned his shirt as he shimmied my dress down over my hips. He stopped and looked down at my near nakedness. He cupped my breasts in their strapless bra, burying his face in my cleavage. He grabbed my hand and rushed me into a bedroom at the end of the hallway, slamming the door behind us. A king-size bed was in the middle of the sunken room. He picked me up and carried me down the two steps, depositing me onto the bed. I watched him, my chest heaving, as he undid his pants letting them drop to the floor. I stared at the bulge in his boxer briefs.

He grinned at me. "Take off your bra."

I seductively unhooked the clasp in the front and tossed the bra to the side.

"Now, your panties."

I lifted up and slid my panties down, throwing them in his direction. He caught them and threw them aside. Hutton dropped to his knees and yanked me to the edge of the bed. "Lie back and put your legs up," he commanded.

I did exactly as he said. He spread my legs in a wide "V" and buried his face in my honeypot. His tongue darted inside of me. I gasped. He flicked and licked at the same time. I moaned my pleasure and my honey trickled. He played with my clit as his tongue massaged me. I placed my feet on his shoulders as my legs trembled.

He lifted his face from between my legs. "Move back."

I scooted back to the middle of the bed. Hutton stood and stepped out of his underwear, exposing his erection. I was gazing at a good eight inches. I bit my bottom lip in anticipation. He stroked himself as I watched. He went to the nightstand and retrieved a condom, setting it on the pillow. He climbed on the bed, lying alongside of me. "Touch it for me."

I looked down at his penis standing at attention. I wrapped my hand around it and began to stroke, firm and slow. He stared at me as my hand moved up and down his member. He moaned and his eyes closed. "Yeah, that feels good," he whispered. He started moving along with the motion of my hand, his chest rising and falling rapidly. In one deft movement, he rolled his body on top of mine. He covered my lips with his mouth. My tongue danced with his. He devoured me with vigor. His kisses trailed down my neck, my chest, to my breasts. He seized my left breast in his hand and sucked it into his mouth. He pulled on my nipple, tracing it with his tongue before sucking my soft mounds back into his mouth.

Hutton reached down and placed one of my legs around his waist. His penis rubbed against my wetness and he half groaned, half cried out. He pressed his pelvis into mine, his hardness bearing down on me. He rocked side to side, his penis sandwiched between us.

"I want to feel your pussy on my dick."

I reached over to the pillow and grabbed the condom. He took it from my hand and raised up on his knees to put it on. He gripped me by the hips and pulled me to him. I wrapped my legs around his back and pulled him down on me. He slid inside, opening me up inch by inch. We moaned together.

"Damn, you feel good," he said.

He pushed himself as deep as he could go and I tightened around him. He moved his face directly in front of mine. I clenched again, watching him flinch. Again and again, I contracted my honeypot walls. Hutton thrust in time with my contractions. I lifted up to meet his thrusts. The intensity of his grunts reverberated throughout the room. I squeezed my legs tighter around his back and rolled my hips into him. He faltered. I took over where he'd left off. I popped my pussy, my clit rubbing on him. I cried out as I chased my orgasm. He clutched me to him, drawing us closer together. My pussy began to spasm. Hutton shuddered. He forcefully moved with me, pushing me to the brink. "Ohhh," I screamed, as my orgasm overtook me.

"So wet," he strained. He pumped faster and harder. "I'm coming."

I helped him along with a twist of the hips. He howled as his body racked with his release. He slowly loosened his grip on my body. I untangled my legs from him and he eased out of me. His body collapsed beside mine.

He smirked at me. "Somehow I knew you wouldn't disappoint."

CHAPTER FORTY

*T*he sunshine poured through the floor-to-ceiling windows. I was perched at the kitchen table in Hutton's oversized pajama shirt. He had ordered breakfast to the suite from room service. Never mind that there was a fully stocked kitchen in the apartment. He explained this was what he always did whenever he stayed. The table was spread with waffles, scrambled eggs, bacon, sausage, toast, coffee, champagne and orange juice. I was picking at a waffle and bacon, and sipping on a mimosa. Hutton was eating everything.

"See, I would've thought I worked up your appetite last night." He grinned at me.

"That's funny. I guess I worked up yours," I said, motioning to his plate.

"Oh, so I didn't do my job. Is that what you're saying? I can take you back in the bedroom right now." He tugged on my sleeve.

I laughed. "You definitely did your job."

"Like employee of the month or I'm about to get my pink slip?"

"Employee of the month two months running."

He beat on his chest. "That's what I'm talking about."

"You didn't need me to tell you last night was good."

"'Good' isn't the word. Last night was incredible. Your pussy was so wet and tight and deep and you tasted so good."

I blushed into my breakfast.

"You made my dick so hard," he continued. "I came with a vengeance."

"So, I get employee of the year?"

"Employee? You're the boss."

I smiled at him. "I'll take it."

"You look good in my PJs." He fiddled with the collar. "I bet you didn't see our evening ending like this."

"No, I can't say that I did. Did you?"

"Maybe not last night, but eventually."

"And you knew that how?"

"Well, you're here…"

"Don't be an ass."

"I go after what I want, Riley, and I get it. I'm not saying that to be an ass. I'm saying it because it's true. You feel the energy between us. I know you felt it last night. Look at our clothes all over the floor. We could barely get in the door without jumping on each other."

"It was kind of wild." I shook my head. One side of my bob fell into my face.

Hutton picked up his phone and snapped my picture. "You're beautiful in the morning." I raked my fingers through my hair and he snapped another picture.

I held my hand up. "Please don't take my picture."

"Don't worry; these are just for me."

"I hope so because we need to be discreet."

Hutton chuckled. "You're big on that."

"I know it doesn't matter to you, but I work for your family."

"Let's not revisit that discussion. I get it. Discretion."

"Thank you."

I hoped he understood. My world and his world were two different things. He lived by his own rules, and I tried to abide by the ones set forth for the rest of us. I didn't need his entire family knowing that we hooked up. I didn't want any of his family knowing.

"I want to spend the day with you."

I looked up from my breakfast. "You do?'

"I'm not ready for our night to end."

"It's daytime."

"It feels like a good long night to me. Let's keep it going. We can do something discreet." His typical mischievous visage returned.

"I don't have any clothes with me. I can't go out in my dress from last night."

"We have a boutique downstairs in the hotel. We'll get you something to wear."

"You have all the answers, don't you?"

"Sometimes I do."

"Okay, let's go down to the boutique."

An hour later we were showered and getting into Hutton's Ferrari. I was dressed in a pair of black wide-leg slacks and a white fitted, off-the-shoulder top. Hutton donned all black. His version of casual was a short-sleeved shirt tucked into a pair of slacks, a leather belt and a pair of expensive loafers with no socks. He sped out of the hotel lot and toward the interstate. Hutton reached over and squeezed my thigh.

He took the exit for the airport ramp.

"Where are we going?" I asked.

"Shopping."

"Shopping where?"

"Fifth Avenue."

"New York?"

"New York."

He pulled into the lot at the private airstrip. A jet was waiting for us when we arrived. I couldn't believe a trip to New York was how he wanted to spend the day. I boarded the plane, taking in the spacious leather seating, sofa and tables. Hutton had a brief conversation with the captain and we got settled. One flight attendant was in the front of the cabin.

As we taxied down the runway, I peered out of the window. I thought about how I hadn't told anyone where I was going, what I was doing or who I was with. I said a silent prayer and gave it to God.

"What are you thinking about?" he asked.

"How crazy this is."

"It's not crazy at all. I do this from time to time."

"You might, but I don't."

"There's a first time for everything. I'm just to glad to have you join me."

"I'm curious how many other women have had the opportunity to join you."

"One or two," he nonchalantly replied. "I don't randomly fly women around the country if that's what you're wondering."

"That's exactly what I was wondering."

"I don't do this all the time, Riley. Have I done it before? Yes, I've taken a couple of women on trips. Never to New York, though."

"Oh, I see. We get different destinations." I chuckled at the thought.

"It has worked out that way, yes."

"Well, I happen to love New York."

"We'll have to get you a tee shirt that says so."

Hutton made me laugh. As much as I wanted to keep my guard up with him, he kept tearing it down. I relaxed back in my seat and enjoyed the ride.

Twelve hours later, I was back in Atlanta with an "I Love New York" tee shirt in a shopping bag. I refused to let Hutton buy me anything else. He, on the other hand, spared no expense on himself, buying clothes, shoes, and jewelry. We waited in front of his family's hotel for the valet to bring my car.

"I had a lovely time," I said.

"You're not the only one."

My car pulled up. Hutton placed a hand on the side of my face and kissed my cheek and then lips.

"Good night, Hutton."

"We have to do this more often." He smirked. "I'll see you tomorrow at Sunday dinner."

CHAPTER FORTY-ONE

I searched through my tote for the second time, feeling like I forgot to pack something. My knives were there, apron, and plastic gloves. I had a separate bag with blueberries, raspberries and strawberries that I wanted to use for a berry tart for dessert. I felt nervous, almost jittery about going to the Carlyles' home.

I'd had some sort of interaction with each of their sons. I'd slept with Hutton. I picked up my phone and dialed Aja.

"Please pick up," I spoke into the air.

"Hey, Riley."

"Aja," I said, dragging out her name.

"What's the matter?" she asked, alarm in her voice.

"Aja…"

"Riley, what's going on?"

"I have to go to the Carlyles' and I don't know if I can do it."

"Why, what happened?"

"What didn't happen is more like it."

"Okay, you have one second to start talking before I hang up on you."

"I went out with Dutton on Friday afternoon and spent Friday night with Hutton…literally."

"You slept with Hutton?" she shouted.

"That's what I said."

"I don't know what to do with you. What happened to keeping things professional?"

"I tried. I don't know what happened myself."

"Okay, you can't keep saying that. Obviously, you know what's happening."

"Aja, I swear. I have the best intentions and then I just get caught up. It's like they have some sort of pull on me." I sat down at my kitchen table and rested my head in my hands.

"You know a part of me wants to high-five you and the other wants to slap you."

"I know. I want to slap me, too."

"Give me the rundown."

"Well, let's see. I went to the rooftop party with Hutton where he ate my box, as you called it. Dutton and I went to an Egyptian art exhibit. I had a makeout session with Preston. Grand and I kissed in his office—"

"What the hell? You turned right around, went to that meeting and ignored what I said?"

"Let me finish."

"Go ahead."

"Like I said, Friday I went to Rome with Dutton and he pecked me on the lips when he dropped me home. And then, on Friday night, I ran into Hutton at an event. We left together, had mad, hot sex and flew to New York yesterday for the day."

"Dayum."

"I know."

"I so want to be mad at you, but girl, you are something. Where did all of this come from?"

"I don't know, Aja. I wish I could put my finger on it, or blame something or somebody, but I can't. It's all me."

"First of all, you need to calm down. You're going to go do your job like you should've been doing in the first place. What's done is done. That doesn't mean you have to keep doing it. Do you understand?"

"Yes, I understand."

"Go over there, cook dinner and bring your hot ass back home."

I started to laugh. "You have a way with words, my friend."

"I've known you forever and this isn't like you. I don't know what you're going through, but you need to take a minute to figure it out. Can you promise me that you will go over there today and just do your job?"

"I promise."

"Okay, one question."

"Yes?"

"The mad hot sex, was it good?"

"Ohhh, it was so good."

"I can't with you! Girl, get off the phone and go do what they are paying you to do. I'll talk to you later."

I hung up with Aja and took a deep breath. I was doing grown woman things, so I needed to handle my business like a grown woman. I would take her advice and really try to figure out why I was behaving so unlike myself. I fought back the one word that kept popping into my head. "Forbidden." My interactions with the Carlyle brothers was forbidden, yet temptation kept getting the best of me. I was rationalizing, avoiding, and ignoring what I knew to be right. I could only think of one time before when I consciously ignored what was right to do what I wanted. That decision cost me the executive chef job at Eden2.

I picked up my bag and headed out to Sunday dinner, hoping everyone would be on their best behavior. Especially me.

CHAPTER FORTY-TWO

*L*ouis opened the door when I arrived. He was on a call and mouthed for me to go right to the kitchen. I was thankful I didn't have to engage in any idle chitchat. The menu for the evening was a simple one. Caesar salad to start, shrimp scampi over chardonnay rice, sautéed swiss chard, and berry tarts. I would have dinner prepared in no time. I started peeling and deveining the shrimp. I wanted to let them marinate before cooking.

"Riley, how are you?" Louis's voice boomed. "I'm sorry, I was on a call when you arrived."

"No problem. I'm already up and running."

"Miriam, Jayla and the boys won't be dining with us tonight. They're at an amusement or water park or something. It's only going to be the men tonight."

"Thanks for letting me know."

"You're welcome. I'll leave you to it."

Louis left me in solitude once again. If I could get through the rest of the evening without interruption, my prayers would be answered. I moved efficiently through the preparation of each course. Still no one had come in to disrupt me. I relaxed a bit more.

I took a deep breath before going to present the salad. I planned to be in and out. It was salad; minimal explanation was required.

I stood next to Louis and all eyes were on me. I ran down the ingredients in the salad dressing and moved to exit the dining room.

Louis looked over at me. "Riley, why don't you join us for dinner tonight?"

"Oh, uh, no, thank you," I stammered.

"I insist. Miriam's not here. We need the feminine perspective."

I hesitated. "Okay, let me plate the main course and I'll join you."

I barreled into the kitchen, clutching my chest. My heart raced. I thought I was in the clear. Louis asking me to join them for dinner was not a part of my strategy to avoid the Carlyles. I took a few deep breaths, inhaling through my nose and exhaling from my mouth. I told myself to pull it together. I could handle it. I plated the main course and walked ahead of the Carlyles' server as he brought it in.

Grand told me to sit next to him, in Jayce's seat. He stood and pulled out my chair. I uneasily joined them at the table. "How was the salad?" I asked, breaking the silence.

"Delicious, as always," Louis said. "Maybe I'll take up cooking when I actually retire."

"That's not a bad idea," I replied.

"I don't see that happening," Grand offered. "Not after Mom banned you from the kitchen."

"She's not lifting that ban," Preston chimed in.

"Unfortunately, I think you're right. After all these years, she still doesn't trust me to make toast."

Louis's sons laughed. They obviously knew firsthand how bad their father was in the kitchen.

"It's all right, Dad. You'll find something to keep busy," Dutton said.

"I'm welcoming my retirement. Your mother threw me a party to force my hand, but she knows I still have work to do before stepping down. I've been thinking lately, I don't know how I'm going to walk away from the company I built from nothing."

Grand shifted in his seat. Hutton stared at him with a smirk on his face.

"I had a vision for the firm," he continued. "I thought when I retired, all four of my sons would be a part of the firm. I wanted to leave my company in all of your hands, not just Grand and Hutton."

"We're capable, Dad," Grand said.

"I'm not questioning that, son. I know you'll do great things. You get it. You understand the importance of family and legacy. You know what duty means. One day you may pass down the company to Jayce and Caleb."

"I'm already grooming them. I know how much this firm means to you. I'll make sure my children know, as well."

Louis nodded and then turned his attention to Hutton. "You've really mastered client relations. More than I thought possible. That's one of the most important elements of our firm and your knack for interacting with our clients is second to none. But, I'm going to caution you. You need to stay focused because it's easy to get caught up in the fast life."

"I may spend time with the high net-worth clients, but I never lose sight that business comes first," Hutton rebutted.

"You know, Dutton..." Louis paused. "I've thought long and hard about why you refused to join the firm. I always come back to the same conclusion. I think your mother coddled you too much. You're probably the smartest out of all my sons. You could have done wonderful and strategic things to advance the firm. But, instead of making money, you want to spend your time with books." Louis shrugged. "I don't know. It's your life."

"Thanks, Dad," Dutton said. "I get a compliment and an insult all in one. If you can acknowledge I'm the smartest, then you should be able to acknowledge that I'm smart enough to make my own decisions." He looked at Grand and Hutton.

Louis shook his head. "At least you made a decision. Preston, what the hell are you doing? You have the world at your fingertips and you're squandering it. So much potential and you're throwing your life away doing nothing. I mean absolutely nothing. What do you want to do with your life? You can't think that you're going to live off of me and your mother forever. That's not going to happen. You need to come work at the firm. Put those degrees to use and earn a living."

"I earn a living with my photography and my music."

Louis cut him off. "I'm done talking about it. You need to join the firm."

I felt like an invader at the table. I didn't want to be present for their discussion. It was personal and should've been private. "I should probably see about dessert." I began to slide my chair back.

"No, stay put," Louis said. "My wife seems to think our sons are all smitten with you. Have they been disrespectful in any way?"

I looked down at my plate and then back at him. "No, they haven't," I softly replied.

"We raised our sons to be respectful and if any of them are doing anything to make you uncomfortable, don't hesitate to let me know." His eyes bore into me. "This is my home and I don't tolerate impropriety. Miriam and I expect all of our sons to be respectful to you and themselves."

He admonished any potential impropriety by his sons, but he looked only at me. I could only assume that in his eyes, the buck stopped with me.

CHAPTER FORTY-THREE

*T*he relief I felt that dinner was over was indescribable. I could not believe that I had to endure such a private family moment. I felt awful for Dutton and Preston. Louis derided their choices not to follow in his footsteps. Dutton was certainly successful in his own right. It was as if he wasn't doing anything worthwhile just because he wasn't at the firm. Louis didn't even give Preston a chance to make a case for himself.

I didn't escape unscathed. The thought that he and Miriam had been discussing me and their sons filled me with worry. She felt they were smitten... What else did she wonder? What had she seen? Heard?

My hand was stinging from the metaphorical smack on the back of my wrist. If I wasn't convinced before dinner that I needed to take a step back from the situation, I was completely convinced afterward. I was thankful Miriam wasn't there. Something told me I would have received a lot more attention. A thought crossed my mind. Maybe Miriam was intentionally absent. Maybe she charged Louis with addressing the issue of their sons' conduct. I moved a bit quicker packing my items. I wanted to get out of there and to my own home.

I sighed at the sound of approaching footsteps. Louis stuck his head in the entryway.

"Uh, Miriam left a check for you in the study."

"Great, thank you." I grabbed my keys and picked up my bag.

"You can leave your bag for now."

I slowly set the tote down on the table. I followed Louis to the study. The fireplace was lit and jazz played in the background.

He handed me a check. "I was about to have a brandy. Would you like one?"

"No, I—"

"An occasional brandy is good for your health. Just one?"

I reluctantly nodded. "Just one."

"Have a seat." He handed me the drink. "You're a talented, beautiful young lady. I know I mentioned before it's admirable that you have your own business at such a young age. You also have your entire life ahead of you. I hope you understand what I was saying about my sons at dinner."

"Yes, I did."

"They all have growing to do. Each and every one of them. I find that I compare them to me at their ages. I have expectations for them and I don't want them to fall short. I definitely don't want them to get sidetracked by a beautiful woman."

There was my affirmation. His speech at dinner was for my benefit.

"Yeah, they still have growing to do," he said. "My sons can't do anything for you. If you want the world, then you see me."

He inched closer to me on the couch. I craned my neck away from him trying to decipher if I actually heard what I thought I did. "I'm sorry, what?"

"I love Miriam. Wouldn't think of being without her. But, I could make your life absolutely astounding."

"Mr. Carlyle…"

"Sometimes you need something to keep you young. I see a fire in you, Riley. Obviously, everyone in this household sees it. Don't you wonder what it's like to be with a real man? Mature. Distinguished. Rich. I could give you the finer things in life." Louis put his arm on the back of the couch behind me. "I can take you on vacations of a lifetime, show you the world."

The study door creaked open. Miriam stood in the doorway, looking from Louis to me. He hurried off the couch and over to his wife, kissing her on the cheek. He removed her jacket and took her purse from her hands. "I was just giving Riley her check. She wanted to wait on you to get home. She has a couple of questions."

Miriam walked further into the study. She peered at the brandy on the table and the lit fireplace. Her eyes darted to me. "What question did you have that held you up from going home?"

I stood up, moving closer to the door. "Oh, I wanted to ask for referrals. I'm officially expanding my catering side of the business and wanted to know if you had any sorority sisters you could refer."

"You could've called me. There was no need for you to stay so late for that."

"Okay, well, I'll do that." I picked up my check and bustled past Miriam. "I'll follow up during the week." I glanced at Louis on my way out of the study.

I rushed down the hall and out of the front door. Impropriety had reached an all new level.

CHAPTER FORTY-FOUR

banged on the door, ringing the doorbell at the same time. If the neighbors were looking, they were probably ready to call the police. Aja opened the door clutching at her robe. I pushed past her, rushing into the house.

"Oh my God, Aja. I had the worst night at the Carlyles. I was doing exactly what I was supposed to and everything went off the rails."

"Sit down, calm down. What happened?"

"Miriam wasn't home. It was Louis and the boys."

"Boys?"

"Aja, please. Not right now."

She put her hands up in surrender.

"I made dinner, no one had bothered me in the kitchen, and then Louis makes me have dinner with them." I gave Aja a play by play of what had happened at the dining room table.

"Wow, they noticed their sons are taken with you."

"It gets worse, Aja. I was wrapping up in the kitchen and Louis tells me my check is in the study. The fireplace is lit, music's playing and he offers to give me the world."

"Wait a minute. He lectures you all on impropriety and then propositions you?"

"That's exactly what happened."

"Are you sure you heard him right?"

"Can you misconstrue someone telling you their sons can't do anything for you but he can? He said I need a mature man in my life. He offered to take me on vacations. That's when Miriam came in."

"She didn't."

"She did."

"Do you think she knew what was going on?"

"I don't know. She saw two glasses of brandy, a burning fireplace and her husband sitting a tad too close to me on the couch."

"Oh, damn."

"I don't think she heard our conversation, though. When she came in, all she saw was us talking. But she was suspicious."

"I was convinced you wouldn't have any problems today."

"I should be so lucky." I leaned back on Aja's chair, resting my head. I could not be blamed for anything that had occurred earlier that night. Louis had never indicated that he saw me in any way other than their personal chef. If Miriam was surprised by the scene, what I felt was akin to utter shock. I may have encouraged or not dissuaded the Carlyles' sons, but never had I urged Louis to pursue me. "Aja, I can't believe he said I needed a real man and he's it."

"He's probably used to getting everything he wants."

"I can't go back there next week."

"I can't tell you what to do, but I would be there making that money. You set the tone with the Carlyles—not the other way around."

"It's not that simple."

"Maybe not, but it doesn't have to be that complicated, either."

CHAPTER FORTY-FIVE

fter a night of fitful sleep, I stayed longer than usual in bed. The news was on the television, but the volume was so low I could barely hear it. As far as I was concerned, there was nothing going on in the local news that could top my own late-breaking story. I replayed the entire weekend over and over in my head. It was on repeat just like the news. Each time it replayed, I thought about what I could have done differently.

I glanced over at the clock. I had things to do and places to be. I forced myself up and into the shower. I stood under the streaming water for far too long, once again thinking about the Carlyles. It was going to be a long day if I couldn't get a handle on my thoughts.

Dressed and my hair done, I went downstairs to start prepping for a client. I started toward the living room to get my knives from my tote bag and it hit me. I left my things sitting in the Carlyles' kitchen. I had run out of Louis's study so fast, I hadn't even thought about my belongings. I cursed out loud.

I plopped down at the kitchen table. Never before had I left my tools of the trade behind. However, never before had I been in a situation like the one I was currently in. I was already thinking that it may be best for me to resign. How could I continue in light of recent developments? How would I face Louis after he propositioned me? I was ecstatically grateful Miriam hadn't heard her husband. I couldn't imagine what would have occurred in that study if she had. My resignation would probably be the best thing for their family and for me.

Never in the past did I have any issues with keeping my business and personal lives separate. Work was work and play was play. It was a given. There was no intermingling of the two. Except the one time... I was in my position as executive chef at Eden2 for about a week. I had attended a charity event with the owner, Cain. He was a gentleman, mature, thoughtful and a glimpse at what kind of man I wanted for myself. At the end of the evening I made the awful decision to kiss him. He had a girlfriend, I had Tyler, and more importantly, Cain was my boss. That single inappropriate action was the undoing of my position at the restaurant. I resigned a week later. If someone told me I'd be considering resigning again, I wouldn't have believed them.

I experienced nothing but challenges in trying to maintain my professionalism with the Carlyles. What was irking me the most was that I had no excuse or rationale for my behavior. I found myself in one precarious situation after another. I wasn't that type of woman. At least, I hadn't been in the past. This was crazy. It was especially crazy because there was something I liked about each of the Carlyle sons. They had distinctive qualities that enticed me in different ways.

My doorbell rang. I looked through the peephole and moved back quickly. "Damn." It rang again. I slowly opened the door.

Preston stood on my front steps, holding my tote bag. "My mother sent me over here with your bag." He reached for my storm door and came in.

I watched him just walk on in and start looking around. He walked into the living room and sat down.

"Okay. Come in, I guess," I said.

"That was some dinner last night."

I rolled my eyes and reluctantly joined him in the living room. "Thanks for bringing me my things."

"No problem. What did you think of your first real Carlyle dinner?"

"I felt like it was none of my business and I shouldn't have been there."

"You had a chance to see the all-powerful Louis Carlyle proselytize."

"Again, I didn't want to."

"Did you hear what he said to me?" Preston didn't wait for a reply. "He basically said I'm throwing my life away."

"He did say that, but he also asked you what you want to do."

"He doesn't care what I want to do. Louis Carlyle asked me a few rhetorical questions. He wants me at the firm. Period."

"I'm not sure I'm the right person to discuss this with. You can't talk to your brothers?"

"If you haven't caught on, we don't have that type of relationship. It's every man for himself when you grow up Carlyle."

"Well, was your father right? Are you squandering your potential?"

"I don't see it that way. Although I could probably stand to get more serious about the things I've been dabbling in."

"Right, I think your father wants you to stop testing the waters and dive in."

"He needs to let me live my life how I want."

I tried not to think about how Louis had preached to his sons and then turned around and propositioned me. They had no idea and I wouldn't be the one to tell them. "You need to tell him that, not me," I said.

"I'm angry because I know he's partially right. I can't live off of them. I live on their property, at no cost to me, and take advantage of the lifestyle he provided for his family. I need to be able to do the same. Messing with these older women in situations that aren't meant to go anywhere is useless."

"Maybe your father's comments served a purpose after all."

"I guess. He definitely got one thing right."

"What's that?"

"I may be smitten with you."

"Let's not go there, Preston."

"We could finish what we started at my place. Let's go to your bedroom."

"I don't think so. I won't be another woman to prevent you from being focused."

He laughed. "There I go testing the waters again."

I shook my head. "Stop testing and start navigating."

"We could at least hang out every once in a while."

I stood up. "I appreciate you bringing my bag, but I have to get ready for a client."

"Fine, just throw me out."

I nudged Preston toward the door. "I'm pushing you out this door and into your life. If you're procrastinating, then stop it. Get on with doing something you find productive."

"Other than you?"

"Goodbye, Preston."

"Enjoy your day." Preston walked down the driveway to his car.

"Oh, Preston," I called. "Do me a favor and tell your mother I have a conflict and can't provide services this week."

CHAPTER FORTY-SIX

*M*idweek at the farmers market was like a different world compared to the weekend. I could move freely from stall to stall without getting bumped about by a throng of shoppers. I wasn't there for anything specific. I was merely browsing the fresh produce to see if there was anything I wanted to purchase.

I'd usually pick up something and think about what I could make with it. If nothing came to me relatively quick, I'd put it back down. I hadn't purchased anything yet. I realized that I may have been feeling uninspired.

I was standing at a stall that was selling a variety of fruits. I mindlessly picked up a peach and sniffed, putting it back immediately.

"Not ripe enough?"

I turned around. Jayla and Caleb were approaching.

"Jayla, hey."

"What a surprise."

"This is my usual location to buy fruits and veggies."

She peeked into my bag. "You haven't bought much."

"Some days it's like that." I bent down. "Hi, Caleb."

He clung to his mother's leg. "Hi."

"Mind if we tag along with you?"

"Not at all."

What was it with this family? I couldn't shake them.

"This is a treat. I get to see what produce our favorite chef thinks is worth buying. Are you making anything special?"

"I don't have anything specific in mind. I'm just looking today." I picked up a cabbage and turned it to look at the leaves. Jayla reached for one and did the same. I replaced mine on the stand.

"How would you prepare something creative and different with an ordinary cabbage?" she asked.

"It would probably depend on what else I was cooking with it. I would use it to elevate the focus of the dish."

I kept walking to the next stall. Large summer squash were on display. I inspected a yellow one.

"Now, I've never cooked a squash. Any suggestions?"

"Oh, I don't know. I would probably make a chilled summer squash soup."

"I wouldn't have thought to do that," she said.

I handed her the squash I was holding. "This is a good one. Take it home and try it."

"Maybe I will. Tomorrow is my wedding anniversary."

"Really?" I was surprised at how surprised I sounded. I dialed it back a bit. "Congratulations."

"Thank you. I still can't believe we've been together for so many years. It feels like we just met yesterday and here we are celebrating eleven years of marriage. I love that man. I want to make him a special romantic dinner. I bought some new sexy lingerie with a lot of straps, and little else, strappy high-heels and warming oils. So, I have the romance part all taken care of. I'm still trying to figure out the dinner part. I guess it was just my luck to run into you."

She wasn't that lucky. I wasn't planning any dinners for Jayla and her husband. If she couldn't pull it together in the kitchen, then she needed to make a reservation somewhere. She was obviously planning to purchase and make something before she ran into me. She needed to stick with that plan. Shadowing me at the market wouldn't make her a skilled professional in her own kitchen.

Hopefully, she had a good cookbook and a game plan. I had a feeling that lingerie would only get her so far. The flirtatious husband she had at home seemed easily distracted.

Jayla's phone rang. "Hello… Hi, baby… I can't wait until tomorrow evening… At the farmers market… Not yet… Yes… I'm planning something special."

I mouthed to Jayla that I was going to head out. She shook her head and put a hand on my arm to stop me.

"I bumped into Riley… What?… Right here standing next to me…" She turned her back and lowered her voice. "I really don't know… No… You do?" Jayla turned around with a strange expression on her face. She held her phone out to me.

I looked at her and then down at her hand. I reached for the phone and slowly put it up to my ear. "I don't think I can… This is an actual meeting?… Tomorrow… It's really last minute… I have clients… I don't know if that's possible… How many people?… There's no one else?… Okay, I can do it…" I handed the phone back to Jayla.

"Hello?" she spoke into the phone.

"He hung up," I said.

"So he needs a meeting catered?"

"It would seem so."

"It also seems like the Carlyles can't stay away from your treats."

CHAPTER FORTY-SEVEN

*T*he chafing dishes were set up and the food hot and ready to be served. I arranged the serving utensils beside each dish and made sure the salad and rolls were positioned for convenient self-service. Grand's assistant entered the dining room. I closed the lids on all of the dishes.

"It looks like everything is set," she said.

"It's ready whenever you are."

"Okay, if you're done, I'll take you to Mr. Carlyle's office."

I followed Ms. Washington down the hall to Grand's office suite. She escorted me inside, closing the door behind me.

Grand was seated on the sofa, one leg crossed over the other.

I sat in the chair next to the sofa. "I'm surprised there's really a meeting this time."

"How do you know there is?"

I got up and started for the door. I reached for the handle and pulled. Grand caught up to me and pushed the door closed. "I'm kidding. There's a meeting today."

I put my hand on my hip. "You could have left my payment with your assistant. I didn't need to come to your office."

"Then I wouldn't have seen your beautiful face. Come on, sit down."

I stood next to the door, tapping my foot. I wasn't in the mood for a game of cat-and-mouse. Grand walked a circle around me—

studying my face and slowly moving down the length of my body. "You really are a beautiful woman."

He kissed the back of my neck.

I moved away. "Stop it."

"I would love for you to give me a beautiful little girl. One that looks just like you." He placed his hands on my hips.

I pushed Grand's hands away, spun around and faced him. "What is your obsession with my womb and me giving you a little girl? Did you forget you're married and, by the way, isn't it your anniversary?"

He just looked at me, taking my hands in his. "I can't help wanting what I see in front of me." He pressed his lips to my palms. "You should be mine." Grand pulled me close to him and kissed my face, next to my lips. "I want you to be mine." He kissed me tenderly, at the same time guiding my hand, placing it on his hardness.

I jerked my hand and pulled away from him. "Grand, you need to control yourself."

"Why do I? I already told you how I feel. I'm putting myself out there," he said, with outstretched arms. "Yes, I'm married. We both know that. I'm also handsome, powerful, rich and I find you to be the most engaging woman I've met in a long time. But, you keep shooting me down. Does this have to do with Hutton?"

"This has nothing to do with Hutton."

"I saw you two in the kitchen that night. You can't possibly think Hutton is the one for you. I know he can't be the man calling to you. Hutton is only about Hutton. He's selfish, doesn't know how to treat women and all you'll find with him is heartache. You can't possibly think, for one minute, that he would treat you right. I would treat you right." He lowered his voice and grabbed my hand again. "I would treat you right."

These brothers did not have each other's back. The way they

disparaged one another was terrible. Grand was in no position to talk about what Hutton would or could do for me. I supposed there would be no heartache involved when dealing with a married man. A man that would not be accessible to me. A man that wouldn't be able to be everything I needed him to be. A man that committed to another woman who would undoubtedly come before me. A man that would spend holidays with his family and not me. A man that couldn't stand in front of God and our families to utter two simple words… "I do." A man that would make promises that would be broken. A man that was not in a position to offer me anything I deserved. Grand could question me about Hutton, but he had no right to tell me what I would be in store for with his brother.

I gazed directly in his eyes. "You're married," I said softly, pulling my hands from his grasp. "And, to add insult to injury, today is your anniversary. What would make you think that I would entertain any of this and on today of all days? Your wife is planning a special evening for the two of you. I saw your son yesterday, your family, and you think I can ignore that? Instead of trying to seduce me, you should be focusing on celebrating your eleven wonderful years together."

"I know my brother is after you, Riley. I see the way he looks at you. I hear the comments he makes."

"Why are you ignoring everything I just said to you? Maybe you can ignore the obvious, but I can't do it. You're married."

Again, Grand approached, placing a hand on my face. "You don't have to keep telling me that. I'm also a man. A man that wants what he wants. And, I want you."

His words were potent and I'd be less than truthful if I said they had no effect. He was all that he proclaimed to be. Handsome. Powerful. Rich. However, married outweighed it all. Maybe I was giving off a certain energy to make him believe I would settle. Settling was not in my vocabulary. Not anymore. "I'm sorry, Grand."

He stroked my cheek and was interrupted by a knock on the door. His assistant poked her head in. "Everyone is assembled for the meeting." She closed the door, once again leaving us alone.

I stepped away from him. "You have to stop with the advances. It's inappropriate. If I've given you any indication that it's okay, then I apologize."

"I hear what you're saying, Riley, but we have chemistry and you can't deny it. I also heard my father's admonishment at dinner. I'm not trying to be disrespectful. I hope you're not perceiving any of my words or actions in that manner. I have a need to be honest and to tell you where I stand. I certainly hope that everything between us stays between us."

"Spoken like a married man." I sighed. "Enjoy your anniversary."

I opened the door and hurried from his office, rushing past Hutton standing next to Ms. Washington's desk. I didn't stop to speak or even wave. I'd had enough of the Carlyle men for one day. If Grand had any more questions, he could ask his brother. I assumed Hutton would do the same. They apparently had a lot to hash out. Either way, I was taking myself out of the middle.

CHAPTER FORTY-EIGHT

I was curled up on the couch in my family room. The Food Network was on and I was only half watching what was on the screen. Every once in a while, I would have an active thought regarding what the chef was doing—I should try that recipe, he chose the wrong seasoning or that looks good. The TV was really just a much-needed distraction and I wasn't sure at that point anything could do the job.

My phone rang. I rolled toward the coffee table and looked at the number before answering.

"This is Riley."

"You were in quite a hurry earlier."

"Yeah, I had somewhere to be."

"You couldn't take a moment to even speak?"

"I was running late."

"No, I think you were rushing because of something that happened between you and my brother."

"Hutton, I catered Grand's meeting, picked up my payment and was leaving when you saw me."

"I was outside of his office for ten minutes, waiting to see him. That's a long time to pick up a check."

"Ten minutes is a long time to wait."

He laughed. "You're not talking. Okay. Grand wouldn't say anything, either."

"That's because there's nothing to talk about."

"I wasn't calling to discuss this, anyway. I wanted to invite you to a tasting at Cezoi tonight. It's open to the public, but a handful of my clients have been asked to promote and attend."

"Let me guess… You neglected to say that one of your clients, who plays for the Hawks, really owns the place. That's why you could get a table without having to make a reservation six months in advance and the chef made you items not on the menu. I get it now."

He chuckled. "You're getting to know me."

"Yeah, I'm starting to see how you operate."

"Hopefully, you also see that I obviously know how to be discreet."

"When it benefits you, yes."

"Will you join me? I would like to have a pretty lady at my table this evening."

"Unfortunately, I can't."

"You're sure?"

"I'm sure."

"You'll be missing out on a culinary fete."

"I can't, Hutton."

"Well, it's your loss, I suppose. Hopefully there's a next time."

We ended our call. I was struck by how quickly his tone changed. My loss? The arrogance may dip out of sight, but it was never too far away. It was always there, lingering. I didn't offer an explanation as to why I couldn't attend and apparently, he wasn't interested in one. I didn't tell him what he wanted to hear, so that was it.

I dialed my sister's number. "Sierra, do you think I was wrong to break up with Tyler?"

"It's tough for me to say what's right or wrong for you. Only you know that."

"How do I know I'm going to find better than him?"

"You don't. That's the risk you take when you opt for something new. At least you knew what you had with Tyler. Who knows what you're going to get next."

"That's true. Hutton invited me to a client event at Cezoi tonight. I didn't even want to go. I don't want to be around a restaurant full of athletes and entitled people with money. I told him I couldn't make it."

"The way you sound, maybe you could use a night out with some drinks."

"I won't be going out with him. I'm not in the least interested in going out with him."

"That's right; you're dating Dutton."

"I'm not dating either of them, Sierra."

"I'm kidding; calm down."

"I am calm."

"Considering you called me asking about Tyler and whether you'll find someone better, you probably should go to the event. Are you opposed to finding a good man? A restaurant full of athletes may be a great place to start."

"So you go. You're always talking about trying to find a man. Take your own advice and see what's out there."

"Not without you."

"I'm not going anywhere. After the day I had, I need to stay home and regroup."

"Okay, get some rest, baby sis. We'll speak over the weekend."

I hung up with my sister and thought about what she'd said. I was taking a risk by opting for something new. I wasn't sure anymore if the risk was worth it.

CHAPTER FORTY-NINE

I glanced over my shoulder toward the hostess station and then checked the time again. When my phone rang early that morning, I didn't expect it to be Miriam. She asked me to meet her for lunch and although I wanted to decline, like I had with Hutton the night before, I agreed to be there at one. I had no idea where she was. She was twenty minutes late and hadn't called.

I turned around again and there she was, making her way through the tables. She leaned down and air-kissed my cheek before taking a seat across from me. She complimented me on my dress, and I on her purse, while I wondered why she'd insisted on meeting with me.

"Preston delivered your message that you're unable to make it on Sunday. I have to be honest; I was a little surprised that I hadn't heard from you myself."

I cleared my throat. "You're right. I should have called and I apologize. It's been a very busy week."

"I invited you to lunch because I wanted to make sure that I didn't come on too strong when I came home last Sunday evening. Louis is always saying that I can be intense sometimes. After all the years we've been together, he knows my ins and outs and I know his. No matter how intense I may get, he loves me just the same. Everyone else may not get me, but he does." She paused. "I hope I didn't offend you."

"No offense taken." I sipped my water.

"I was surprised to see you were still at the house."

"I was waiting to speak with you."

"Well, just so you know, I did put the feelers out to my sorority and may have a few referrals coming your way."

"That would be great, thank you."

The waiter approached and Miriam waved him off. "Louis mentioned that he had a discussion with you and my sons…"

I met her gaze full on. "Yes, he did."

"My boys. I love them, but sometimes they don't know what's good for them. I watch Grand working himself to the bone to be like his father. He thinks he has so much to prove. Sometimes I watch him and realize that he feels so entitled because Louis has thrust so much upon him. He works him hard, but he gives him praise when it's due. Sometimes Grand runs away with it."

I looked around, hoping the waiter was in the vicinity poised to return.

"Hutton has done great things at the firm. My husband couldn't be happier with his results. It's unfortunate he operates from the wrong place. He's not concerned with his father's or our family's legacy. He's motivated by greed. I keep telling him that greed will be his downfall. Now, Preston's downfall," she quickly added, "is that he's a dreamer. He won't commit to anything. He goes on about not living a life others have chosen for him, but he's not even making a living. I don't understand. Oh, and here's my other son now."

I was briefly confused by her words. I thought she was about to say something about Dutton. I followed her eyes and looked behind me. Dutton was walking over to our table. He seemed just as surprised to see me as I was to see him.

"Hey, Mom." I could hear the question in his voice. "Hi, Riley."

I spoke to Dutton as he sat down to join us.

"Mom, I didn't realize we weren't dining alone."

Miriam looked at me. "I hope you don't mind."

I shook my head, still confused that Dutton had joined us.

"Have you ordered yet?" Dutton asked.

"Not yet," I said, wondering if that would ever happen.

"Riley and I were just catching up. The waiter should be back in a minute. They have a delicious roast squab on the menu. You should try it."

"I think I'll have a salad," he said.

"That sounds good," I said.

"You all are so health-conscious. I know Dutton stays in the gym; what about you, Riley?"

"I try to get there when I can and unfortunately, I don't get there nearly enough."

"I can go on campus, so it's convenient for me," he offered.

"Maybe I should start going. Your father will be fully retired soon. I can drag him along with me. This way we won't gain any extra pounds from your delicious dinners, Riley."

I laughed politely.

"I think her meals are worth the weight," he said. "As in pounds, not wait as in waiting for it."

Miriam looked at her son and shook her head. "We get it, son." She turned to me. "He's too smart for his own good. Or, maybe he doesn't think his mother is smart enough. I don't know which one."

"It's neither." A look of embarrassment spread across his face.

"Riley, I was hoping you could resolve your conflict for Sunday," Miriam said. "Dinner won't be the same without you there to prepare your specialties."

"I'll have to see."

"I won't take no for an answer. Will you be there?"

I nodded. "I can be there."

"Great. The family will be pleased." Miriam glanced at her watch. "Well, I have an appointment. You two stay for lunch. It's on me." She got up from the table and graced us with a prolonged look before walking away.

"Are you just as confused as me?" Dutton asked.

"Even more so."

CHAPTER FIFTY

utton and I were baffled by our unplanned lunch together. His mother had asked him to meet her for lunch just because. I was invited with no explanation other than she wanted to discuss something with me. Yet, here we were together with no Miriam in sight.

I flipped through the menu. "You better order that delicious squab your mother suggested."

Dutton erupted in laughter. "Squab? Not quite what I had in mind for lunch. A burger or a sandwich, maybe. Squab, I don't think so."

"We'll both have salads like we told your mother. She approved of the salad."

"Don't talk about my mama."

We laughed together.

"I owed you one. Now we're even."

Dutton stopped laughing, a serious expression coming over his face. "This really is a pleasant surprise."

"I guess your mom is full of surprises. We've been set up."

"Apparently so, but I was glad to see you sitting here. I hope you're not upset."

"Not at all. I'm going to enjoy my free lunch with good company."

"You mean me, right?" He looked over his shoulders. "You're not expecting someone else?"

I nudged his arm. "Stop it."

"I'm kidding."

"I hope so."

"The last time we were at a table together wasn't this enjoyable."

"There was definitely a different tone."

"You got an earful. I'm curious about what you thought."

"I thought it was a father talking to his sons."

"I know you thought it was more than that."

I didn't know what to tell him I thought. All I knew was that I viewed his father in a different light. I searched for a reply that would take my experience with Louis that night out of the equation. "I feel like he wants his sons to succeed and he wants you to do it his way."

"You don't have any thoughts about what he said specifically about me?"

"No, Dutton, I don't."

"My father thinks I'm a mama's boy."

"Is that what you think?"

"All I know is that I've never been the apple of his eye."

"Is that what you want?"

"Not when I see what it does to Grand. He lives for my father's approval."

"Most sons do. However, it's all right if you don't."

"I used to. It just stopped mattering when I finally realized that nothing I did was good enough."

"Are you proud of what you've managed to accomplish? If so, that should be all that matters."

We ordered lunch and continued our conversation. I could appreciate that Dutton felt comfortable enough to open up to me, but in the back of my mind, all I could think about was keeping my distance. I was used to some level of personal relationship with my clients, but it was abundantly clear that I had far exceeded that level with the Carlyle family. If I was employed by someone else, I would have been in breach of their code of conduct. Maybe I needed to create my own, for myself, for my company of one. I'd have to fire myself. I stifled a giggle.

I could tell Dutton enjoyed being around me and I honestly liked spending time with him, too. I didn't feel like he wanted anything from me other than to be with me in that moment. It was nice. My guard had never been up with him. Not like it was with his brothers.

"You're smiling."

"I am?" I replied. "I didn't even realize it."

"That means you're having a good time with me."

"Is that what it means?"

"Do you have a better explanation?"

"Maybe my food tastes so good that I can't help but smile about it."

"I refuse to believe that a salad rates higher than me. I put that smile on your face." He grinned at me. "Just admit it."

"I think it's the salad," I kidded.

"Okay, then let me take you out to prove it's me."

My smile faded. "I don't think that's a good idea, Dutton."

"What is it? You didn't enjoy our first date?"

"No, it's not that."

"You're not attracted to me?"

I peered at the man across from me in his blazer and jeans. Clean-cut and handsome at the same time. The good guy. No, he was definitely attractive. "You're a good guy, Dutton. It has nothing to do with—"

"Then let me show you how a real Carlyle man treats a woman."

I leaned back in my chair and sighed. "Okay, I'll go out with you."

"Tomorrow night. I'll pick you up."

I figured what the hell. Why not give the good guy a chance.

CHAPTER FIFTY-ONE

stopped in front of the mirror and gave myself a once-over. The doorbell chimed again. I opened the door and let Dutton in. He looked extremely handsome in a charcoal suit and a crisp, white French-cuffed shirt. His attire played nicely off my crimson, one-shoulder jumpsuit. Dutton handed me a small square box. I hesitated before removing the lid. A sparkling scarab on a necklace glittered from the cushion.

"This is beautiful, Dutton. You shouldn't have."

"I wanted you to have it." He reached into the box and removed the necklace. I turned around so he could put it on me.

I went over to the mirror and touched the glittering bauble. "Thank you."

"You're welcome.

I looked over at the handsome man in my foyer and smiled. "I will definitely give you credit for putting this one on my face."

"I told you I'd prove it to you."

"Where are we going tonight?"

"You will see when we get there."

"What makes you think I like surprises?"

"That smile on your face."

We left my house already in good spirits and casually conversed as he drove us to our destination.

As he navigated the downtown streets, I had an inkling. "We're going to Piedmont Park, aren't we?"

"How'd you know?" he said, with a chuckle.

"I heard something on the radio about a concert beneath the stars tonight in the park."

"That's where we'll be—front row center."

"Are you trying to impress me?"

"Only if it's working."

We spent the evening being serenaded by smooth R&B sounds. It wasn't the type of show where people got out of their chairs to dance, but there was plenty of rocking back and forth in our seats. Dutton's arm was behind the back of my chair for most of the evening. There was a slight breeze in the air and he offered me his jacket.

After the show, we decided to take a stroll around the park. He reached for my hand and I obliged, our fingers interlinked.

"How'd you like the show?" he said.

"It was great. Live music is one of my favorite things."

"I could tell by the way you were moving in your seat."

"You were watching me?"

"More than the show."

I glanced at him. "It's a beautiful night. Look at all those stars in the sky."

He was eyeing me. "Why look up when I have one right next to me."

"Are you trying to charm me?"

"I'm just saying how I feel. You make me want to say how I feel."

"Why me? What did I do?"

"By just being you. From the first time we spoke and you offered to make me a separate dessert, there was something about you. Your kindness and openness was evident. You probably don't even know, but you opened me up."

"And that's a good thing?"

"For me, it's a great thing." Dutton stopped walking and turned to me. "I want you to go out with me again tomorrow night."

"I'd love to."

"No cajoling or convincing this time?"

"Not one bit."

"Then you and I have a date."

"Since you're so fond of surprises, I won't bother to ask where we're going, only what I should wear?"

He threw his head back and laughed. "Something elegant, like you."

CHAPTER FIFTY-TWO

We drove up to my house and I immediately realized Tyler's car was parked in my driveway. Yet again, Tyler arrived at my home unannounced. It wasn't okay the first time and even worse this time. Dutton looked over at me as he pulled up behind him.

"That's my ex-boyfriend's car. I don't know what he's doing here."

"Are you going to be okay? Do you want me to come in with you?"

"No, thanks, I'll be fine. Thank you for a wonderful evening."

"You're more than welcome."

We leaned in, our lips meeting for one brief, soft and sweet kiss.

"Good night, Dutton."

"I'll see you tomorrow night."

I got out of his car and walked over to Tyler's. I rapped on the passenger window and he unlocked the door for me to get in.

"You look nice," he said.

"What are you doing here, Tyler?" I asked nicely, but I wanted to get straight to the point.

"I was on my way home from the studio and decided to stop by."

"And when you arrived, what did you discover?"

"That you weren't home, of course."

"So why are you in my driveway?"

"I wanted to see your face. I thought I'd wait a little while to see if you returned."

I could tell he was going through something. My walking away from our relationship was affecting him. "This is not okay."

"I know. Were you out on a date?"

"Yes," I whispered.

"I thought so. That's probably why I waited—to see for myself."

He could've called later and asked me where I was. Obviously, Tyler was a "seeing is believing" type of guy. He needed those hard facts. I assumed that was why he was in the news business. I wanted to tell him he couldn't treat me like he did work, popping up on the scene for a story. I refrained because I wanted to take a more delicate approach with him and our situation.

"I think it would be best for both of us if you called before coming over here."

"Because you're dating."

"No, because we're not together anymore. We have to be respectful of one another's space."

"I know you're one hundred percent right and I'm sorry."

"It's all right."

"Maybe we can talk sometime soon."

"Maybe."

"I'd better get going."

"Take care, Tyler."

I got out of the car and went into the house. He was still sitting in the driveway five minutes later. I wasn't going to bother him. I knew he'd leave eventually. He needed to process, whatever he needed to process. If he had to gather his thoughts before driving off, that was fine with me.

I went upstairs to get ready for bed. As I undressed, I reflected on how nice it had been to get dressed up for a Friday night date on the town. Headlights shone through my window as Tyler backed out and finally drove away.

CHAPTER FIFTY-THREE

utton opened my door and extended his hand to help me from the car. My heels were high, my black strapless dress was fitted and I looked like elegance, per his request. We walked hand in hand up to the entrance of a mansion. Expensive cars were being parked and guests were arriving in streams.

We entered the building and it was like a wonderland. Staff outfitted in tuxes, lavish displays of white flowers and green plants, soft lighting, black and silver balloons, a red carpet leading further into the mansion, music playing and photographers snapping pictures as guests arrived.

"What is this fabulous function, Dutton?" I asked, as we walked down the red carpet.

"It's my father's official retirement party hosted by the firm."

My gait slowed. "A party for your dad?"

"This is the big event the firm planned. All of his colleagues from over the years—employees, clients, you name it—will be here tonight. The party my mother hosted at the house was a more intimate precursor to the main event."

We entered the cavernous hall. There were tables upon tables of guests. A live band played from the stage in front. I scanned the room to see where we were heading. Dutton stopped. Louis and Miriam were walking in our direction. I put a smile on my face and held my breath.

Miriam looked at me, nodded, and then smiled. "Riley, you're stunning." She turned her attention to her son. "Dutton, you look very handsome tonight."

"Hi, Miriam. Mr. Carlyle."

"Hello, Riley." Louis was a blank slate. No smile in sight. He shook Dutton's hand with the sternest of expressions on his face.

"Nice turnout, Dad." Dutton clapped his father on the back. "Mom, where are we sitting?"

"The front table on the right side of the room."

"We'll see you a bit later," Dutton said. He grabbed my hand and headed toward the table. He seemed unfazed by his father's less than warm reception.

As we navigated our way from the back toward the front of the room, we bumped into Preston. He was grinning from ear to ear.

"Dutton, we obviously need to talk." He gave his brother a fist bump and me a kiss on the cheek. "You two look nice."

"So do you, man. We're headed to the table now. Where are you going?"

"I'm taking in the scenery." Preston winked at me. "I see plenty of beautiful scenery here tonight. I should've brought my camera. I'll see you at the table in a minute." Preston continued moving on.

I took a couple of cleansing breaths as Dutton approached the table. Grand and Jayla were seated at the table engaged in conversation. Grand looked up and saw us and it was as if every bit of color drained from his face. He appeared confused, eyes squinting like they were refocusing. Jayla draped an arm around her husband's shoulder. He glanced at her and then back at us.

"Dutton, Riley, you came together?"

We sat across from them. "Yeah we did," Dutton replied.

"This is a pleasant surprise," Grand commented. Nothing about his tone or grimace was pleasant.

Dutton pivoted his chair on an angle facing me. "Can you believe all of this grandeur?"

"I'm speechless."

"Should I have told you I was bringing you to a family affair?"

I dramatically stretched my eyes wide and nodded. "Uh, yeah."

He chuckled. "I'm sorry. I figured you know my family… You're with us every week… I really just wanted you by my side."

I shook my head, a reluctant smile tugging at the corners of my mouth. "We'll discuss this later."

He took my hand and kissed it. "I'm in trouble, I know."

I looked up and Grand was staring at us. Jayla was watching him.

"We're going to have a good time," Dutton said. "There's live music. We know how you love that."

There was no way Dutton would have ever known how I felt about distancing myself from his family. I couldn't even get mad at him for bringing me there. "I do love my live music," I responded.

"We can even dance tonight if you want."

"We'll see."

"We will. I want to see more of what you had going on last night at the concert. No chairs involved this time."

I laughed. "Fine, no chairs."

Grand resumed his conversation with his wife, but watched us from the corner of his eye.

Dutton leaned in closer. "Maybe after the party we can take a drive to Stone Mountain Park."

"What are we going to do there all dressed up?" I whispered back.

"Park and look at the stars. We can recline our seats and gaze out the panoramic roof."

"Good evening, Grand and Jayla."

Dutton and I raised our heads simultaneously. Hutton was standing next to the table glaring at us.

"My twin, it must be a really good evening. Riley. How's everybody doing tonight?" Hutton walked by Dutton and sat in the empty chair on my other side. I was sandwiched in between them. "So what do we have here?" Hutton said.

"Riley's my date."

"Is that so?"

"Well, we came together, so I think that's pretty accurate."

Hutton put his arm behind my chair and leaned in. "You are looking beautiful tonight, Riley."

"Thank you." I moved forward slightly in my chair.

"Do you want me to sit there?" Dutton asked.

"Why would she want you to do that?"

"I'm talking to Riley."

"Maybe I should talk to her, too," Hutton said. "Riley, why would you want to change seats with my twin?"

"I'm fine where I am," I said to Dutton. I didn't even look in Hutton's direction.

"You are fine," Hutton stated.

I glanced across the table. Grand was silently watching the exchange. He was sneering at his brothers and me, I supposed.

"So what do you think," Dutton asked. "Stone Mountain?"

I lowered my voice. "Maybe."

"Your date isn't interested in your plans for the evening?"

"Knock it off, Hutton."

Dutton tried to carry on as if his brother wasn't there. "Didn't we hear that song the band is playing at the concert last night?"

"Oh, you two went to a concert?" Hutton asked.

"I think so," I said.

"You think you went to a concert?"

"She's talking to me, Hutton."

I didn't like the energy coming off of Hutton. A chill ran through me and I shivered.

"Are you cold?" Dutton asked.

"No, I'm fine."

Hutton stroked my bare shoulders. "Your skin feels a little chilly to me. I can warm you up."

Dutton banged on the table and I jumped. "Do you always need to be an asshole, Hutton?"

"I'm the asshole?"

"Isn't that what I said? You're sitting here touching Riley and making inappropriate comments. What's wrong with you?"

"You're asking what's wrong me? That's hilarious. My antisocial twin brother wants to know what's wrong with me. What the hell is wrong with you? Better yet, what's been wrong with you? Ever since we were kids, there's been something wrong with you."

"Why, because I'm not you? Because I'm not a fucking asshole like you?"

"Oh, so now I'm a fucking asshole?"

"No, not now. You've been a fucking asshole."

Grand leaned forward. "Knock it off, both of you. This is not the time or the place."

It was nice of him to finally realize he needed to step in. I looked around to see where Louis and Miriam were. I caught a glimpse of them on the dance floor.

Jayla was watching everything with her arms folded in front of her, resting on the table. "Are you enjoying yourself, Riley?"

I wondered what kind of question was that to ask in the midst of what was going on. "As much as could be expected."

"I find it interesting that you're not only making our Sunday dinners, but you're catering meetings at the firm, and attending family functions. The Carlyles seem to love you." She glanced at her husband.

"I'm a great chef. Miriam hired me to provide services based on my skills."

"Which skills would that be?"

I glared at her. "Culinary. The same reason Grand hired me to cater his meeting."

"You're not catering tonight…"

"I invited Riley tonight," Dutton said.

"You're proud of yourself, aren't you? You're finally feeling like a man."

"Knock it off, Hutton," Grand warned.

Hutton's eyes darted to his older brother. "I know you're gunning to run Dad's company, but you're not the boss of me."

"Right now I'm the boss of you because you're being an ass at our father's event."

"You will never be the boss of me. You keep trying to be Dad's mini-me."

"I'm not his mini anything. I don't have to be him to run the firm."

"You act like you do. If for one moment you stopped acting like him and tried to be yourself, you would have to face some harsh realities."

"Oh yeah, why don't you enlighten me, Hutton."

"The only reason our father thinks so highly of you is because you try to act just like him. Act like yourself for one minute and you know what he'll realize?"

"What's that?"

"That I'm much better at the firm than you."

"You're a self-absorbed, delusional ass," Grand replied.

Hutton ticked off with his fingers. "I bring in more money than you. I work with the clients better than you do. And, I know more about the firm, and how it runs, than you do. Dad may put you in charge, but let's see how long you stay there."

"Oh, I'll remain in charge while you're waiting in the wings, hoping to one day be where I am."

"That day may come sooner than you think. But, hey, don't worry. You can always turn to teaching like Dutton."

"I live my life on my own terms," Dutton said. "Maybe you're envious you don't know what that's like."

Hutton scoffed. "You get a date and now you've got some balls to speak up for yourself?"

"You fucking asshole!"

In a flash the twins jumped up, shouting and shoving one another. I rushed to get out of the way. Dutton had Hutton hemmed up by the shirt collar. Hutton's arm was locked around his brother's neck. A chair toppled to the floor. They scuffled back and forth, profanities flying from their mouths. Grand ran from around the table, trying to pull them apart. Preston sprinted over and grabbed Dutton. Grand wrestled Hutton free and wrapped his arms around his chest, pinning his arms at his side.

Preston locked Dutton's arms behind his back keeping him at a safe distance.

"You call yourself a brother?" Dutton shouted. "You've never been a brother to me."

"Don't talk to me about what I've been to you. When have you ever stepped outside of your own private world to be there for me or anyone else in this family?"

A crowd had formed around the brothers. Louis and Miriam rushed over, pushing their way through the throng of people. They looked at their sons, restrained and clothes disheveled.

"What is going on?" Miriam cried.

"These two fools got into a dust-up," Grand roared.

"You started this because you think you run me and you don't! I keep telling you, you don't!" Hutton shouted at Grand.

"Hutton was being a disrespectful asshole, as usual," Dutton yelled.

"You're all acting like idiots," Preston hollered.

"Stop this right now!" Louis thundered, standing in the middle of his sons. "I don't believe you all. Preston, let him go. Grand, turn him loose. My sons are at my retirement party, for a company I built for all of you and you're fighting like strangers in the street? You choose to do this here and now for everyone to see? My peers… my colleagues…friends…family? Your mother is over there in tears because her children are acting like fools."

Miriam crumpled in a chair, tears streaming down her face. Jayla was rubbing her back, attempting to console her. Louis's guests started to disperse, going back to their tables to give the illusion of privacy in a very public space.

"I would have never expected this from my sons." Louis shook his head. "Not the boys I raised."

Dutton grabbed my hand. "That's the problem. We're not boys anymore and some of us don't even know it."

He shoved through the last of the guests encircling the family and stormed out of the party.

CHAPTER FIFTY-FOUR

The silence was deafening. Dutton hadn't spoken a word since we'd left the party. My role in their altercation was weighing heavily on me. Hutton kept poking at his twin— poking and poking and poking. He saw us together and was on a mission to prove that Dutton wasn't the man for me. I would have never willingly attended that event. Had I known that was what Dutton had in store, I would have told him I was unable to attend.

We had been sitting in my driveway for five minutes. I stared at Dutton waiting for him to say something. He finally turned his head in my direction and acknowledged my presence. I noticed his left eye was bruised and puffy. I reached out and gently touched it. He winced and pulled away.

"Come inside and let me put something on that eye for you." He didn't respond. "Dutton…"

He took his keys out of the ignition and opened his car door. I took that as my signal that he was going to let me tend to his eye.

I led him inside to the family room. "Have a seat. I'll be right back."

I went to the kitchen and got an ice pack from the freezer. I wrapped it in a clean kitchen towel and returned with it. "Lay your head back." He reclined his head on the oversized sofa pillows. I gently applied the pack to his eye.

He winced again. "Ugh," he uttered.

"I know it hurts, but this will help." I stood over him, holding the ice pack to his swollen area. "Are you all right?"

"No, I'm not." He took the ice pack from my hand and held it.

I came around to the other side of the sofa and sat next to him. I reached down and slipped off his shoes. "Do you want to talk about it?"

He sighed. "I don't know what happened tonight. Why tonight of all nights? I have been dealing with my brother's bullshit my entire life, but I let him get the best of me tonight. I ruined my father's party. A man who already thinks I'm a failure."

"He never said you were a failure."

"No, but I can see it in his eyes. I've never lived up to his expectations. It's that simple. You heard what he said tonight. He didn't raise his boys to be… That's his thing, you know. How he raised us. He raised us to do this. He raised us to do that. He didn't raise us to do this or that. He thinks he can control us like he did when we were kids. We're still supposed to behave how he wants because he raised us a certain way. I'm a grown-ass man." He lifted his head. "What did I do, Riley?"

"Nothing that can't be fixed."

"I had a physical altercation with my brother. We haven't fought since we were kids."

"I'm sure after you let things cool down for a while…"

"Maybe Hutton's right. I haven't been a good brother. I've been so focused on how different we are, I haven't really let any of them in." He leaned forward, his head hanging low. "I messed up."

"We all mess up sometimes."

"I really messed up."

I started to rub his back. "You'll get through it."

Dutton put the ice pack on the table and touched my face. He traced his fingers along my jaw and around to the back of my neck.

He drew me to him, gently, and kissed me. We moved closer to each other and he wrapped his arms around me. My arms encircled his waist. He pulled away and looked into my eyes. I placed my hand on the back of his neck and pulled him to me. I kissed him, planting the sweetest of kisses on his face, his cheeks, his lips. I nibbled on his mouth, licking and nipping his bottom lip. I eased my tongue into his mouth and lured him to me. I slipped my hands inside his jacket, peeling it away from his shoulders and arms. He tugged on the sleeves, taking it off completely. I trailed kisses down his neck as I slowly unbuttoned his shirt. With each open button, I kissed his exposed skin. My hands massaged his pecs. His hand was in my hair, cradling my head as I descended lower. I licked his abdomen muscles and they flexed. I looked up with a seductive smile, unbuttoning the rest of his shirt. "Take this off."

I stared at his muscular, bare chest. He watched me, waiting. I extended my hand to him. He took it and let me lead him upstairs to my bedroom. I turned around in front of Dutton, my back facing him. "Can you unzip me?"

He unzipped my dress, holding it up for me to step out of it. I took it from his hands and let it drop to the floor. I unfastened his pants, pulled down the zipper and let them drop. He stepped out of them, pulling his socks off, as well. We were face to face. Me, braless, in a thong. Him, naked. He didn't wear any underwear. I stepped out of my panties so we were one in the same. He reached for me and I wrapped my arms around his neck. I hugged him to my body, rubbing against him. His hands ran through hair, down my neck, over my shoulders, down my arms, to my waist, over my hips, to my thighs. He hoisted me up and I wrapped my legs around his waist. He grabbed my ass and lifted me higher, maneuvering to enter me. I slowly gyrated, easing as much of him as I could inside. He held my weight as he stroked with measured movements.

In and out. In and out. The friction was building. "Keep it right there," I whispered. In and out. In and out. I was getting wetter and wetter.

"Tell me what you want," he said.

"Keep doing that."

"This?" He dipped a little deeper.

"Yes," I moaned.

"Like this?" He pulled out almost to the tip and thrust upward.

"Yes," I whined.

"Do it like this?" He increased the tempo, pumping my pussy in long strokes.

"Yes," I cried.

He carried me to the bed, still inside of me. He lay me on my back and pulled my arms above my head, holding me by my wrists. He thrust down and then upward, rocking my body back and forth. My legs were on either side of his body, bent at the knees. I looked down the length of our bodies at him pulling out and plunging back in. He couldn't get all of his inches inside. I spread my legs wider to grant him more access. He pushed, but he hit the end of me, before reaching the beginning of him. He pulled out of me. My juices glistened all over him. He positioned me where he wanted me, on all fours. Holding his penis with one hand, he slid himself inside. He gripped my hips and with a smooth pop-like stroke he made my pussy oh so wet. I was biting my bottom lip stifling my cries so I could hear him. He moaned with each stroke. It was like a song, different ranges and octaves. It was deep and intense, raspy and gruff, prolonged and short. The sound of him made me vibrate from within.

"Is it good to you, Riley?"

"It's good."

"Do you want me to stop?"

"No, don't stop."

"I want to hear you. What do I need to do so I can hear you?"

He thrust harder. I stopped holding back. "Harder," I said.

He pumped hard, his skin slapping against mine. Dutton smacked my ass. I let go and let him hear what I sounded like when I was getting good love. I yelled out with each thrust. I tried to warn him that I was coming, but I couldn't catch my breath.

"Ooh," he shouted, as I dripped all over him. He thrust twice and quickly pulled out of me, releasing on my back.

I looked over my shoulder at him. "I definitely need a shower. Do you have my back?"

"Absolutely."

CHAPTER FIFTY-FIVE

utton stroked my face as we lay in bed, facing one another. We spent the night in each other's arms. It was the best sleep I'd had in weeks. No tossing and turning. No fitful dreams. Just the strength of his arms around me, holding me close. My leg was in between his, anchoring me to him. I kissed him on the lips and he smiled. I touched his chin, feeling the smoothness of his beard. He jutted his chin out.

"What do you think about me shaving it off?"

"No, keep it. It's sexy."

"You're just saying that because you're imagining you have Omari Hardwick in the bed."

"I am not!" I pinched his arm, laughing. "I know who's in my bed."

"Any regrets?"

"Not one."

"Was it good for you?"

"You couldn't tell?"

"I don't want to assume."

"Now you're playing modest. You know it was great."

He kissed me on the forehead and settled back on his pillow. I reached up and touched his bruised eye. "It doesn't look as swollen. We should probably put some more ice on it."

"I guess Sunday dinner is cancelled tonight." He chuckled, yet it didn't quite reach his eyes. "I wouldn't have gone anyway. I don't want to see anyone."

"That's understandable, but you know you can't avoid your family forever."

"Not forever, but for now."

"Don't let too much time pass. Sometimes we—"

Dutton kissed my lips, interrupting me. "I really like you, Riley, and I want to keep seeing you." He paused, waiting for me to respond.

I hadn't thought past the night before, or the moment we were in, but I liked the way being together felt and the possibilities it presented. "That would be nice."

"I think so, too."

"How about some breakfast?" I asked, springing from the bed.

He sat up. "You took care of me last night; why don't you let me make you breakfast?"

"No, that's okay, I can make breakfast."

"Let me cater to you for a change." He stood in front of me and took my hands in his. "Let me treat you to something special."

"I like the way that sounds."

We were downstairs in my kitchen. Dutton was in his slacks, top button undone, shirtless and barefoot. I sat at the kitchen table while he whipped up his self-proclaimed famous French toast. I thought about his nakedness underneath the pants. "I wouldn't have taken you as a commando type of guy."

He raised his eyebrows. "What are you thinking about over there?"

"Just how surprised I was that you weren't wearing any underwear and that you don't have any on right now."

"Sometimes a man needs to let it hang."

I bit my bottom lip. "I can see that." He had some serious hang time. Dutton was a well-endowed brother and very good at working his assets. I had made some assumptions of my own about Dutton.

I was judging the book by its cover. He was much more than the intelligent professor. He was also very manly and passionate.

"How do you like your eggs?" he asked.

"What's your specialty?"

"Soft scrambled."

"That's how I'll take mine."

"Coming right up."

It was cute that he was in my kitchen cooking for me. It was rare for anyone to cook for me. Everyone always thinks that the professional should do all the cooking. It's nice to get a break every once in a while. Dutton said he wanted to cater to me for taking care of him last night. He was appreciative and for that I appreciated him more.

My phone vibrated on the table. I picked it up and saw there was a new text message. It was from Miriam.

Confirming Sunday dinner.

I stared at the screen in disbelief. "Your mother just texted me."

"What did she say?"

"Confirming Sunday dinner."

"That's it?"

"Yup. Let me respond." I spoke my reply out loud. *"Miriam, I will not be able to make it tonight."*

Dutton was whisking the eggs, looking at me, not the bowl. "Any response?"

"Not yet. Oh, wait, here it is. It says we really need your services. Dutton, what am I supposed to tell her?"

"I don't know."

"She's your mother."

The phone vibrated in my hand. "She's insisting that I need to be there and can't cancel on her without any notice."

"Tell her no."

"I can't do that."

"Then I don't know what to tell you because I won't be going."

CHAPTER FIFTY-SIX

Melba opened the door when I arrived. I was caught off guard, having not seen her in some weeks. Miriam approached from down the hall. "Riley, you made it."

"Here I am."

"Let's go in the living room."

I would have rather gone straight to the kitchen. She showed me into the living room and asked me to have a seat. I sat in a high-back chair and Miriam settled into the identical one across from me.

"It's funny," she said. "I couldn't get any of my sons to come here today. Something that was supposed to bring them together has pulled them apart." She watched me. "What's going on with you and my boys? They aren't talking much about what happened last night."

I didn't answer. I wasn't trying to be disrespectful; I didn't know what to say.

She sighed. "I did speak to Jayla, though. And, she recounted what happened at the table."

"So, you really didn't need me here to cook today?"

"What's going on with you and my sons?" she repeated.

Louis strode into the room. "Miriam, you know what's going on."

"I don't, Louis," she said, her voice raised. "That's why I'm asking."

"This young lady has been involved with each of our sons; isn't that right?" He glowered at me.

I couldn't speak a word. I was at a loss.

"I've spoken to Grand, Hutton and Preston today. I left Dutton a message, but he hasn't returned my call. The others, each one of them, told me what was going on."

Miriam moved to the edge of her seat. "Well, what is it exactly?"

"Grand told me that he pursued her and they kissed, but it hadn't gone any further than that. Preston said he had Riley at his place. Hutton, well, Hutton basically let me know that he slept with her, too."

"I didn't sleep with Preston." I finally spoke up in an attempt to defend myself.

"But you consorted with my married son and slept with Hutton?" Miriam asked, confusion painting her face. "And, here I was trying to pair you with Dutton. You aren't good enough."

Louis picked up where Miriam left off. "I'm disappointed. I thought you were worthy, the cream of the crop."

Miriam turned her head toward her husband, her forehead wrinkling.

I looked from one to the other. There was nothing I could say. I was embarrassed, upset and had heard enough. "Excuse me, I have to go." I got up and quickly walked away from them.

I rounded the corner and bumped into Dutton, leaning against the wall outside of the living room. He was shaking his head and could barely look at me.

I reached for his arm, my hands trembling. "Dutton…" I said, my voice almost inaudible.

He stepped away, turned his back on me and walked down the hallway.

I bolted in the opposite direction, toward the front door. There was no reason for me to stay. I may not have cooked for the Carlyles, but Miriam and Louis had me for dinner, chewed me up and spat me out.

CHAPTER FIFTY-SEVEN

As soon as I left the Carlyles, I dialed Aja. I asked her to meet me at the bar in our favorite restaurant. My hands were still trembling from my exchange with Miriam and Louis. I banged on my steering wheel. Dutton standing in the hallway was the last thing I expected. If he'd heard everything his parents had said, I could only imagine what he was thinking about me. I didn't even speak up for myself. I sat there like a child being reprimanded. I bore the brunt of this debacle, as if their sons played no part. I sped faster through traffic. I needed to talk to my best friend.

Aja was waiting for me when I arrived. I climbed onto the bar chair and looked at her. Tears were on the brink of falling. I had been holding them back ever since leaving the Carlyles and they were threatening to overtake me.

She rubbed my back. "Don't do it. Be strong."

I inhaled a few shaky breaths and then nodded. "Aja, that was the most embarrassing moment of my life. I'm mortified." I relayed to Aja everything that had happened at the party, afterward with Dutton and the scene from which I'd just fled. She listened without interruption. Shaking her head from time to time and sipping on her drink.

Hearing myself retell the story, I felt ashamed for being in such a predicament. Louis harped on how he raised his sons. Well, I knew I hadn't been raised to behave as I had. If my father was looking down on me, he surely wouldn't be proud of his daughter. I was missing him more than ever. I had a thought. "Do you think I was so taken with this family because my father is no longer here?" I asked.

"What makes you think that?"

"Well, when I first met Louis Carlyle, I was so in awe of who he was, what he had accomplished and that he had this great family. I felt like he was this wonderful father figure to his sons. Maybe I was idolizing what I thought he was like and what his family was like. I miss that sense of family ever since my dad died."

"That may be how you view Louis, but that doesn't explain what you were doing with his sons."

"I didn't say I had all of the answers. I'm still trying to figure that out. Maybe I was attracted to the possibilities with each of them. I wasn't happy with Tyler and felt something was missing. I may have been trying to fill a void."

"Anything is possible," Aja said. "What's important is that you don't repeat this in the future."

I twisted my lips. "Do you really think I would do that?"

"I didn't think you would do this…"

"Please don't lecture me tonight. I don't think I could handle it."

"I know, I know." She leaned over and hugged me. "It'll be all right. You'll see. Now order me another drink. I have to visit the ladies' room."

I swirled the ice in my glass with my stirrer. What a mess I made of a great opportunity. I had damaged my professional and personal reputation with a client. The Carlyles weren't blameless, either. I thought about Louis's condemnation of my character. He had no right. A flash of anger passed over me. This titan of finance had asked me to have an affair and had the audacity to condemn me for my actions. Unbelievable.

Aja had been gone a long while for a bathroom break. Her drink had been sitting and the ice starting to melt.

I was ordering my second round when she slid back into her seat. "What took you so long?"

"Your sister is here having dinner with this fine brother. When I saw her, I stopped at her table to chat."

"Really? That's a shocker but good for her. She needs to get out more. Where's she sitting?" Aja pointed me in Sierra's direction. "Let me go say hello. I'll be right back."

I walked through the restaurant and spotted Sierra's table. I approached slowly, my hand moving to my chest. "My day just keeps getting better," I said.

"Hey!" Sierra said excitedly. "You know Hutton."

Hutton looked at me and smiled.

"What are you doing with him?"

The smile disappeared from my sister's face. "I decided to go to the tasting event you told me about. I saw him there and he invited me to join him. We've been talking ever since the event."

"Why would you do that?" I asked.

"You said you weren't in the least interested in going out with him."

"Sierra, I was talking to Hutton."

"What do you mean?" he said.

"You know what I mean, Hutton."

"I didn't think you would mind if I pursued your sister, since you obviously had no boundaries when it came to me and my brothers."

"What is he talking about, Riley?"

"Hutton and I were fucking around, Sierra."

Sierra's mouth opened as she looked from one of us to the other. "You were with my sister and intentionally pursued me?"

Hutton smirked. "Why wouldn't I? You're beautiful, smart and I want to get to know you better."

"And you invited me back to your place…" She started gathering her things. "This is messy and I'm not with it." Sierra stood up. "Riley, I'll call you later."

My sister hugged me tightly and left the table. Hutton stared up at me with his typical arrogance shining through.

"What did you think you were doing?" I asked.

"How are we any different?"

"I didn't intentionally pursue any of your brothers."

"Any? Don't you mean all?"

I sat down in Sierra's abandoned seat. "You have a lot of nerve. You pursued me, just like your brothers. I didn't seek any of you out. And, you didn't seem to care about what any of them thought. You were out for yourself. Every chance you got, you tried to stick out your chest and prove that you could be with me over them."

"What did you do every chance you got? Spend time with each one of us."

"Hutton, I really didn't plan for any of this to happen. I've wrestled with it from the beginning. I tried to disengage myself numerous times, but you still kept pursuing and something kept drawing me back. I'm willing to apologize for my part in all of this. I never wanted to mislead and definitely not hurt anyone."

"I'm not hurt. I had a good time. I was curious about what adventures we could've gotten into next."

I shook my head and laughed. He was all about the adventure. I knew that wasn't what I was looking for. Hutton leaned over and tried to kiss me. I moved out of the way.

"I was only saying goodbye." He stood up, tossed money on the table for his ruined dinner and headed out of the restaurant.

I rested my head in my hands. How this situation continued to spiral downward I could not understand. I felt a tap on my shoulder. Aja was peering down at me.

"What the hell is going on?"

I sighed. "You don't want to know."

CHAPTER FIFTY-EIGHT

had to go check on my sister. I apologized to Aja for dragging her out, but I needed to leave. Sierra opened the door and motioned for me to come inside. Her zombie show was on the television again, but I dared not complain. She waited for me to start talking.

"I'm sorry about that spectacle at the restaurant."

"Do you want to tell me what's going on?"

"Not really, but I will."

"I'm listening."

I explained to my sister how I'd managed to get into my current mess of a situation. She mostly just nodded or shook her head as I spoke. I didn't want to disappoint my sister, but I saw in her eyes that was exactly what I had done.

"I just don't understand why you seemed to dig yourself deeper and deeper with these men," she said.

"I was drawn to all four of them in different ways. I knew it wasn't right, but it didn't necessarily feel wrong. I know that probably sounds crazy, but that's what it was."

"Are you done with it now?"

"Yes."

"I mean all of it, Riley. All of them."

"I have to be. Just as I was developing feelings—"

"If you're done, then be done and move on."

I nodded. I knew my older sister was right. I had no choice but to move forward. I sat back on her couch relieved to watch someone else's drama unfold.

I was having a rough Monday morning. I wasn't in the mood to deal with any clients, but it was too late to reschedule. I was in my kitchen doing as much prep as I could for my first client, before I had to head to his house.

As I chopped vegetables, I flashed back to Dutton cooking for me the day before. We had shared a wonderful night together and in the morning it felt right. I didn't have any regrets, no feelings that I shouldn't have been with him. From the beginning, he treated me with respect and tried to get to know me. I wondered what he thought of me now.

My doorbell rang, interrupting my thoughts. I answered, but kept the storm door closed. Preston looked at me, waiting for me to let him in.

"What are you doing here, Preston?"

"I came to check on you."

"I'm fine."

"Are you going to let me in?"

"I just told you that I'm fine. You can see I'm fine. I don't think we have anything else to discuss."

"That's not fair, Riley. I haven't done anything to you."

Technically, he was right. He hadn't done anything to me. I was taking my frustration out on him. I unlocked the storm door and let him come inside. We went into my living room and sat down.

"Are you all right?" he asked.

"I'm hanging in there."

"I heard you were by the house on Sunday."

"Your parents wanted to have a word with me."

"I could only imagine how that went."

"If you imagined not good, you'd be right."

"I wanted to check on you, but I also wanted to offer you a word of advice."

"You have advice for me? This is going to be good."

Preston laughed. "You could use a little advice, too, you know."

"Maybe I can."

"If you care for my brother, which I think you do, you should do whatever it takes to make it right."

"Why are you saying this?"

"On Saturday, at the party, I saw something between you. You two had a real connection."

"You saw that?"

"Am I wrong?"

I shook my head. "No, I don't think so."

"You have to know that out of all of us, Dutton is the real deal. My brother is a sincere guy and worthy to be with you."

"At this point I'm sure he doesn't think I'm worthy of him."

"You never know, but are you willing to not try and find out what he thinks?"

"I have to give that some thought."

He chuckled. "I was actually proud of Dutton on Saturday. He went toe to toe with Hutton. Not that I want to see my brothers fight, but I loved seeing him stand up for himself."

"Sometimes people reach their breaking point."

"Trust me. It was long overdue. It was a good thing you two left when you did."

"Why, what happened? Grand and Jayla got into it. She was accusing him of taking way too much interest in you. Accused him of having an affair and everything."

"What did he say?"

"Denied it, of course. My father ended up sending all of us home. He couldn't believe we were such an embarrassment."

"I feel awful and partly responsible."

"You can't worry about that. The only thing you should be concerned with is talking to Dutton."

"But what about your parents? They aren't going to want me anywhere near him, especially your mother."

"Dutton is a grown man, his own man, and this family is far from perfect. I think you've seen that firsthand."

Preston was right. His family had shown me their many imperfections.

CHAPTER FIFTY-NINE

stood outside the door to the anthropology department deciding whether to go in. I finally stepped inside the office and asked a woman at the first desk I saw if Dutton Carlyle was in his office. She told me he was teaching a class, but it should be wrapping up soon. She wasn't sure if he'd be returning to the office for the day. I asked if she could tell me in which building and room I could find him.

I crossed the campus rehearsing what I wanted to say. I was still unsure about even being there, but I kept going back to my conversation with Preston. I needed to make things right. I waited in the hallway, standing off to the side of Dutton's classroom. I kept checking my watch. The minutes were ticking by slowly and I was nervous. I tried to calm my racing thoughts.

The classroom door opened and students began to file out of the room. I waited, looking expectantly at every face that exited. Then, I saw him. He was wearing a blazer and a pair of jeans, his glasses adding a distinguished flair.

I called out to him. Dutton looked over in my direction, hesitated, and kept walking. My stomach dropped. I told myself to get over it and go talk to him. I hurried to catch up to him.

"Dutton, I need to talk to you."

He looked straight ahead. "I can't. I have a class."

We headed down the stairs and out of the building. I was walking fast to try to keep up with him. "I only need a minute."

"I don't have a minute. I have a class."

"Can you slow down for a moment?"

He stopped short. "Riley, I have a class."

I stared up at him. In that moment, I didn't know what else to say. Dutton turned around and left me standing on the quad as he jetted into another building. I started to wander slowly over to a bench near the lawn to collect my thoughts. I sat down and thought how that didn't go as planned. He didn't want to talk to me. I showed up on campus assuming he would listen to me. I couldn't have been more wrong. I sat on that bench, thinking. Thinking about what went wrong and whether it was even possible to make it right. I put myself in Dutton's shoes and wondered if I would be so willing to forgive. Knowing me, I wouldn't.

He was one of the good ones. I felt awful that I had messed over one of the good ones. Intelligent, handsome, adventurous, caring, thoughtful, and loved his mother—though that point wasn't at the top of my list at the moment. Sitting on that bench I realized Dutton was the man that called to me. I wanted him.

An hour passed. Students began to exit the building Dutton had entered. I stood up, watching the door. He came outside looking around, as if searching for something or someone. I waved to him. He stopped walking, then slowly headed in my direction. My pulse sped up. He stopped a few feet away from me.

"Hi," I said, smiling nervously.

"Hello."

"Can I talk to you for a moment?" I motioned for him to sit down. He came over to the bench and we sat side by side.

"I can't believe what was going on with you and my brothers." He dived right in.

"I'm sorry, Dutton."

"I made a fool of myself."

"No, you didn't. I made the fool of myself."

"I'm supposed to be the smart one, right? Why didn't I see this?" He shook his head. "I've been trying to make sense of this and I'm coming up with nothing."

"Dutton, I was missing something in my life. When I started working for your family, I started to get to know all of you in different ways. I've always been a stickler for keeping my personal and professional lives separate. I wasn't even going to attend the art exhibit with you because I feared I'd be crossing a line. Slowly, your family started to work their way into my life. I know it's no excuse for any of my behavior, but I never intended for any of this to happen."

"Even with me?"

"Not at first. I enjoyed spending time with you, yes, but I wanted keep things between us casual. You were my clients' son."

"What changed?"

"I began to realize that I liked the way I felt when I was with you. You made me begin to think that perhaps I should reevaluate what I wanted from a man. Maybe I didn't need a long list of qualities. When I was with you, I didn't feel like anything was missing."

"My brothers didn't make you feel that way?"

"Grand is married and Hutton might as well be married to himself."

He smiled and my heart skipped.

"What about Preston?"

"Preston is throwing his life away doing nothing." That time I got a laugh out of him.

"Okay, Louis."

"I'm trying to make a joke, but I have no interest in Preston. I have no interest in any of the Carlyle men, except you." I clasped his hand. "I came here to ask you to forgive me. We were getting to know each other and I would love to see what could happen between us…if you could move past this."

"That's not going to be easy to do."

"I know it wouldn't. I could only prove to you through my actions that you're the man I want. I won't pressure you, but I hope that you will consider starting over with me. This time I'll be the one to pursue you. I'll make my intentions clear to your entire family. You're the man I want and no one else can do a thing for me."

A strand of my hair blew across my face. Dutton reached up and tucked it behind my ear. I held his hand to my cheek. Gradually, a smile appeared on his face.

"You're smiling," I said.

"Am I?" he replied.

"You are."

"I didn't realize."

"I think I put that smile on your face," I said.

"I don't know if you're responsible."

"Okay, then let me take you out to prove it's me."

"Sounds familiar." He grinned. "Okay, I'll go out with you."

I leaned in and gave him one brief, soft and sweet kiss on the cheek.

CHAPTER SIXTY

*D*utton's fingers were interlocked with mine. He gave my hand a squeeze. The driveway was filled with cars. We stood on the doorstep, gazing at each other. He pulled me close and kissed me on the lips.

"Are you ready?" he asked.

I nodded.

He rang the doorbell. The classic Westminster chime rang out. He squeezed my hand again. The door opened and we smiled.

"We're here for Sunday dinner."

ACKNOWLEDGMENTS

I guess it's time to get out of Riley's head and reclaim my own thoughts. I'm watching the sunrise and the beauty is inspiring. The air is crisp, the sky is littered with fluffy grayish-blue clouds, and I'm thinking how wonderful it would be to sit outside with my laptop to write. I immediately wonder would it be too chilly to a point of distraction. I'm not fond of feeling cold. Regardless of the chill, what strikes me is that while admiring the beauty of nature, I'm thinking about writing. In the midst of taking in God's glorious wonders, I'm thinking of what I love to do, my passion. And, living my passion gives me a sense of purpose and brings me joy. It's as simple as the rising sun.

There's nothing like creating a story and a cast of characters in which others want to spend time. I've spent countless hours with these characters and to introduce them is a personally rewarding experiencing. I accomplished something I set out to do and I'm able to share it with you.

I appreciate each and every reader that gives of their time to read my work. Let's face it, we can spend our free time in any way we choose. I thank you for choosing *Cater to You*. I especially thank you for your support. I hope you enjoyed meeting Riley and the Carlyles. Maybe you've taken something away from their experiences. I sure hope so. I know I have and, no, I'm not telling you what! At the very least, always remember to cater to *you*.

I must thank Zane. Through your vision, you have given my passion an audience. I am forever grateful. Charmaine, you are the calm in the storm. Your ability to relate was more helpful than you know. Sara Camilli, I appreciate you! What more can I say? Well, maybe one more thing—thank you.

Over the years, I've been blessed with the most amazing friends. I never have to look far because I know they're there for me. My partners in crime, MC, OA, XB, JM, & DW, when's the next caper?

My dynamic Sorors of Delta Sigma Theta Sorority, Inc., Nassau Alumnae Chapter, thank you for your support. Divas will be divas!

All my love and devotion goes to my family. You. Are. My. Everything.

Well, I'm eager to see where this passion of mine leads me next. I'm inviting you to join me on the journey. You can bring the snacks! Until then, let's keep in touch...

www.ShamaraRay.com
www.facebook.com/ Shamara-Ray
Twitter: @ShamaraRay
Instagram @ShamaraRay

ABOUT THE AUTHOR

Shamara Ray is a graduate of Syracuse University. She first enticed readers with her debut novel, *Recipe for Love*. Her next offerings, *Close Quarters, You Might Just Get Burned* and *Rituals for Love*, continued to delight audiences. Ray has a penchant for the culinary arts and enjoys entertaining friends and family in her Long Island home. She is currently working on her next novel. Visit the author at www.shamararay.com

IF YOU ENJOYED "CATER TO YOU," BE SURE TO CHECK OUT
RILEY'S PAST IN

RITUALS FOR LOVE

BY SHAMARA RAY
AVAILABLE FROM STREBOR BOOKS

CHAPTER TWENTY-THREE

CAIN

When I stopped laughing, I heard the front door opening and heels striking the hardwood floor. I peered at my watch. It was almost nine. "I'm in the kitchen, Jade," I called out.

"Hey, ba—," she said, coming to a halt in the doorway.

"Jade, this is Riley. Riley, this is my girlfriend, Jade."

Jade looked from me to Riley. A confused look quickly replaced by a smile. She approached the table. "Riley," she pleasantly sang, "nice to meet you."

"You, as well."

"Have a seat, honey."

Jade surveyed the table as she sat down. "What do we have here?"

"Peppercorn seared filet mignon with a merlot glaze, chicken sautéed in a garlic, lemon, caper butter, and crispy honey-chipotle shrimp," Riley replied.

"It looks and smells amazing."

"When I arrived at Eden to have dinner with Riley, she offered to show off some of her skill. I thought it was a good idea, but the kitchen was busy tonight and Jeremiah didn't want us in the way. So we came back here."

"Although, I didn't offer to show off. I was *showcasing* my skills," she quipped.

"I guess you really want that job," Jade commented.

"Actually, I do."

"It's always a pleasure to meet a fellow chef and clearly a talented one. Where did you train?"

"Johnson & Wales and I also studied at Le Cordon Bleu in Paris."

"The famed Le Cordon Bleu? Impressive." Jade slowly nodded. "Where did you study?"

"The Culinary Institute of America."

"CIA is a great school."

"Jade is a great chef," I offered. "She owns her own restaurant here in Long Island."

"That must be interesting. Both of you being restaurateurs."

"It's great because we relate on *many* levels," Jade responded. "Are you currently working in a restaurant in Atlanta?"

"No, I'm actually a personal chef. I have worked in restaurants in the past, but for the last few years I've had my own clients to which I provide services."

"Why the transition?"

"A chef friend of mine mentioned the position at Eden2. I thought it would be a wonderful opportunity and would give me a chance to exercise my culinary chops."

"Well, you did a fine job here tonight," I said.

Riley reached over and touched my arm. "I'm glad you enjoyed it. There's much more where that came from."

"Keep up the good work. Jeremiah will be giving me his feedback at the end of the week."

Riley got up from the table and went over to the counter. She returned to the table with two bowls. "Merlot poached pears with delicately sweetened mascarpone." She placed one in front of me and the other in front of Jade. "I'm going to be leaving, but enjoy your dessert."

"You're not going to have any?" I asked.

"No, I want to get back to the hotel. I few calls to make before I call it a night."

I stood to show her to the door. "Well, thank you for dinner."

"You're welcome. It was great to get to know you better. Nice meeting you, Jade."

"The pleasure was mine."

I walked Riley to her car and gave her instructions to the parkway. She assured me the rental car had navigation and she'd find her way just fine. I returned to the house and back into the kitchen. Jade was moving her pear around the bowl with her spoon. I sat next to her. "Is it good? You should try some of this other stuff."

"I grabbed a bite in the city."

"Have just a taste. I'd love your opinion."

She sighed. "Okay, I'll take one bite of each." Jade reached over and took the fork from my plate. She sampled the beef, chicken and then the shrimp. "It's delicious."

"I thought so, too."

"I was surprised to see this spread when I came in."

"We decided on a whim to use my kitchen."

"I was even more surprised to see a tall, beautiful woman sitting at the table."

"You think five feet eight is tall?"

Her forehead wrinkled. "You know how tall she is?"

"It came up when she mentioned playing basketball in high school."

"I had no idea it was a female chef you were considering. I thought Riley was a man."

"I never mentioned Riley was a woman?"

"Not a word."

"I guess that's because it really doesn't matter. Male chef, female chef—I want the best *person* for the job."

"Did you think she was a bit touchy-feely?"

"I didn't notice anything."

"She grabbed your arm a couple of times and touched your shoulder when she put the dessert in front of you."

I started to clear the table. "I was focused on this meal and getting to know the potential future chef of my establishment. Those were the only two things that had my undivided attention. At least until you came in. I'm going to put away this food and clean the kitchen. Why don't you go up and get settled? I'll be up in a minute."

I had to shake my head once Jade went upstairs. If I didn't know any better, I'd say she seemed a little jealous. I could understand her being slightly thrown for a loop when she saw a cinnamon-complected beauty with a long bob sitting with me at the table. Especially if she didn't know I had company and thought Riley was a man. But she had no reason to be jealous.

I set the alarm and turned off the lights downstairs. I entered my bedroom and sat next to Jade on the edge of the bed. "So what do you think?"

"Ultimately, it's your decision. I will say Riley makes a tempting dessert."

CHAPTER TWENTY-FOUR

CAIN

I was up before Jade. She was just coming out of the bathroom as I was getting dressed. The news was on the television. I waited to hear the weather and traffic report. She was driving into the city to Genesis and wanted to know the traffic situation.

"You might want to head into the city a little later. The traffic is crazy at this hour."

"I'm going to Rituals first. I should miss any of the congestion by the time I travel into the city." She disappeared into the closet.

"If you need me, I'll be at my offices today," I called out. "I may go over to Eden at lunchtime. I have a good feeling about Riley. I think she'd make a great executive chef at Eden2."

She peeked her head out. "Oh really? You know that already?"

"I'll know by the end of the week, but I like what I see."

Jade came out of the closet and sat on the bed. "Don't you want Jeremiah's feedback?"

"His preliminary feedback is good. The complete opposite of what he thought of the first chef. If I hire Riley, I'll probably head to Atlanta for a week to get her settled in as the executive chef."

"Can you spare a week in Atlanta with all the work we're doing for Genesis?"

I stepped into my slacks. "Genesis is in more than capable hands with you at the helm."

"I'm capable, but with the rapid pace that Hal is progressing with the build-out, it's important for you to be here. This week he's already doing the floors in the dining room and the marble flooring in the upstairs lounge and reception areas. Next week, he'll be on to the steam rooms and vitality pools. Not to mention, the light fixtures are going up in the treatment rooms as soon as they complete the electrical work."

"You've just verified what I already knew. You have everything under control. If I have to go to Atlanta, you have Genesis covered. Remember, this is your vision. I trust that you'll manage the build-out exceptionally."

She muted the television. "One thing I've been thinking about since spending time on-site is either a Genesis chain or franchise. We're on to something with this venture and should consider taking it nationwide. What are your thoughts on opening not just one, but many, Genesis locations?"

"In my professional opinion, I think we need to start small with a single location. Franchising is not an option for us right now. If we were to even consider a chain or franchise, it would be years from now. We need a proven business model before we expand."

"Hypothetically speaking, what if a consortium of investors funded a Genesis chain?"

"My opinion has nothing to do with funding. Without a proven business model, I wouldn't dive into an expansion of that magnitude. That's just not how I do business. Trust me, you don't want to either." I went over to the bed and kissed Jade on her forehead. "I have to get to the office. Drive safely into the city. I'll talk to you later."

"Okay," she distractedly replied.

"That's all I get?"

"Have a great day." She craned her neck for a kiss.

I kissed her lips softly. "You, too."

I left the house, and on my way to the office I dialed Jeremiah to share my thoughts on Riley.